PRIDE BY THE BOOK

LOVE IN MAPLEWOOD
BOOK 6

JEFF ADAMS

BIG GAY Media

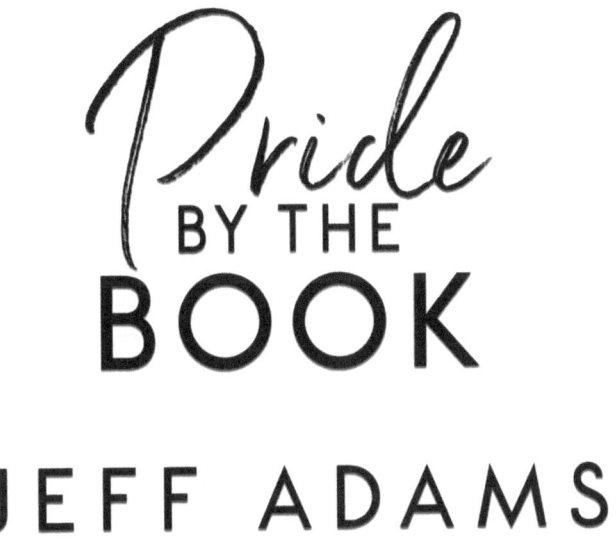

Pride BY THE BOOK

JEFF ADAMS

Pride by the Book
Copyright © 2025 by Jeff Adams
All rights reserved.

Editor: Jennifer Smith

Proofreader: Lori Parks

Cover Art: Morningstar Ashley Designs

Maplewood map by The Illustrated Page The website:
TheIllustratedPage.net/design/

Excerpt from *Finding My Rainbow, A Journey of Courage, Acceptance,
and Pride* by Josh Coleman used with permission of the author

ONE

ETHAN

As I turned onto the long, tree-lined driveway to the Montgomery place, childhood memories flashed through my mind. I hadn't been out here in six years, not since the funeral for Nicolas's mom. When I was a kid, though, and all the way through high school, this was one of the places I hung out, especially in the winter.

Nicolas was a couple of years older, but we'd met because his dad coached hockey and through that we became friends. The pond here wasn't too deep and usually provided playable ice for three months, more or less. Anyone who knew the Montgomerys and played hockey took full advantage of the outdoor playtime.

Hockey and school were my primary focuses back then. One fed the other.

I needed good grades to stay on the team.

I needed to be a great player to get into a college with a top hockey program.

The end goal was an education and the chance to go pro.

The work had paid off. I put college on hold after my first year to play. And last week I'd wrapped my fifteenth NHL season with a conference final loss in the Stanley Cup playoffs.

As much as I loved playing, returning to Maplewood for the summer was something I looked forward to. Although I preferred it when I came back in July rather than May or June.

Nicolas sat on the porch swing, looking toward the pond in the distance. It reminded me of his dad sitting there, coffee in hand, watching us play. In the winter when the trees were bare, he'd had a perfect view.

The house looked great, even better than the pictures he'd sent along a month ago. The two-story mid-century-modern-inspired house had been well maintained, and I intended to keep that tradition up.

Nicolas came off the porch as I got out of my SUV. He appeared haggard and older than I would've imagined. At his temples, gray flecked his auburn hair, and dark circles under his eyes suggested he wasn't getting enough rest. His attempt at a welcoming smile didn't mask the weariness in his movements.

"Ethan, it's good to see you." He gave me a warm hug. "I really could've met you in town."

"I couldn't wait to come out here, especially on a gorgeous morning like this."

Summer started tomorrow and even though it was a little warmer than usual, the sky was crystal blue and the breeze was just right, making it an ideal day to make my first visit back.

Sadness tinged Nicolas's eyes. "I'm glad you wanted this place. I know you'll look after it. Dad smiled when I told him you were the buyer."

That meant a lot.

Nicolas's father had struggled since his stroke a couple of years ago, so seeing his dad smile must've been a relief for Nicolas. I hoped it'd let him release some of the stress he carried.

I nodded. "It'll be in good hands. And there'll always be a room for you and Angel when you visit. In fact, I hope you can get here during the holidays for some hockey." I gestured with my head toward the pond.

"Let's make that happen. As long as you promise not to trounce me too badly."

"A friendly pickup game is yours anytime you want it." I clapped him on the back as we headed inside.

As we crossed from the foyer into the living room, one of the floorboards creaked just like it always had. Entering the space, I was hit with a wave of nostalgia at the sight of the stone and wood-paneled floor-to-ceiling fireplace. My heart ached for Nicolas, having to give up this place.

I knew from the pictures I'd seen that the kitchen had undergone a radical transformation. Gone were the vintage wood cabinets and patterned linoleum floor in favor of sleek walnut cabinetry, quartz countertops, and stainless steel appliances, but the pendant lights over the island and the starburst wallpaper reminded me of the kitchen where so much hot chocolate had been served.

"The place looks wonderful. Seeing it in person is…" I didn't have the words to describe my feelings to him. "I honestly can't believe I get to live here."

"I think it was meant to be. Elena hearing about it from Janice and then telling you. We didn't expect to sell so quick and easy." Nicolas paused and looked at me. His eyes glistened as he blinked and struggled to hold back his emotions. "It really helps."

"I'm glad." I drew him into another hug since it looked like he needed it.

I released him as there was a knock on the door. "That must be the notary. I've got everything on the big table. I'll be right back."

I nodded and headed into the dining room. I traced my fingers over the smooth surface of the weathered oak table. The view through the tall windows out to the woods captivated me, just like it always had.

I greeted Ms. Easton as Nicolas took a seat and started signing. She took out her notary supplies as I sat in what was my usual spot.

"I remember sitting here telling your dad that I was sure we could turn the basement into a mini hockey rink so we could play year-round." I smiled at the random memory.

Nicolas chuckled, shaking his head. "I bet you could do that if you wanted to."

"Can you imagine?"

His laughter increased. "If you pull that off, I expect to be invited to the opening game."

"You know it." I began signing the papers he handed over. I'd read them all over the past couple of days, as had my attorney, who'd initialed the top right corner of each so I'd know she'd reviewed it. "Say, are you sure you don't want any more of the furniture?"

"We don't really have room for more than the couple of chairs we took. If there's anything you don't want, I'm sure there are plenty of people in town who will take it off your hands."

"Everything fits the house so well, I don't imagine I'll get rid of anything. It'll also make moving in super easy."

Our eyes met for a moment as I handed over the stack of paperwork to Ms. Easton, a final acknowledgement that Nicolas's family place was safe with me.

The house symbolized far more than just a place to live. It held as many memories as the home I grew up in with my moms. I planned to fill this forever home with friends and family just like the Montgomerys had.

I pulled my phone from my jeans pocket. "I'll have Caroline do the transfer."

"Great. I'll—" His phone sounded from his pocket. "Sorry." He sighed when he saw the screen. "I've got to get this."

He started to get up, but I raised my hand. "You stay. I'm gonna go look around."

He nodded and answered the call. "Hi. This is Nicolas."

Outside I headed for the pond, which shimmered in the morning sun just beyond a line of trees.

I opened the messaging app on my phone and brought up my texts with Caroline, my attorney for the past five years. Tapping the microphone icon, I said, "Good morning, Caroline. Everything's signed. You can transfer the money." I thumbed send.

Swiping over to the camera, I brought the phone up to frame myself with the lake and trees in the background. The sun couldn't have been more perfect for how the light danced on the water and in the leaves. I smiled and snapped a few images, selecting my favorite and adding it to the group chat I had with Mom Elena and Momma Grace.

I tapped the mic icon again. "It's all mine."

I sent that message on its way.

As much as I loved playing hockey, being back in Maplewood was the best. This summer promised to be fantastic. I'd settle into this house, and hockey camp was always a blast. I loved working with the kids, and this year many of my friends were coming in to be guest coaches. Of course, Pride in Maplewood was always an incredible time.

This year I had some anxiety associated with Pride, though. Although being named grand marshal was an honor, the role came with expectations during the weekend.

What if I let everyone down?

Being the center of attention was never easy.

Yes, I was in the spotlight all the time playing for

Seattle—but I knew how to play hockey. It also wasn't all about me, but about the team.

Grand marshal meant not only being in the parade, but also judging some competitions and maybe more. I didn't have the full rundown yet.

As if she sensed my anxiety, Mom called. I connected the video call and held up the phone, framing myself much like I had with the selfie.

"Good morning!"

"Hey, sweetheart!" Mom's voice immediately reduced the tightness in my chest. "You look so happy. It's gorgeous out there this morning."

"I was just out looking around, taking it all in."

"Everything okay?" Mom asked.

It was impossible to hide anything from Elena with her counselor skills. My voice must have given a little something away.

"Just in my head a bit about the festival." We'd talked about this several times since the invitation to be grand marshal had come in.

"I understand." Mom's voice shifted to the soothing tone she'd used anytime I was stressed. "Remember, you're loved here and people want to honor your hockey accomplishments and all you contribute to this community. Just take it all one step at a time and remember to breathe. And try to have some fun with it. It is Pride after all."

"You always know just what to say. Will I see you before the festival meeting tonight?"

"We're headed to the theater since some of the

performers arrive today," Mom said. "Drop by if you've got time. Otherwise we'll see you tonight."

"Will do. Love you both."

"Love you too," she said back.

I disconnected the call and headed back to the house.

Beyond my anxiety about the festival activities, it was the first time since high school I was going to be around Andre Thompson for more than a nod of acknowledgment.

The difficult dynamics between us had started back then. He'd had a fiery enthusiasm, rallying the student body to show its school spirit or to get behind causes. In his world, everyone had to be involved. He hadn't hidden his frustration that I never took part.

I'd wanted to help Andre so many times, but I couldn't make the commitment between studies and practice.

Having to work with him during the festival was weighing on me more than any other aspect of the weekend.

In the house Nicolas stood at the large windows, taking in everything.

"Sorry I was gone for longer than I expected." I joined him at the windows.

"No problem. Ms. Easton finalized everything and I left your stack of papers on the table. And these are yours." He handed me four keys. "The alarm code is with the contracts too."

"Thanks." Something caught my eye out in the woods. I focused deep into the trees at a cut tree stump.

A brown, red, and orange painted bowl was on top of it. "Is that what I think it is?" I pointed to where I was looking.

Nicolas grinned and nodded. "Yup. It's still there."

"Oh, wow. We built that when I was"—I had to think a moment—"ten?"

"Sounds about right."

Nicolas, our friend Liam, Nicolas's dad, and I had built a place for Mabel's food. Mabel was a legend in these parts. No one had ever captured actual evidence of the cryptid, but the Montgomerys believed.

So did I after Nicolas's dad told a story about Mabel one night we were all camping in the woods. I was pretty sure I'd caught glimpses of her three times on visits.

"I went and filled the bowl this morning," Nicolas said. "We've been paying Tommy Harrington to bring food every couple of weeks. Dad wanted to keep Mabel happy, even though we weren't here."

"I'll continue that tradition. Make sure to stay in her good graces."

"Right? Don't want an angry Mabel on your hands." Nicolas knocked into my shoulder and smirked at me.

"How long are you staying in town?" I asked.

"Headed home after a breakfast meeting with the banker."

I nodded. "Coming back for Pride?"

"I'm bummed to miss out, but Angel has a lot going on for Boston Pride, and I need to be there for him."

"You'll be missed. Say hi to Angel and your dad for me."

"I'll do that." He looked at his watch. "I should get going."

I followed him across the room to the foyer. I hadn't noticed when I came back in that he'd put a backpack and a duffel by the door.

"Thanks again for making all this so easy." Nicolas came in for another hug. "I hope camp is fantastic. And enjoy Pride. You'll be a perfect grand marshal."

"Thanks, man."

He knew me well enough to know my struggles, and I appreciated that he kept his support simple.

We walked out to the porch and he headed down the stairs to his car.

"Drive safe." I waved as he tossed his bags in the back seat.

"Take care."

As he disappeared down the driveway, I sank into the same rocking chair Nicolas had occupied when I'd arrived. This would be the perfect place to start the day, sipping coffee and soaking in the view.

TWO

ANDRE

I stepped into Red's and the familiar scent of coffee, maple syrup, and bacon hit me as I made my way to our usual table in the back. Olivia was already there, her vibrant green hair a stark contrast to the others in the diner.

"Morning, sunshine," she chirped, sliding a steaming mug toward me.

"Thanks," I said before taking a sip. I'd been up too late between library work and festival details. "Where's Wade?"

As if on cue, the bell above the door chimed and Wade rushed in, their laptop bag slung over one shoulder.

"Sorry I'm late," they panted, sliding into the booth next to Olivia. "My alarm took the morning off."

"Don't worry about it," I said, stifling a yawn. "I've only been here about a minute. Olivia, of course, beat us both. How are you two this morning?"

Olivia smiled brightly. "I should be sleepier, but I'm doing great. I got carried away designing last night."

"I'm good. Psyched that we've got less than a week to go." Wade drank from the coffee Olivia put in front of them. "What about you, boss?"

"Trying not to be worried that we've bitten off more than we can chew. This is our most ambitious Pride celebration yet."

Ingrid came over to get our order. "What can I get you all?" She looked at me.

"I'll have my usual veggie omelet and toast, please."

Ingrid nodded.

Olivia went next. "Blueberry waffles and maple sausage for me."

"And I'll take the maple bacon pancake stack special." Wade sounded eager.

"Half or full?" Ingrid asked.

"It's gotta be a full stack."

Olivia's mouth dropped open. "You're going to fall back asleep before we're even done with this meeting."

"Nah, I'm only going to eat half. The rest will be for dinner."

"Uh-huh." Olivia shot a doubting look to me and I shrugged while Wade rolled their eyes.

"Don't judge me." Wade got their bag off the floor and pulled out their laptop. "So it's pretty last minute, but I had an idea." They looked at Olivia and me before they continued. "We're already planning to stream the main stage events but there are so many other amazing things happening. What if we could stream more?"

That was a fantastic idea. "How would we even do that?"

"Well..." Wade paused.

I shot them a smile and nodded. Wade had shared with me last year that they sometimes feared their enthusiasm overshadowed the ideas they had. I did everything I could to encourage their big thoughts.

"I'm pretty sure we could turn it into a media project for some friends I have at school. I was helping a couple of them out last night and told them what I was doing here with the streaming and the VR history project. That triggered a whole discussion about streaming more to show off the festival, the town, everything that makes Maplewood special."

Ingrid brought the food, and Wade quickly moved the laptop out of the way. While Olivia and I had one plate each, three plates with pancakes, bacon, hash browns, and eggs landed in front of Wade. Their eyes lit up as they surveyed the food.

"I love the idea. It could be an amazing showcase. What did you and your friends come up with?"

As we dug in, Wade explained that there'd be a mix of computer science and journalism students here to run the streams. For events that might not stream well on their own, the journalists could provide commentary, maybe interview people and such. It would not only showcase the festival but also be something for the students' portfolios as well.

"I like it." I reached down to pull my tablet from my backpack. With the pencil, I scribbled a few notes. "Can you put together a full proposal including how many people would be involved, the plan, and what tasks there are to pull it all together? And I kind of need that before the meeting tonight."

"Already on it." Wade didn't even stop to think about it. "I've got most of it ready. I'll have it to you by noon."

"Great. Good job."

"That's very cool." Olivia stole some hash browns from one of Wade's plates. "Let me know if there's anything I can do."

"Will do."

"And everything's set with the VR project?" I wanted to make sure that was still good to go. The expansive project, chronicling Maplewood's history and its Pride celebrations, was a central part of Thursday and Friday's educational sessions. We couldn't lose focus on that while adding more streaming.

"It is. I'm doing the final check today and I'll have the demo units for you and Mayor Axelrod to try out tomorrow as planned."

"I'm looking forward to that." I smiled. I knew they'd have it ready, but it eased my mind to hear them say it.

"So I've got something new too." Olivia rummaged in her bag and brought out a notebook. She handed me folded pages that made up a program. "This is what I came up with last night."

Her artistic flair had transformed our basic program into a vibrant, eye-catching one that captured the spirit of Maplewood's Pride. Small illustrations brought each event to life, using a palette of warm oranges, deep reds, and rich purples reminiscent of autumn maple leaves interspersed with the rainbow colors of Pride.

Some of the drawings stood out. For the parade, she created a procession of colorful floats and at the front a tiny Ethan Gallagher waved from a convertible adorned with maple leaves and rainbow flags. The dance performance featured one man lifting another, a scene I recognized from one of the promo photographs we had. For the exhibition hockey game, she'd created an action-packed scene with players mid-motion on the ice. Intricate maple leaf patterns morphing into various Pride symbols decorated the margins of every page.

The result was a program that was not just informative but a work of art in itself. It wasn't a surprise. Olivia created all sorts of designs for Maplewood festivals, but this one was above and beyond. Each individual drawing could easily hang in The Wild Palette's gallery, alongside the other artwork she curated from Maplewood artists.

"I don't know what to say." I handed the mock-up to Wade. "It's stunning. You did that last night?"

She nodded. "I had one idea for the parade, and then I just kept coming up with more."

"I wish we'd charged more for the ads since they're going to be surrounded by your gorgeous art."

"Wow," Wade said under their breath.

Olivia beamed. "Thank you. I'm glad you like it." She took it back from Wade. "I'll talk to the printer to see what this version costs and if it can be done in time."

"It'll be worth the money. I'm sure we can shift funds if we need to."

We spent another hour talking about all the events and the status of everything. In the midst of it, Ingrid cleared away our dishes and boxed up Wade's leftovers.

"Now, about the grand marshal duties..." I trailed off, unable to keep the edge from my voice. The thought of working with Ethan frustrated me despite my best efforts to remain professional.

Olivia raised an eyebrow. "Has something happened?"

I forced a smile, shoving my personal feelings aside. Selecting the grand marshal was a community decision, and I had to work with whoever was chosen.

"No. He arrived yesterday as planned. It's just... a lot of moving parts to coordinate. He's got his hockey camp starting too. And honestly, we don't normally have someone of his status as the GM."

Wade looked up from their screen. "He's certainly a big draw. There's a lot of buzz because he's got some of his NHL friends with him for the charity game."

"Yes, the extra attention's great," I said quickly, not wanting to dampen their enthusiasm. "I'm sure he'll be fine. I just want to make sure we brief him properly on all his activities."

Olivia leaned forward, her expression thoughtful. She knew our history and that I wasn't happy about his selection. "I can meet with him if that helps."

I sighed, running a hand over the top of my shaved

head. "I appreciate it, but I'll take care of it. As the lead organizer, it's my responsibility."

She nodded. "Well, tell me if you need anything."

"Thanks." I tried to give her a reassuring smile. "I think that'll do it. I feel good about where we are. Can we meet up in the mornings at this same time over the next few days, just to check in?"

"And more pancakes!" Wade said.

Their enthusiasm helped me put aside any concerns.

As we packed up, Mickey, my best friend and the son of the diner's owner, came over. "Sorry I couldn't join in this morning. How's everything?"

"It's looking good," I said. "Thanks for organizing all the food vendors and sponsoring the picnic."

He beamed. "Always! Oh, and congrats on that award you and the library are up for. That's amazing."

My face heated in a flush of pride. "Thank you. It's an honor to be recognized for the banned books initiative."

Olivia leaned in, her curiosity piqued. "How do I not know about this?"

"It only got announced late yesterday afternoon, and the library is getting a release out today." I couldn't hold in a big smile.

"Good job, boss," Wade said. "It's great what you're doing."

"Thanks." I was at a loss for words. The announcement had been unexpected and I was still taking it in alongside everything else going on. "I need to get going and open up the library. We're meeting the next few mornings. Can you hold our table for us?"

"Will do." A bell rang and Mickey looked over to find one of the servers with a big order. "I'm going to help them. I'll see you all tomorrow."

As we were settling the bill, the bell above the door chimed, and Nicolas Montgomery walked in with Mr. Barclay.

"Andre!" Nicolas called out, his face lighting up with recognition. "How are you?"

I went to him and we hugged. "It's all good. How's life in Boston?"

"Busy but good." I heard the weight he carried in his voice. "Just taking care of some business here."

That was fortuitous. "How long are you around? I heard you're selling your family's place. I'd love to talk to you about that."

Nicolas looked sheepish. "I actually sold it this morning. That's why I'm here."

"Oh. I didn't know it'd been officially listed."

"It came together really quickly with Ethan Gallagher."

My stomach dropped, and I hoped I kept my expression neutral. "Ethan. Well, that's... unexpected."

Nicolas nodded, oblivious to my inner turmoil. "He spent a lot of time there and he wanted to keep that part of his childhood. I didn't know you were interested."

"Don't worry about it. I had some ideas bouncing around. I'm glad you were able to get that wrapped up quickly."

"Yeah. It was for the best. I wish we had time to catch up, but I need to get to my meeting." He gestured to where Mr. Barclay sat reading his phone. "Good luck with the festival. I'm sad to miss it this year."

"Thanks." I hugged him again. "You might even be able to watch it from Boston if Wade's plan comes together." Wade smiled as I nodded in their direction.

"That would be amazing. Send me the details."

After we said our goodbyes, I headed out.

My mind reeled. Ethan Gallagher bought the Montgomery place? How did that happen so quickly? I took a deep breath, trying to quell my frustration.

My phone buzzed in my pocket. Dad's smiling face lit up the screen, and I answered.

"Hey, Dad!" Hearing from him improved my mood. "Didn't expect to hear from you today."

"We had to call. Just heard about your nomination. Congratulations!" Dad's voice radiated happiness. "We're so proud of you."

"You're amazing!" Sato, my stepdad, called out from somewhere in the background.

"Thanks, both of you. I'm still processing it, to be honest."

"You deserve it. Your banned books initiative has made significant impact." Dad paused. "How's the festival prep going? You holding up okay?"

I forced brightness into my voice. They didn't need to know about the challenges, especially since they were halfway around the world in Tokyo. "Everything's on track. Just finished a planning meeting, actually. Lots of exciting things coming together. Grandma's going to be able to watch at least some of it from there."

"She would love that," Sato said, closer to the phone now.

"Speaking of Grandma, how's the birthday celebration?"

"She's having the time of her life," Dad said. "She sends her love."

"Tell her I love her right back, and happy birthday again."

We chatted for a few more minutes, and they mentioned they were looking forward to being home before the festival began. Right after we disconnected, Dad sent me a picture from earlier in the evening showing Sato's mom surrounded by friends and family, beaming with joy.

The moment with my dads and seeing the terrific family photo provided a needed reset for my mood so that I could get on with the rest of the day.

THREE

ETHAN

The walk toward Town Hall was a perfect transition after going over hockey camp details with Liam, my best friend since forever. We'd met the first day of kindergarten, bonded over hockey trading cards, and become instant best friends. Luckily, we survived a misguided attempt at dating in high school, and we kept our strong friendship. We'd co-founded the camp five years ago, and he was also Maplewood's youth hockey coach.

Maplewood buzzed with pre-festival energy as a team of people moved along the sidewalk using a bucket lift to hang Pride banners from the lampposts. Many of the storefronts featured vibrant rainbow displays at various stages of completion.

My hometown was always a comfortable place to be, which I needed since a persistent anxiety picked away at me. The grand marshal role was an honor, but thinking about working with Andre and the events of the festival set off a fresh wave of dread that I did my best to keep in check.

I waved and smiled at several familiar people as I walked, invigorated by the small-town camaraderie. Living in a town where everyone knew everyone was something I never tired of, and that connection eased the nerves that crept in as the festival approached. No matter how many visitors came to Maplewood for the celebration, I represented this community, and they would take care of me. That sense of belonging felt like armor, offering the same protection I found on the ice as part of a team.

"Coach Ethan," called someone from behind me.

I turned to find Tommy Harrington and Mimi Abbott running in my direction. They had attended camp since we started and were always part of the first session.

"Hey! How've you been?"

"Great," Tommy said. "I had a personal best for goals this season."

I offered him a fist bump. "Well done. Sounds like the work with Liam paid off. How about you?" I looked at Mimi.

"I got a hockey scholarship to Ohio State." Mimi bounced, unable to contain her excitement.

"Oh my God, Mimi! I'm so proud of you. Can I give you a hug?" Even though I was pretty sure she'd say yes, it was important to ask.

She nodded, smiling as she stepped in, and we embraced briefly.

"That's amazing. Congratulations."

"Thanks, Coach. I still can't believe it."

"Listen, I need to get to a meeting for the festival but looking forward to being on the ice with you for a couple of weeks."

"Is there any help you or Coach Liam need for setup or check-in tomorrow?" Tommy asked.

I loved the campers so much, always asking questions like this. "Everything is set, so just come ready to play. But if anything comes up, one of us will shoot you a text."

"Cool. See you in the morning," Tommy said.

"Have a good night, Coach Ethan," Mimi added. "Or should I say Grand Marshal Ethan?"

I shook my head but smiled. I doubted I'd get used to that title. "Coach Ethan is fine."

At Town Hall, I paused, doing some breathing exercises to help me stay centered. I could do this.

Before I got inside, another voice—one I knew well —called out. "Gallagher! How's my favorite nemesis?"

I turned to find Dixon Cliff, my friend and rival from New York, striding toward me with a grin. Beside him was a shorter man with a lithe physique and a calm smile.

"Dix, hey!" We clasped hands and pulled each other into a hug. "Glad you made it in okay."

"You were right. This town is gorgeous. I'm glad to spend a couple of weeks here." He gestured to his companion. "This is my boyfriend, Oscar Salazar. Oscar, meet the infamous Ethan Gallagher."

Oscar's handshake was firm. "Nice to finally meet you. I've heard a lot about you from this guy."

I chuckled. "I can only imagine. Most of it was good, I hope."

"Mostly," Oscar teased, nudging Dix playfully.

Dix rolled his eyes. "We're headed to the theater so he can check in. What are you up to?"

"I've got a meeting about the festival. Catch up with you after?"

"Love to. Once Oscar's done, we're just chilling."

"I'll text you and we can meet up for dinner. I'll check if Liam's free too. We're so glad you're here. The kids are going to love learning from you."

Dixon smiled. "I'm looking forward to it."

Oscar put his arm around his boyfriend.

We said our goodbyes, and I finally went inside. As I entered the main auditorium, the excited chatter of townspeople surrounded me. Among the voices, I picked out Andre's, his tone clipped with frustration.

"... still no sign of him. I swear, if he's not taking this seriously..."

I paused, wondering again why I'd accepted. Andre's words stung, making me feel sixteen again.

He stood near the front of the room, deep in conversation with Olivia. He was scowling, tension evident in the set of his shoulders. I approached, clearing my throat when I was close enough to be heard.

Andre's head snapped up, surprise flickering across his face before it settled into a neutral expression. "Ethan. Glad you could make it."

The words were polite, but the undercurrent of annoyance came through loud and clear.

"Andre." I nodded at him, and then approached Olivia with a hug. "Olivia, good to see you. How are you? How are Hayworth and Felix?"

"I'm fabulous. You know I love this time of year. It's great to have you back home." She released the hug. "And Hayworth and Felix are better than I could've ever hoped."

"That's terrific." I was happy that Olivia's son had finally found someone after years of saying love wasn't real. "I look forward to catching up with them."

"They'll be at the festival, so I'm sure you'll run into them at some point."

I turned to meet Andre's steely gaze. "Can we talk for a minute? In private?"

He hesitated, then nodded.

"Sorry to steal him away," I said to Olivia.

"No problem. You guys should talk." She gave Andre a pointed look.

Andre and I moved to a quiet corner, hopefully away from curious ears. We didn't need to become fodder for the *Maplewood Matters* town gossip machine.

"Look," I began, keeping my voice low, "I overheard what you said. If you don't think I'm right for this, I can step back."

Andre's eyes widened slightly, then narrowed. "You can't just back out now. Do you have any idea how much work has gone into the planning? How much you're a part of it?"

I ran a hand through my hair, frustrated. I had no idea on either count. It didn't help my anxiety, knowing that it was a lot. "I can imagine, and I'm not trying to disrupt the plan. But I also don't want to cause you or anyone else stress."

"It's not about me," Andre said, his voice tight. "It's about what's best for the festival and Maplewood."

Trying to find the right words, I took a deep breath. "I know grand marshal is an honor. I do. And I want to do right by Maplewood. But this... being in the spotlight like this... It's not easy for me."

Something in Andre's expression softened, even if his voice stayed tense. "You're the center of attention all the time. You have been for years."

I shook my head. "It's not the same. Not even close. This?" I gestured behind me to the still gathering crowd. "I'm way out of my comfort zone."

He was quiet for a moment, then sighed. "Look, we're both here for the same reason—to make this festival a success. Can we agree to work together? Put aside our... history?"

None of my tension subsided, but I nodded. If we put that behind us, it would ease some of the stress. "Yeah," I mumbled and then found my confidence. "Yeah, we can do that."

"Great. Let's talk after the meeting. I'll take you through everything."

"Sounds good." I'd have to delay meeting up with Dixon and Oscar, but I'd find out what I was in for over the next week.

As Andre returned to Olivia, I spotted Liam across the room and headed over to him.

"Glad to see you here," I said as we fist-bumped. "I'm not sure what I've gotten myself into."

"It'll be fine. You already know I'm happy to help if you need it."

I could always count on Liam to put me at ease. Just the way he'd said that calmed me.

"So, I ran into Dix and his boyfriend on the way here. We decided to meet up for dinner. Love to have you join us if you're free."

"That'd be great."

"Cool. I'll let him know."

Andre called the meeting to order. I started to follow Liam to the seats in the back when Andre waved me up to the front. I hesitated, but I'd said we'd work together and I'd meant it. Setting aside my doubts, I took the seat Andre had indicated.

I listened as he laid out the festival schedule, my eyes widening as I heard the extent of my duties. Judging competitions, the parade... the list seemed endless.

"And now," Andre said, his voice carrying across the room, "I'd like to introduce our grand marshal and winner of this year's Lady Byng Memorial Trophy for his outstanding sportsmanship and skill as a member of the Seattle Riptide, Ethan Gallagher."

I stood, feeling the warmth of a blush creeping up my neck as applause and cheers filled the room. Looking out at the friends and neighbors I'd known my whole life, a mix of pride and apprehension settled in my chest. I smiled and waved at them. Thankfully, I didn't have to say anything.

As the meeting continued, I kept zoning out, the magnitude of what I'd agreed to sinking in. This was the biggest Pride festival Maplewood had ever staged, and I seemed to be at the center of a lot of it.

I discreetly ran through my calming routine. I closed my eyes and focused on my breathing.

In for four counts, hold for four, out for four.

I flexed and relaxed my hands, then my shoulders, grounding myself in the present moment. These subtle exercises brought me a little calm.

Andre wrapped up the meeting, promising to keep everyone updated on the events through the Maplewood Pride website and with volunteer needs and other logistics on the Maplewood Pride social media channels. How was he able to sound so confident about all of this?

As people departed, Mrs. Goddard, one of my favorite English teachers, came over. "Ethan! It's wonderful to see you back."

I smiled genuinely. "Thank you. How have you been?"

"Oh, just fine. Excited about the authors coming in for the festival. Andre put together a fantastic lineup. And of course thrilled to see you get the grand marshal title. You deserve it."

"Thank you."

"I read on *Maplewood Matters* that you bought the Montgomery place. That's exciting."

"News travels as fast as ever I see." I smiled as she nodded. "I'm looking forward to settling in there."

"Mrs. Goddard, do you mind if I steal him away?" Andre's voice sounded warm, a tone he never used with me.

"Of course. I'm sure you two have a lot to get organized. Have a good night."

"'Night, Mrs. Goddard."

"I've got everything up there at the table"—he gestured to where he'd been speaking before—"if you want to just go over things here."

"Sure."

Liam approached me as Andre went to the table. "Hey, man, when do you want to meet up?"

"I need to take care of some things here. Would you mind texting Dix and letting him know to meet up at Red's? I can join you all when I'm done."

"You got it." Liam and I traded fist bumps and he headed out.

As I approached Andre, he looked at me with his warm light brown eyes that drew me in. The hardness from earlier was gone. Instead, he had a confidence about him. It struck me how handsome he was too. With his smooth head, dark brown skin, appealing lips, and those eyes, he'd become quite attractive.

I didn't know what to do with those thoughts or why I was having them at this inconvenient time.

FOUR

ANDRE

As Ethan talked with Liam, I settled into a chair at the front table and pulled out my tablet along with one of the printed schedules. Meanwhile, my mind was a whirlwind of thoughts. The meeting had gone well, and the town was buzzing with excitement.

Ethan, though. His unease was palpable.

I doubted anyone seated behind him noticed, but I'd clocked at least one relaxation exercise. His words from earlier echoed in my head.

Being in the spotlight like this... It's not easy for me.

We had so much riding on this festival, and he was such a crucial part. If it would cause so much stress, why had he said yes? He'd never hesitated to say no before.

As he made his way toward me, he rolled his shoulders and flexed his hands. Another relaxation exercise perhaps.

I'd make this as simple as I could, and hopefully he'd

tell me what he needed. We'd agreed to work together, and I was committed to that.

"Ready to dive in?" I asked as Ethan took the seat across from me.

He nodded, a tight smile on his face. "As ready as I'll ever be."

"I get your concerns," I said, hoping to put him at ease. "This year's festival is twice as long as before—four days instead of two. It seems daunting to me at times, and I've been planning these for a few years now. Whatever you need to feel comfortable, please let me know."

He nodded, though I wasn't sure I'd provided him with any sense of calm.

I handed him a festival schedule. Unfortunately, I didn't have a mock-up of Olivia's gorgeous program that would let him see how much care we were putting into the weekend. I gave him a moment to read it over, noticing that he ran his finger under each line of text, some lines more slowly than others.

"Do you mind if I record our talk so I've got good notes?" He pulled his phone from his pocket and held it up.

"No, of course not." Once he set the phone between us, I continued. "Let's start with the opening ceremony. You'll give a brief speech and take part in the usual tree planting."

Ethan's eyes widened. "Speech?"

"Just a few words to kick things off. We added that last year as a way for everyone to hear from the grand marshal."

He nodded. "Ah. That's what I get for missing the opening last year. I didn't know that was a thing."

"We can work on it together if you'd like."

He nodded, relief evident in his expression. "I might take you up on that. Thanks."

As we went through the schedule, Ethan's anxiety seemed to fluctuate. The fingers on his left hand lightly tapped an irregular rhythm on the table. It was oddly endearing.

The way he looked at me as he listened to the event details, on the other hand, was a little distracting. A small crease kept forming between his eyebrows, and I inexplicably wanted to smooth it away.

I mentally shook myself. Why was I noticing these things?

This was Ethan Gallagher, the guy who'd infuriated me in high school because he didn't want to take part in anything that wasn't hockey.

And yet I couldn't deny the flutter in my chest as his blue eyes reflected a vulnerability I hadn't expected. There were also the freckles sprinkled across his nose, and how the stood out against his pale skin.

"On Saturday you've got a couple of things. Before the hockey game, you'll help judge the crafts competition. You've seen that before, right? The Pride-themed things that people create?"

Ethan's tapping intensified. "Yeah. I've seen that before. But what am I judging on? I'm not sure I'm qualified to judge anything."

"Creativity, originality, use of a maple element, and

relevance to the Pride theme. Don't worry, you're always one of three judges and there's specific instruction on the categories. If it helps, I can email you the rubrics tomorrow." I paused, studying him. "Are you okay?"

He closed his eyes and took a deep breath. "Yeah, I'm fine. It's just... more than I expected. Getting the criteria tomorrow would be great so I can study."

"Will do." I made a note in my digital notebook. "And I don't think you're going to have to study. Plus the judging forms will have the criteria listed too."

Ethan fidgeted with the schedule papers I'd given him. "Any chance you can send the forms too? It'll help to be familiar with them since this is my first time."

"We should have those ready by Tuesday, and then I can get them to you." I made another note. "Is that okay?"

"I appreciate that."

I hesitated but decided to ask the question that was nagging at me. "Is this stress why you never participated in events back in high school? Other athletes did events all the time, especially captains. But you avoided them."

Ethan's posture stiffened. He took his hands off the table and crossed his arms over his chest. "I was busy. Balancing studying and hockey took up a lot of time."

His response seemed evasive, and I couldn't let it go. It was practically the same response I got back then. "But surely you could have made time in the offseason? It seemed... out of character for someone in your position. I mean..."

Ethan's eyes flashed with—anger? Hurt?

"Look, Andre, I get that you're trying to understand." His voice was tight with frustration and weariness. "I don't need to be bullied all over again about the choices I made in school. I'm here now, aren't I?"

His words hit hard, and I almost put my hands up in defense.

Bully him? Was that how he saw our interactions? I hadn't realized. Bullying was the last thing I'd ever want to do. I took a deep breath, tamping down my confusion and hurt, not to mention some anger at the accusation.

"Ethan, I'm sorry." My voice cracked, a well of emotion bubbling up from my chest. "That was never my intention. I didn't know that's how I came across. I can't apologize enough for causing you that pain."

So many questions swirled in my head, but I kept them to myself. It was a struggle since a part of me wanted to know how he could think such a thing. But, the important thing was to get through the next few days.

It was a relief that he'd resumed tapping the tabletop.

"I really want us to work well together for the festival. Let's focus on that, okay?"

Ethan left me hanging for what felt like an eternity before he finally nodded. "Okay."

We continued going through the schedule that wrapped up on Sunday with him leading the parade and hosting the closing concert. I made a conscious effort to be more supportive. There was nothing I could do to remove events from his schedule, though. He'd already been announced for them, which had sponsors and participants excited.

"Thank you for doing all of this. I realize now we should've communicated more since the festival expanded this year. The committee will do better in the future."

"It's all good for the community." He sounded more relaxed than he had at any other time since we'd started talking. "The events are good, as always. And the new ones sound fun, especially the art walk."

"The last thing you should know, even though it's not finalized yet, is we're hoping to stream many of the events. That'll allow anyone who can't be here to be connected virtually. As that comes together, I'll make sure you get details."

"That's a terrific idea. If there's anything I can do to support that, let me know."

Ethan's offer confused me. The stream would only add to the people watching him. "I appreciate that. I'll keep you posted."

I puzzled over his response. It seemed a one-eighty from his reluctance to be in the spotlight. Why would he support potentially more public attention? Was it genuine interest or perhaps an attempt to smooth over the earlier tension?

"Anything else we should discuss?" Ethan asked.

"That's it for now." I snapped the stylus in place on my tablet and closed its cover. "How about we meet up on Tuesday to go over all the judging stuff. I'll email you what I already have, but we can sit and discuss it all then."

"Let me know a good time and I'll work it out with the camp schedule." Ethan thumbed off his phone and pocketed it.

"So, I heard you bought the Montgomery place. Any big plans for it?" I dropped the question before I could second-guess asking it.

Ethan's face lit up. "Nothing big. I'm planning to keep it pretty much as is. I have so many memories of spending time there as a kid that when I heard it was going up for sale, I jumped at the chance for it."

Hearing it from Ethan brought a finality to the dream I'd had, even more than getting the news from Nicolas. Tension coiled in my chest as he made it seem so easy to buy something that big.

Ethan caught whatever disappointment I was showing. "What's wrong?"

"I... I had hoped to buy that property. It'd be the perfect place to develop a summer camp for queer youth."

"Oh." Ethan sounded remorseful. "I had no idea."

"No, of course you didn't." Bitterness flowed through my voice as I couldn't hold back my feelings. "Must be nice to be able to swoop in with your hockey money and grab up whatever you want."

My disappointment over the property was raw, but it wasn't just about that. Years of unresolved feelings from high school rushed back, not to mention his comment about feeling bullied that had caught me off guard. All of it fueled my outburst.

"That's not fair." Ethan's voice was low and angry as he stood up, shoving the chair back hard enough that I thought it might flip over.

"Isn't it?" I shot back as I stood too. "You're a pro hockey player. You've got wealth and opportunity. It's easy for you to do anything. After all, you did that a few years ago, buying the theater for your moms."

Ethan recoiled. The hurt in his eyes was unmistakable and sent a pang of guilt through me. Buying the theater like he'd done was a good thing for the town. It was also an example of how he can just do things.

Sometimes I didn't know when to shut myself up.

Mixed with that guilt was a confusing swirl of other emotions—resentment but also an undeniable attraction. Even angry, Ethan was maddeningly handsome, especially with how a lock of hair had dropped across his forehead.

"I'm sorry the success I've worked for offends you so much." Ethan ran a hand through his hair, which caused more to fall toward his eyes. "And I'm sorry if I've disrupted your plans." He grabbed the chair and shoved it against the table. "I'm going to go before one of us says anything else. Just... reach out if there's something you need for the festival."

As I watched Ethan go, a battle waged within me. Lingering frustration and regret over my harsh words swirled within me. Underneath it all sat a spark of attraction that I couldn't shake or explain.

I dropped back into my chair, resting my face in my hands. Things had gone so wrong so quickly. We'd started the evening with a tentative truce, and now I wasn't sure where we stood.

FIVE
ETHAN

The familiar scent of freshly cut ice greeted me as I stepped into the rink. The atmosphere always transported me back to good times. I smiled, taking it all in, a mix of nostalgia and excitement for the beginning of camp. This was also a safe place, free of all the responsibilities I'd taken on with the Pride festival.

I made my way toward the registration area, two cups of coffee from Special Blend in hand. Liam had sung the cafe's praises since Caspian Lane had reopened it in January. He swore by the coffee, which I'd already found to be some of the best in town.

The coffee's warmth seeped through the cardboard sleeve, a contrast to the cool air. Liam sat at the registration table organizing welcome packets.

"Morning!" I read the side of the cup, checking for the *3* before holding out one of the cups. "I come bearing fuel."

Liam's face lit up as he saw me approach. "Yes!" he said, reaching for the cup. "Perfect timing."

"One triple pump maple latte." I handed it over. "Just the way you like it, even if it might put you in a sugar coma later."

Liam took a long sip, fluttering his eyelashes in satisfaction. "Worth it." He raised the cup.

"I don't know how you drink that. On the way in, I accidentally had a sip and I swear my eyes almost bugged out."

"Lightweight." He chuckled and made a show of taking another large drink.

We fell into a well-rehearsed rhythm, finalizing everything for the campers who would arrive in the next few minutes.

"How are you doing? You didn't say much after dinner, and I didn't want to push."

I sighed, shaking my head. "I thought through a lot of things last night, about the festival and Andre too."

Liam nodded, encouraging me to continue. He'd let me say as much or as little as I wanted to.

"There's a speech. I wasn't expecting that." Like with my moms, I didn't have to hide anything from Liam. "It's just a few words, but the idea of standing up there in front of the town and visitors..." Not even being at the rink could hold back the anxiety that tightened in my chest like a vise.

Liam nodded and squeezed my shoulder. He knew my struggles with reading and the stress that had followed me into adulthood.

"I'm happy to practice with you so it's memorized."

He'd helped a lot back in school, as had my moms and other friends. "Thanks, man. There's other stuff I may need help with too."

"I'm sure I speak for all your friends when I say that we're here to help. How much are you doing anyway?"

I gave him the full rundown.

"Wow. I didn't realize what the bigger festival meant for you."

"Yeah, it's pretty amazing. If I wasn't in it, it'd be great to attend." I took a sip of coffee.

"You mentioned Andre too."

"Oh, man." I shook my head. "We almost found some peace, but then he laid into me about buying the Montgomery place."

Liam's eyes widened. "Really? Why would that matter?"

"He wanted to turn it into a queer youth camp, which is amazing. But I couldn't even discuss that because he went off about how easy it is for me to get whatever I want with my *hockey money*." I put up air quotes to make it clear he called it that.

Liam let out a low whistle. "Damn. That's rough."

I shrugged, trying to shake off the lingering frustration. "It's fine. I mean, it's not fine, but... I don't know. One thing at a time."

"Have you considered telling him about what you were juggling in school? It's not his business, but it might help clear the air."

I hesitated, considering Liam's suggestion. I'd already

said more to Andre than I'd intended. These days I navigated reading with the help of technology, but it didn't reduce the flashbacks of how it had been in school when studying was difficult and talking in front of the class was nightmarish.

"I'll think about it."

As if the universe knew I needed a subject change, the doors to the rink opened and the first campers arrived. The energy shifted with excited chatter and the clatter of hockey gear being lugged in.

Liam and I seamlessly transitioned into greeting campers and parents, checking registrations, giving out packets, and directing everyone to the locker rooms. My mood improved as I welcomed returning players and introduced myself to first-timers.

Dix arrived as registration continued, his presence causing a stir among the campers who recognized him. He made his way over to us, looking around the busy lobby with a huge smile on his face.

"Morning, coaches." He was dressed in the coaching outfit we'd provided—jacket, insulated shirt, and pants all emblazoned with a rainbow puck that featured the words Maplewood Hockey Camp. "Anything I can do to help?"

I glanced at Liam, who shrugged. "If you want to mingle with the campers, introduce yourself, that'd be great. You can also hit the ice whenever you want."

Dix nodded, already scanning the crowd. "You got it." He immediately started talking to some of the campers who were nearby.

Two familiar faces approached.

"Mimi! Tommy! Good morning."

Mimi beamed, her excitement on display. "Coach Ethan! Coach Liam! Can't wait to get started."

Tommy nodded in agreement. "Is the ice open?"

"Of course." I was sure Mimi and Tommy would live on the ice if they could. "You can go out anytime you're ready."

"Awesome," Tommy said.

I handed over their information packets. "See you out there."

They headed back to the locker rooms, stopping to chat along the way. Watching these kids grow and improve year after year was one of the best parts of running the camp.

A new camper stepped up, dragging his gear bag behind him and holding two sticks along with his phone. He appeared to be about sixteen, and his eyes darted all over, taking in the scene.

"Good morning," I said as he leaned the sticks against the edge of the table, taking a moment to make sure they weren't going to fall. "I'm Coach Ethan. Let's get you checked in."

The young man smiled. "Good morning." He tapped his phone before he continued. "Hi, I'm Milo Joss." He paused again, seeming nervous. "I'm deaf and my hearing aids are off right now because of the rink noise. I signed up last night because I found out Dixon Cliff is here. I know it's last minute and you probably weren't expecting a deaf player, but I'd love to do this. I play for my high school in Montpelier, and my coach there could talk to you about how we make it work." He held the phone so I could see the screen for a moment. "I'm not sure these captions are going to work well with the noise, but we can try. I can read lips too." He looked hopeful.

I held up a finger. "One moment."

I pulled up my messaging app and spoke. "Hi, Milo. Great to meet you. I'm Coach Ethan. It's great to have you here. To talk right now, we can text, go somewhere quieter so you can use your hearing aids, or I can sign. What works best for you so you don't have to rely on lip reading?"

I handed my phone to Milo, and his face lit up as he read. He returned the phone to me and quickly signed back, his movements fluid and expressive. "You can sign?" He looked pleasantly surprised as he also spoke the words.

I nodded, my hands moving to form the words as I spoke aloud. "I learned in college. One of my roommates was deaf and he preferred signing."

Milo's smile widened. "That's awesome. I usually sign if I can, even when my hearing aids are on. Is it okay if we talk like this for now?"

"Absolutely." I continued to reply in sign and speak just as he was. "Tell me more about your last-minute decision."

Milo's hands moved expressively as he explained. "My coach mentioned yesterday that Mr. Cliff was going to be here. I'm a fan and I'd love to learn from him. Luckily, my parents said yes. But I know you might not be able to fit me in."

Liam handed me Milo's packet and the form with his details. "I apologize. I printed the form off this morning without reading it."

"Just a second," I signed to Milo. He nodded.

"There is a note here in the 'what can we do to make this camp the best it can be for you' field." Liam pointed to that part of the page. "It says that Milo's deaf and that he hoped it'd be okay to be here. His coach's number is here too."

"We can make this work," I said to Liam. "We can talk to his coach this afternoon."

"For sure." He didn't hesitate.

I returned my attention to Milo. "We're happy to have you and we're sure this can be a great experience for you. Can you tell me a bit about how you usually communicate during practices and games?"

Milo's hands flew as he explained his usual setup— hearing aids during quieter off-ice moments, lip-reading, and a combination of hand signals and visual cues during play. "For on-ice coaching and other times where there's a lot of talking, I use my phone for real-time captions. If a coach can have it in their pocket and hand it to me during discussions, I'll be set."

I nodded, already thinking about how we could adapt our coaching style to fully include Milo. "We can do that," I signed. "We'll make sure to face you when we're speaking too, and you can teach us some of the signals you use. Is there anything else you need from us?"

Milo hesitated for a moment. "I just hope I can keep up. I've never been to a camp like this before."

The vulnerability tugged at my heart. I was familiar with that kind of worry.

"I have no doubt you'll be successful. Your coach wouldn't send you here if he didn't think you could excel." I looked around and found Tommy heading for the ice. "Hey, Tommy!"

He looked my way and I waved him over.

"What's up, Coach Ethan?"

"Tommy, this is Milo," I spoke and signed. He nodded at Milo. "Milo's joining us for the first time. He's deaf and often uses hearing aids, but it's too noisy in here to have them on. He also reads lips and sometimes uses his phone for captions. Can you please show him where the locker rooms are and make sure he gets settled?"

"Nice to meet you, Tommy," Milo said and signed to Tommy.

"You too, man." Tommy faced Milo as he spoke. "Come on, I'll show you so you can get changed and then you can come warm up with us."

"Cool." Milo turned back to me. "Thanks, Coach Ethan."

Tommy and Milo sped across the lobby to the locker rooms. Once they disappeared from view, a man in his early forties approached the registration table, his expression warm and grateful.

"Hi there, I'm Adam Joss, Milo's father." He extended his hand to each of us in turn. "Thank you so much for making this smooth for him. He insisted on doing check-in on his own, but I wanted to introduce myself."

"We're happy to have him." I smiled. "And I think Dix is going to be thrilled to have someone who's such a big fan too."

"He's always breaking down his plays. There was no way we could say no to him coming here." Adam leaned slightly on the table. "I noticed there's a billeting program, but it's closed for this session. Is there any chance there might be something available? He's done summer camps the past two years with billet families, and it's always been good. If not, we'll make the drive each day, but I figured it couldn't hurt to ask."

Liam glanced at me before addressing Adam. "We might be able to work something out, but we'd need a day or so to see what's possible."

"That would be fantastic." Adam pulled out his business card and handed it to Liam. "Whatever you can do, we'd appreciate it. I'll be back this afternoon to pick him up, but please call if you need anything."

"Will do, Mr. Joss. Thanks for trusting us with him," I said.

"Please, call me Adam." He checked his watch. "I should get going. See you this afternoon!"

The lobby had emptied quickly as the top of the hour approached. Liam and I went into the rink and saw

Dixon passing the puck with some of the campers. Milo was stretching with Tommy, Mimi, and a couple of others.

Despite the stress of the festival, sharing the ice with these kids and coaching them would help keep me grounded for the week.

SIX

ANDRE

The quiet peace of the library was a stark contrast to the chaos in my office. Stacks of papers, brochures, and sticky notes covered every available surface. My desk, usually neatly organized, looked like a rainbow tornado had hit it. I sighed as I surveyed the mess.

My gaze drifted to the schedule I'd reviewed with Ethan last night. The memory of our conversation sent a sharp pang through my chest. I'd spent half the night tossing and turning, my mind stubbornly replaying every moment in an endless loop. How had I allowed those awful words to escape my mouth?

What gnawed at me most was his accusation that I'd bullied him. I'd always prided myself on being the organized planner who brought students together for events they wanted. The thought that I might have caused anyone pain made my stomach churn.

Setting aside the guilt, I attempted to focus on the mountain of festival tasks before my shift at the circulation desk. As I opened my laptop, I steeled myself for the inevitable flood of emails. As I scrolled through my inbox, one subject line made my heart plummet—Urgent: Author Cancellation.

The message came from the publicist for one of Friday's featured authors. A family emergency had forced her to withdraw. While the publicist promised to seek a replacement, she couldn't guarantee success on such short notice.

I understood completely, but it was one more fire demanding attention.

In my tablet's notebook, I added *Find new author panelist* to the expanding to-do list, right under *Meet with security* and *Get the list of featured artists for the theater performances*.

A knock at my office door interrupted my spiral of worry. I glanced up to see Wade practically vibrating with excitement.

"Hey, boss!" Their enthusiasm radiated like sunshine. "I've got excellent news about the live streaming project."

I gestured them inside and managed a smile, silently praying this wouldn't add to my workload. "What's up?"

Wade dropped into one of the chairs across from my desk. "My friends are ready to run the streaming for the event. We've got six people confirmed and possibly two more joining. Whether it's six or eight, we can provide fantastic coverage. The team's buzzing with ideas to make it awesome for both the festival and their portfolios."

"Excellent work pulling that together so quickly."

Wade's enthusiasm dimmed. "There's just one tiny hiccup. They can manage transportation, but accommodation is tricky with all the hotels booked solid."

Of course, there had to be a catch.

"Right. I'll see what I can do." I kept my voice steady, not wanting Wade to sense my mounting stress. "Perhaps we could reach out to locals with spare rooms? We could offer festival perks in exchange."

Wade nodded eagerly. "I'll compile a list of potential hosts. Olivia and I can work with some other volunteers to brainstorm options."

"Perfect. I appreciate you taking that on." Relief washed over me at their initiative. "Could you send me details about any equipment the team needs? I want to ensure we're prepared."

"No worries there. They've got their own gear or they're borrowing from school. Plus Maplewood's wireless network is solid." Wade bounced to their feet.

"You might have just saved my morning."

"Happy to help. I'm off to find Olivia. See you at the security meeting this afternoon."

My stomach clenched at the reminder. I still needed to prepare for that. "Yes, see you there."

After Wade departed, I sank back in my chair and closed my eyes. The library's silence enveloped me, but my thoughts remained loud. Despite the tower of tasks awaiting my attention, my mind drifted back to Ethan.

That spark when our eyes met, the unexpected flutter in my chest.

It was ridiculous.

Ethan and I were opposites in so many ways, and he wasn't even my type. Yet something in the vulnerability he'd displayed, in his admission of anxiety, had made me truly see him.

Perhaps for the first time.

Had I been so blinded by my preconceptions of who I'd expected him to be?

Another knock at the door cut short that unsettling thought.

Before I could respond, Mickey peered inside.

"Hey. Thought you could use this." He extended a cup in my direction. "I come bearing hibiscus tea and updates about festival food."

"Just what I needed. Come in."

Mickey settled into the recently vacated chair, his eyes widening at the chaos spread across my desk. That subtle reaction was his only comment on the disorder.

"You'll be pleased to hear that I've organized the food vendors—which ones will have booths in the park and which ones will set up in front of their establishments."

"Wonderful. Can you forward that to Olivia for the program she's assembling?"

"Consider it done." His expression softened as he studied my face. "Everything alright? You've got that look you get when something's eating at you."

I hesitated, uncertain whether to confide in Mickey. Though he'd become a close friend since my return, his long-standing friendship with Ethan complicated things.

Yet that connection also made him the ideal person to ask.

"Mickey, do you..." My voice emerged barely above a whisper. "Do you think I was a bully in high school?"

His eyebrows shot up. "Where's this coming from?"

Running a hand over my head, I exhaled. "Something Ethan said. We argued, and he accused me of being a bully. Was I?"

Mickey leaned back, contemplating. "That's quite a loaded question. Can you give me some context?"

I explained the situation, omitting my worst behavior. With each word, tension crept further into my shoulders as the weight of everything settled over me.

Mickey remained silent for a moment.

I shouldn't have brought it up. Too awkward.

"Look, I wouldn't say you were a bully exactly. But you've always been... intense. Particularly about organizing events. You've definitely mellowed since high school." He paused, choosing his words carefully. "I can imagine that sometimes the intensity might have felt pushy or intimidating."

The knot in my stomach tightened. "So Ethan's right?"

Mickey shrugged. "I didn't say that. Perception is complex. What you saw as enthusiasm and rallying people, Ethan might have experienced differently."

"But I never intended to..."

Intent and impact—they weren't always aligned, were they?

"I know," Mickey said gently. "But perhaps this is an

opportunity to sit with Ethan and understand his perspective. You'll be working closely this week. A genuine conversation might prevent further misunderstandings."

Horror struck me as the memory of how harsh I'd been about his purchase of the Montgomery place flashed through my mind. "Oh God. What if he withdraws? The entire event could collapse!"

Mickey raised a calming hand. "Don't create problems that don't exist. Ethan won't back out. His commitment to Maplewood runs too deep to risk the festival's success."

"How can you be so certain?" The desperation in my voice was embarrassing.

Mickey leaned forward, expression serious. "Consider this: despite whatever happened in high school, Ethan said yes to being grand marshal even though he knew he'd be working with you. He also consistently supports community projects and returns every summer for the hockey camp."

I frowned, trying to recall specific instances of him backing the town beyond seeing him at summer events like Pride or setting his moms up with the theater. "Support?"

"Let's discuss the library for a moment. Who are your major donors?"

The abrupt topic shift caught me off guard. "We have many individual contributors, with the largest giving a couple thousand annually. Several local businesses, like yours, donate. The biggest is the Maplewood Foundation, which supports several organizations."

He raised an eyebrow expectantly. "Have you never wondered about the foundation?"

I shrugged. "It was already in place when I took over here. I submit the required annual report. I assumed it was established by the founding families as their way of giving back."

Mickey's lips curved into a knowing smile as he shook his head.

My mind raced, connecting the dots. "Ethan?"

He nodded. "He set it up during his first NHL season. You know he shies away from attention, so he didn't want his name plastered everywhere. But he's deeply committed to his hometown."

This revelation rattled me to my very core. The Maplewood Foundation appeared in virtually every local organization's donor list. Foundation funds comprised nearly half the library's annual budget. Without that support, the banned books initiative wouldn't exist.

And I'd thoughtlessly accused Ethan of selfishness.

Shame washed over me.

"I'm not sharing this to make you feel worse." Mickey reached across and squeezed my arm. "But you and Ethan need to have an honest conversation. Get to know who you both are now, not who you remember from high school."

I nodded, still processing. "I owe him so many apologies."

Mickey stood, stretching. "I should get back. But

Andre, don't let this fester. Talk to him. You might be surprised what else you discover."

After Mickey left, closing the door behind him, my thoughts churned. Clearly, he'd held back information—it wasn't his story to tell after all. I hoped sharing the Foundation information hadn't betrayed a confidence. I certainly wouldn't mention it to Ethan.

Opening a new email, I contemplated my words. After several false starts and deletions, I figured out what to send.

Hi Ethan.

Here are the judging details for your review. Please let me know if you have any questions. Also, if you can spare some time today, I'd like to apologize in person. My behavior last night was inexcusable, and you deserve better. I'll be at or near the library most of the day. If I'm not here, the staff can reach me and I can come right back. I hope we can talk to ensure the next week, and beyond, goes smoothly.

Thanks, Andre.

I clicked send and hoped he'd grant me another chance, even though I hadn't earned it.

SEVEN

ETHAN

I hadn't expected to see Andre today after the way things ended last night, but his email and a nudge from Liam found me at the library once camp wrapped up for the day.

Camp had put me in a great mood, so at least I was in a good frame of mind for the visit. The campers were psyched to be there, and it was a fun day for them and the coaches. I could already tell that the exhibition game featuring the campers and my friends would be outstanding.

Inside the library the scent of books took me back. It was as familiar as the smell of the rink. The library had changed little since I was a kid, other than adding several more computers and listening stations. It still had the cozy vibe I remembered. There was a new couch in the corner where I used to work on the exercises Mrs. Goddard recommended, but it looked just as comfy.

I approached the circulation desk where Clara, a woman with curly red hair and bright green glasses, typed away at a computer.

"Hi, Clara," I said, using my library voice. The last thing I wanted was to have to be shushed. "Is Andre around?"

Clara looked up, her eyes widening slightly in recognition. "Oh! Ethan, hello. Andre mentioned you might stop by." She glanced at her computer screen. "He's in a festival meeting right now but should be back soon. I'll text him so he knows you're here."

"Thanks." I smiled, appreciating how exuberant she was while also being quiet.

"You can have a seat anywhere or feel free to browse."

A colorful poster caught my eye as I turned away. I studied the text carefully and discovered it was about the library's banned book project with a photo of Andre speaking at what looked like a conference. Below the image was a call for community members to write letters of support for Andre's nomination for an award.

I'd heard something about the library being up for an award but hadn't had a moment to get the details.

"Sorry to interrupt." I paused for Clara to look up from her work at the computer. "Can you tell me more about the award Andre's up for?"

Her face lit up. "It's for the Library Association of America's Freedom to Read award. Andre organized our banned book project three years ago. The program's been incredibly successful and not just here in Maplewood. It even inspired similar programs across the country."

It wasn't a surprise that Andre started something like that. "That's amazing. What does the project involve?"

"It started as a simple display of frequently banned books that we already carried. It's grown so that we have every book that's landed on a banned book list in the U.S. Most of them are in our digital catalog since it's over four thousand titles. Andre expanded it into a series of events too. We have book clubs, author talks, and a writing workshop for teens and adults so they can explore themes from banned books in their own work." Clara's enthusiasm was contagious.

Incredible. I knew my contributions through the Maplewood Foundation funded banned book programs for the library, but I hadn't investigated the breadth of it.

The front door swung open and Andre rushed in. There was a hint of tension on his face, but he gave me a welcoming smile. That was something I didn't think I'd ever received from him before. It sent a flutter through my chest.

I didn't know what to do with these feelings about Andre.

"Ethan, hey." He was slightly out of breath. "Sorry to keep you waiting. The festival security meeting ran long."

"No worries," I said as he came over to the desk. "I was chatting with Clara about the banned book project. Congratulations on the award nomination."

"Thanks. It's been a labor of love for all of us."

I gave him a quizzical look. "Clara was telling me about the work you've put into it, and not just for Maplewood."

Andre looked at Clara with half exasperation, half amusement.

She grinned unrepentantly. "Just spreading the good word."

Andre shook his head, but he couldn't hide the fondness in his expression. He scrubbed his hand over his face.

"Anyway," he said, turning back to me. "Did you want to talk here, or…"

I glanced around the library. It didn't feel comfortable having what might be a personal conversation in such a public space.

"Actually, it's a beautiful day out. Want to grab a coffee and sit outside somewhere?"

Andre looked relieved. "That sounds perfect." He took his tablet out of his bag before handing it over to Clara to put behind the desk.

Special Blend was a short walk away. On the sidewalk, we fell into step beside each other, a comfortable silence between us.

As we walked, I snuck glances at Andre. He looked tired, with faint shadows under his eyes, but there was an energy about him that was undeniable. Even stressed, he had a certain charm and charisma.

I wondered what it would be like to really get to know him, beyond the superficial level we were used to.

At the cafe we joined the short line. When we reached the counter, Caspian took our order. Andre asked for his usual, hibiscus tea. I tried something different with the rainbow-spiced latte, a special for

Pride. Caspian also apologized for being out of Andre's favorite, maple pecan scones.

When I reached for my wallet, he waved me off. "This one's on me. Consider it part of my apology." Andre tapped his phone on the payment terminal.

I hesitated, not wanting to dwell on our argument, but Andre's expression was earnest. "Thanks."

We grabbed our drinks and found a small table outside. The warm breeze made it a perfect early summer afternoon.

"Thanks for sending over the judging details. I'll look those over tonight and let you know if I have any questions." I blew across the top of my drink to cool it down. "So, we didn't talk much about the overall festival planning. How's it going?"

Andre sucked in a breath. "Honestly, I think we might have expanded too far. It looks excellent on paper, but pulling it off is more than I expected. There's always something new popping up. But I do think we'll pull it off."

I nodded encouragingly. "That's good news. Anything major giving you trouble?"

Andre ran a hand across his face. "A couple of things came up this morning. Remember I told you about the streaming project?"

"Yeah."

"Well, we've got a team of college students who can do it, but we need a place to put them up. And an author for the book festival had to cancel."

I nodded, considering potential solutions. "I think I can help. After all, I've got two houses right now." I hoped bringing up my recent purchase wouldn't stir up trouble, but it could certainly help.

Andre's eyes widened. "Are you sure? That would be incredibly helpful."

"Of course. How many people are we talking about?"

Andre flipped digital pages. "Six for sure, possibly eight. But we don't want to impose…"

I waved off his concern. "You won't. I'm already planning to be living out at the Montgomery place within the next couple of days, which leaves one house unoccupied. There's space at the new house too if you need it. We can make it work"—I paused and shifted into a conspiratorial whisper—"as long as they're not planning to throw raging parties."

Relief washed over Andre's face. I hadn't expected to be so thrilled at being able to take care of that for him.

"That would be amazing. Thank you so much. And I'll make them promise no parties." He chuckled, picking up that I was only kidding.

"Glad to do it. Just have whoever is leading the team contact me for the keys." I shifted topics. "About the author cancellation, I might be able to help with that too. What are you looking for?"

Andre looked surprised but intrigued. I didn't think he expected me to be friends with an author. "We need someone who is queer and writing queer fiction or nonfiction. Name recognition would be great, but at this point we'd be grateful for anyone who can step in on short notice."

"How about Kendrick Sanderson?"

Andre's mouth dropped open. "Seriously? The author of the *Rainbow Rivers* series? We tried to get him, but we were told he wasn't doing events right now."

"I can make a call. His boyfriend is one of the players we haven't announced yet for Saturday's game. I don't know if Kendrick's coming with him, but I can find out and if he'd be into doing the event."

Andre put his hand over the top of mine, squeezed it, and then left it there. "He would be an incredible addition. I don't want to get my hopes up, but... wow."

He pulled his hand away suddenly, seemingly startled that he was still touching me.

The warmth of his hand was gentle and reassuring in a way I didn't expect, and I wished he'd kept it there longer.

"I'll make a call as soon as we're done and see what he says."

We sipped our drinks in companionable silence for a moment before Andre turned serious.

"Ethan, I want to apologize again for last night," he said, his voice low and sincere. "I was out of line, and I said so many things I regret. It was wrong to take my frustration out on you. I'm truly sorry."

I took a deep breath, a mix of emotions pinging around in my head. Part of me wanted to brush it off, to say it was all in the past. But this was a pivotal moment.

"I appreciate that," I said carefully. "I think we have

some misconceptions about each other, and I'd like to get those behind us."

Andre nodded, looking relieved. "If it's okay, I'd like to understand better so I don't make the same mistakes."

I hesitated, old insecurities rising up about discussing my reading problems, but Andre's expression was open and curious. I took another sip of my latte, gathering my thoughts.

"Calling it bullying might have been a poor choice of words. It was more..." I had to pause because I wanted this to come out right. "I always thought I was disappointing you. You were so passionate about events and causes, and I could never measure up to what you wanted."

Andre's forehead creased. I imagined he was replaying our past in his mind. "I suppose I wanted—expected—you to do the same that other athletes did. To attend events. Rally other students."

Looking into my coffee cup, I ran through my relaxation exercises since it was time to lay everything out for him. I looked up before I spoke. "School was a struggle. I have pretty severe dyslexia, making reading very difficult, so much of my energy went into studying to keep my grades up. And I needed good grades so I could stay on the hockey team."

"Ethan, I had no idea." His hand was back on mine and that sent goose bumps up my arm. "Why didn't you say anything?"

I shrugged, a familiar mix of embarrassment and

defensiveness trying to rise up. "I was self-conscious, so I kept it only to my family and close friends."

His voice wavered a bit as he responded. "I wish I'd known. I'd like to think I would've tried to help or at least been more understanding."

"It's okay," I said, surprised to find that I meant it. "We were kids. The experience taught me a lot about asking for help and offering help as much as I can. My moms were great through it all, and I had some very supportive teachers and friends."

"Still, I feel terrible that I added to the stress. You hid all that so well." He paused, his gaze shifting to the ceiling. "I always admired you. It seemed like you had everything together."

"You did?" I couldn't hide my surprise.

"You were this amazing athlete, popular, and always kind. If I'm honest, I wanted to be around you more. That's one of the reasons I kept asking you to work on projects and was so disappointed when you wouldn't."

Warmth spread through me, coming directly from where his hand touched mine. "I thought you saw me as a dumb jock who didn't care about anything important."

Andre looked down at the table and shook his head. "I can't say sorry enough." He looked back at me, his gorgeous brown eyes—when did I start thinking of his eyes that way?—appearing on the verge of tears. "Talk about misconceptions."

The weight I'd been carrying about working with Andre started to lift. "I'm glad we talked. Not just to get through the festival but to put all that firmly in the past."

Andre's smile widened. "The festival is going to be epic."

"And maybe after the festival madness, we could grab coffee again or dinner? Get to know each other in the present."

A slow smile spread across Andre's face, making my heart do a little flip. "I'd like that."

EIGHT
ANDRE

Arriving at Red's, I spotted Mickey, who was settled at the booth farthest from the door. He was sipping coffee, no doubt his maple blend, while reading on his phone.

The diner radiated its typical easygoing Sunday afternoon energy—that lull between brunch and dinner when people indulged in coffee and snacks. Despite our festival discussion, the vibe offered a respite from the whirlwind of preparations.

"Hey." I slid in across from Mickey. "Sorry I'm late. Got caught up with Grace about the theater's programming. She and Elena have put together something incredible."

Mickey waved off my apology. "No worries. Just sat down. Once I give you my update, perhaps you can relax and put the festival aside for a few minutes."

"You've met me, right?" I quirked my eyebrow comically high, wiggling it up and down until Mickey snorted with laughter. The moment of levity felt good. "I'm not sure I can go more than thirty seconds without festival thoughts." I leaned forward, lowering my voice. "Last night I dreamed the parade made a wrong turn and ended up going right out of town. I couldn't run fast enough to catch it."

Mickey shook his head. "Not sure if that's a sign you need reassurance or a year off after being in charge for three."

I grunted but kept smiling. "For now I'll settle for lunch. I'm starving."

Mickey caught Ingrid's eye, and she took our orders —a club sandwich and ginger ale for me, a burger and root beer for Mickey. As he ordered, my gaze drifted out the window. People strolled by, basking in the beautiful day. The kind that made you want to linger over lunch and forget responsibilities. I'd have more time for that in eight days.

"So, how are things with the food? Any last-minute hiccups?"

Mickey's eyes gleamed with confidence. "Everything's set, unless someone changes something up. Found out today that Special Blend is doing special maple bacon donuts, which will have rainbow colors. I got to sample one. It's next level." He looked for a moment like he was experiencing the flavor again. "They need to be on the regular menu."

My stomach growled in anticipation. "They sound yummy. I wish you'd brought me one?"

"Duly noted for next time. Bring Andre all of the next-level treats to sample." Mickey smirked at me as he continued scrolling through his phone notes. "And Mrs. Nguyen is debuting a maple-infused kimchi that's amazing. And we've got a food truck bringing in maple pulled pork sliders."

"Sounds like we'll need to hand out stretchy pants at the entrance." I was only half joking. Maplewood's festivals always tempted me to overindulge. Not only would there be amazing food for Pride, but just a week later there was the Fourth of July and so much amazing ice cream. "But seriously, great job."

"I'm proud that we've got so many options. You could eat something different every day of the festival. All the vendors are also on board for being at the picnic."

Our food arrived and we dug in, our conversation on pause as we savored our meal. My mind drifted from the festival to its other favorite topic: Ethan Gallagher.

Heat crept up my neck as I imagined his smile, his laugh...

"What?" I asked, catching Mickey studying me. "Do I have mayo on my face?" I grabbed my napkin, self-consciously wiping my mouth.

Mickey's brow furrowed. "No, nothing like that. You just seem... distracted. And I don't think it's the festival."

The flush deepened. Was I that transparent? "I'm just eating," I mumbled, taking another bite.

"Uh-huh." Mickey wasn't buying it. "This wouldn't have anything to do with a certain hockey player turned grand marshal, would it?"

"What? No, of course not." Even I didn't believe how that sounded.

Mickey's expression softened. "Andre, come on. I've known you both since high school. You two talked, didn't you?" Concern flashed in his eyes. "That didn't make things worse, did it?"

I set down my sandwich, shoulders sagging. "No. I mean, yes, we talked. But no, things didn't get worse. It's all so... complicated."

I wiped my mouth, trying to hide the smile that had formed. It was such a change that thinking about Ethan now triggered more smiles than frowns.

"What happened?"

With a deep breath, I tried to organize my thoughts. "We had this... moment. We talked—really talked—for the first time ever. And I realized how wrong I'd been about him all these years. This image I had of the perfect, popular athlete who got everything? So off base. I had no idea what life was like for him."

"Ethan shares a lot with close friends, but he's not one to bare his soul to everyone. It's not your fault you didn't see past the facade he put up back then."

"But I should have," I insisted. "I was so caught up in my own world that I didn't even bother to ask. Instead, I assumed things and missed out on knowing someone I actually admired."

"You can now, though, right?"

"Maybe. He said he wants to get together after the festival. But why would he want to get to know me after how crappy I made him feel?"

"Do I need to make a list? You're both amazing people. Why wouldn't you want to know each other?"

Mickey's eyes widened as he leaned across the table and lowered his voice. "Wait, is there more going on than a possible friendship?"

My heart raced and I shrugged. "The thought terrifies me."

"Why?" Mickey asked softly.

"Because it's Ethan." I paused, hoping that explained everything, but Mickey's expectant gaze forced me to continue. "We have all this terrible history. What if I'm reading too much into things and he doesn't feel the same way?"

Mickey was quiet for a moment. "Can I tell you something? Something only one other person knows?"

"Of course."

"Back in college, I had the biggest crush on this musician, Fred." Mickey's voice softened. "He was hot, charming, and smart. Watching him play piano was mesmerizing, the emotions crossing his face... We had a couple of classes together and I got to know him. But I never took the chance to ask him out. I told myself someone as creative as him wouldn't want a small-town boy like me."

"That's on my mind too. Why on earth would he want to be with a librarian from his hometown? What kind of heartbreak am I setting myself up for?"

"What if you're setting yourself up for the best thing ever? Ethan asked me that question when I told him about my crush, and it's something you should think about."

I sat back, mulling over Mickey's words. It seemed

simple, but it would be an enormous leap. "So you think I should tell Ethan how I feel?"

Mickey shrugged. "I'm not saying declare your undying love right now. But you should give yourself a chance to see what might happen."

The bell over the diner door chimed, and Olivia walked in. We traded smiles as she stopped at the counter to chat with Ingrid before coming over.

"Hey, you two. Mind if I join you for a minute while I wait for my order?"

"Of course not," I said. "We were just talking about the festival."

"Why am I not surprised?" Olivia grabbed a chair from one of the nearby tables. "A couple of artists arrived today to set up their larger installations. Oh, and did you guys catch the press conference about Ethan's charity hockey game?"

I shook my head. "I couldn't make it over there. How did it go?"

"It was great." Olivia pulled out her phone, showing me a photo. "I happened to be near the rink and stopped by. Ethan was there with Dixon Cliff, who's already in town. Ethan talked about how important events like the game and the festival are for bringing the community together, celebrating diversity, and raising money for a great cause. Alex was there, just like always, snapping pics for the town socials. TV and newspapers from out of town were there too."

Alex covered every town event and was incredibly fast getting posts up on the city's website and social media.

Between him and Wade the festival would be well covered.

"That's great there was out-of-town coverage," I said.

"Did you know how many players he's got coming in?" Olivia looked between us. We both shook our heads. "It's like ten. I might not have counted right, but it's a lot. Plus, they'll have autographed jerseys and other stuff in an auction. Tickets are almost sold out."

"I'd heard that," I said. "And that was just with Ethan and Dixon on the website. There was a mention of more guest players to be announced, but I hadn't expected so many."

"He's going to put the rest of us who organize festival events to shame." Mickey's tone was light.

"Right?" Olivia added.

Her order was called, and she hopped up. "I better get going. See you two later."

We nodded and said our goodbyes as she pushed her chair back in.

Mickey turned to me with a raised eyebrow. "So, back to Ethan."

Hope fluttered in my chest, quickly followed by anxiety. "I don't know. Even if he is into it... what if it all goes wrong?"

"It might work out or it won't," Mickey said, matter-of-factly. "But isn't it worth finding out? Don't even get me started on how long it's been since you had a date."

I groaned and shook my head.

"You can make that noise all you want but I stand by what I said about it being worth finding out."

I gazed out the window again, watching a couple stroll by hand in hand. My heart skipped a beat, imagining Ethan's fingers intertwined with mine.

Sighing, I gave in to the idea. "Maybe."

We finished lunch, chatting about the upcoming film screenings and what we hoped to see.

"Thanks for listening and for the advice," I said as we got up.

Mickey pulled me into a quick hug. "Anytime. Just promise me one thing?"

"What's that?"

"Don't hold back from exploring what might be. It's cliché but true that life's too short for what-ifs and maybes."

I nodded, determination swelling in my chest. "I'll try."

On the way back to the library, my mind raced. The festival was days away, bringing countless opportunities to be near Ethan. So many maybes ran through my mind.

There might be a spark there. Could I let myself be open to where it might lead?

If nothing else, perhaps we could actually become friends like we were with so many others in town. But deep down, I had to admit that a part of me hoped for more.

NINE

ETHAN

My living room looked like a box fort construction site. We were gathering what I needed to start living at my new place. Once the festival was over, I'd get everything else moved.

Liam and Mickey had come over after camp, with Tommy and Milo pitching in to speed up the packing.

"Hey, E," Liam called from the kitchen. "Which mugs besides the Bears one?"

I'd already set aside the Bears hockey mug, my constant companion since age ten. I'd played for the Cubs, and then the Bears, through school. I was so proud when I'd bought that mug with my own money at a team fundraiser. "Pack four extras for now. Actually, four of all the dishes can come with me. I want to leave some kitchen stuff for the streamers."

Mickey emerged from my bedroom, arms full of clothes. "For a guy who's not here much, you've got a lot of clothes in there."

"Should we check out *your* closet next?" I teased.

Laughter drew my attention to Tommy and Milo across the room. Tommy was talking and partially signing to Milo, who responded with an enthusiastic nod and grin. Tommy's family, no doubt with encouragement from their son, had become Milo's billet family and that had only added to their connection.

"Those two have become quite the duo," Liam said as he joined me.

"Yeah. One of the fastest friendships I've ever seen. Tommy's even learning sign, which is so cool."

"I wonder if there might be something more there." He'd lowered his voice so they wouldn't hear.

Tommy playfully bumped Milo's shoulder before they grabbed up boxes to take to the truck.

"Young love, perhaps?" Mickey dramatically clasped his hands over his heart as he joined us. "Remember when we were that age?"

I rolled my eyes. "And how terrifying declaring feelings was? Yes."

My current feelings for Andre illustrated that the terror hadn't faded with age. Asking him out seemed impossible. Why would he even want that?

My phone buzzed, a welcome distraction. Nick Lawson's name flashed on the screen. Nick played for Boston, and was coming in for Pride and the exhibition game.

"Hey, Nick." I moved to an empty room. "What's up?"

"Ethan! Shawn's here too."

"Oh, cool. Hey, Shawn."

"Hey, Ethan," said Shawn, who was Nick's boyfriend and wrote romances under the name Kendrick Sanderson. "Nick told me about the book event and I'm in. I was coming for the game and to check out Pride in a small town, so I'd be happy to help."

This was the news Andre needed. "That's fantastic! Thanks so much, Shawn. It'll mean a lot to the organizers, and I appreciate it too."

We worked out some details and after hanging up, I dictated a text to Andre.

Ethan: *Great news! Kendrick Sanderson is confirmed for Friday's book event.*

A grin spread across my face as I watched the three dots of Andre's response dance across the screen.

I headed back to the living room as my phone finally buzzed.

Andre: *That's amazing! Thank you so much. BTW, I saw a post about the game too. I'm sorry I wasn't at the press conference. You've gone above and beyond with all the players you've assembled.*

I basked in the praise. I hadn't expected how much I wanted to do something good for him.

Ethan: *Glad I could help arrange it. And thanks. I'm looking forward to the game. It's going to raise a lot of money for some worthwhile organizations.*

Andre: *Yes it is! If you need help with final prep for that, let me know, ok?*

Ethan: *Will do. Thanks. Talk to you later.*

"Earth to Ethan." Liam waved his hand in front of

my face. "You planning on finishing up here, or are you just going to grin at your phone?"

Heat rose in my cheeks. "Sorry, I was just texting Andre about the book event. Kendrick Sanderson's confirmed for Friday."

Liam cocked his head, his favorite smirk spread across his face. "Uh-huh. And that's why you're blushing?"

"I am not." My face grew warmer, betraying me.

Mickey came in with a box. "Who's blushing? What did I miss?"

"Nothing," I said quickly.

"Ethan's got a crush on Andre," Liam added.

I groaned, burying my face in my hands. "I do not have a crush."

Mickey set the box down. "So there's absolutely nothing going on between you two?"

I hesitated, remembering my coffee with Andre.

The warmth of his hand on mine.

The feeling when his brown eyes locked on me.

"Maybe there's something. It's just... nice, you know? Working together, talking. And he's... well, he's pretty handsome."

I couldn't believe I said all that—I sounded like a love-struck teenager.

Liam clapped me on the back. "It's about time. How long has it been since you dated anyone seriously?"

Self-consciousness kicked in. "You know exactly how long it's been. But come on, this is me and Andre. We need to see if we can get along for more than twenty-four hours."

"Sometimes the best relationships start with people at odds," Mickey said softly. I wondered if he'd already talked to Andre about this since they were friends too.

I nodded. "We should get through the festival first." I shifted the conversation. "By the way, I heard Andre wanted to start some kind of youth camp. Do you know anything about that?"

"He's been wanting to do a queer summer camp with sports and arts," Mickey said. "Weekend stuff in the spring and fall too. It's pretty ambitious. He's scouted potential locations for months, but it hasn't been easy. I think he even talked to Zeke about trying to use the festival grounds. It's been a while since he's brought it up, though."

"It's a terrific idea." I closed a box of clothes and put tape across it. "Something that would fit right in around here."

As we continued packing, the camp idea kept churning in my mind. I'd wrecked one of his possibilities for it. Could we team up and sort out a plan?

A knock interrupted my thoughts. Wade stood at the open front door, fidgeting with the strap of their messenger bag.

"Hi, Mr. Gallagher. I mean Ethan." They corrected themselves before I could. "Thank you again for letting us use your place. We won't mess up anything."

"I'm happy this worked out. And don't stress. I'm sure it's in excellent hands with you."

Wade relaxed, grinning.

I handed over a ring of keys. "There's nine keys, one

for you and each person on the team. I figure everyone will need to come and go at different times."

"That's perfect. I'm glad you thought of that. Some people will arrive tomorrow to set up and scout the event locations."

"Sounds good. I'll be out of here in a few minutes. If you need anything while your team's here, don't hesitate to ask. And if it turns out you need more room, we can make that work too."

Wade pocketed the keys. "I think we'll be fine, but I'll let you know. See you later. Hope the move goes well."

As Wade left, I looked around at the now box-free living room. Liam, Mickey, Tommy, and Milo came in. "I think that's everything."

"It is," Liam confirmed.

"Fantastic. Let's get going. The sooner we're unpacked, the sooner there can be pizza."

We caravanned over to the new place, with Mickey taking a quick detour to Red's.

I looked forward to my first morning coffee on the porch.

Liam, Tommy, Milo, and I unloaded the cars, stacking things in the appropriate rooms. I'd deal with unpacking later, getting out essentials as needed.

As Tommy and Milo set down the last of their boxes in the living room, they approached me.

"Is it okay if we go check out the pond?" Milo asked while also signing.

"Of course. Just don't fall in or anything." I spoke

and signed, always matching Milo's communication style even when he had his hearing aids on.

They thanked me and headed out. As they walked away, it looked like Milo was teaching Tommy how to sign *pond hockey*.

"Alright, this is the last of it." Liam came up the steps holding a box. "What do you say we order that pizza you promised?"

I pulled out my phone and checked the delivery app. "It's about five minutes away."

"Advanced ordering for the win," Mickey said as he came in with two drink holders with five cups. "I'll set these in the kitchen."

"Oooh, what'd you bring?" Liam asked, going over to inspect the cups.

"The only drink appropriate to christen Ethan's new home?"

I had a sharp intake of breath. "You didn't!"

"Of course I did. Twenty-sevens for everyone. And bourbon'd versions for the adults."

I'd only had one 27 since I'd been back, and it wasn't one with bourbon. I'd developed what became The 27 back in elementary school when I mixed peanut butter and maple syrup into vanilla ice cream. Mickey had tried it at my place one afternoon and loved it. He'd gotten his dad, Joe, to add a maple and peanut butter shake to Red's menu shortly after that.

Joe renamed the shake to The 27, my jersey number, after my first NHL season. It was just one of the things that made Red's my favorite diner.

It was Mickey who discovered the extra kick bourbon brought to the shake, so that had become an adult alternative. He'd declared its name to be The 27B, though that was not on Red's official menu.

"You're the best." I went to Mickey and carefully gave him a side hug to avoid jostling the shakes. "Thank you and thanks for helping out."

"Anytime."

We followed Mickey into the kitchen, and he set the drinks down. He handed us each a shake, the ones marked with a *B*.

We stepped out on the porch, dropped into the rocking chairs, and took in the view. The late afternoon sun cast a golden glow over the water. Tommy and Milo skipped stones at the edge, sometimes jostling each other to cause a bad throw. Their laughter drifted up to the house.

"Penny for your thoughts?" Liam asked after we'd sat quietly for a moment.

I gestured out at Tommy and Milo. "I wish I could start from square one with Andre like those two are with a new friendship."

The pizza delivery car came into view, putting a swift end to that discussion.

"Hey, guys," I called out toward the pond. Tommy turned. "Pizza's here."

As they came up to the house, the driver brought up the four pies. The aroma of sauce, melted cheese, pepperoni, and other toppings filled the air.

We laid the pizzas out in the kitchen as Tommy introduced Milo to The 27. Milo had a look of bliss as he took his first pull from the straw.

"That's amazing," he said, only signing with one hand as he kept the shake in the other. He immediately drank some more. "Where do these come from?"

"Red's," Tommy finger-spelled.

"We need to go there more." Milo barely had the straw out of his mouth and didn't bother to sign. He sipped more through the straw.

"Careful or you're going to freeze your brain," Mickey said.

"I kinda don't care." Milo laughed.

We ate on the porch since it was so nice out. Milo and Tommy sat on the steps, leaving the chairs for the rest of us.

"So, Ethan," Liam said between bites, "have you thought about what you're going to say in your speech?"

I groaned because I was worried about saying the right things in front of everyone. I set my plate in my lap so I could sign. "There are a lot of notes on my phone that I'm trying to make into something good."

"Coach Ethan," Milo interjected, "don't worry about signing while we eat. I appreciate that you do it, but I've got my hearing aids on, so I can hear everyone fine. If I miss anything, I'll ask for a repeat."

"Will do," I said, and we traded a smile.

"You always give the best pep talks at camp," Tommy said. "The speech will be like that but with more rainbows."

We all laughed.

"I'm going to work on it tonight. Who knows. Maybe I'll try it out on you all tomorrow."

"Cool. A sneak peek," Milo said.

"Tommy, Nicolas told me he had you feeding Mabel. Would you be interested in doing that when I'm out of town?"

"For sure. Anytime. Just let me know when."

"Mabel?" Milo looked confused, drawing smiles from Mickey and Liam.

"She lives in the woods. Sorta like bigfoot, but instead of hairy she's leafy."

Milo cocked his head, and looked at each of us. "Seriously?"

"For sure. My dad swears Mabel helped him find his way out of the woods when he ended up lost and had no phone signal."

"Coach, this is a joke right?"

"Nope. We're all believers here and have been for years." Mickey and Liam nodded to back me up.

"Maybe we could go camping sometime this summer and see if she comes to visit. You want to?" Tommy asked.

Milo looked skeptical. "I'm all in for camping, but I'm not so sure about a big leafy beast."

"She's harmless. Not a beast at all." Tommy bumped into Milo's shoulder. "We'll figure out when to camp once hockey's over."

After we'd eaten more pizza than we probably should've, Tommy and Milo left with Liam. Mickey hung back to help clean up the kitchen before heading out. The sun was still setting, so I returned to the porch to watch the colors paint the sky.

My phone buzzed with a text.

Andre: *Just wanted to say thanks again for everything you're doing for the festival. It means a lot. Hope the move went well!*

A smile tugged at my lips, and a flutter filled my chest at his random text.

Ethan: *Happy to help. And the move was smooth. Lots of boxes of course, and still more to come. But things are good, and the other place is ready for Wade and their team.*

I hesitated for a moment, then sent another message.

Ethan: *Look forward to seeing you tomorrow to go over the judging stuff.*

His response came fast.

Andre: *Me too. Get some rest. We've got a big week ahead of us.*

He wasn't kidding about that. The festival, the speech, the game, not to mention camp—it was a bit overwhelming.

I brought up the notes app on my phone and had it read out what I'd put in so far for the speech. The sooner I had it completed, the sooner I could memorize it. The quiet, pleasant evening was the perfect time to work on it.

TEN
ANDRE

I loved mornings in the library. Usually just a few people, all of them regulars, came in to read newspapers we'd received from out of the area, use the computers, or get a new book or two to read. Few things made me as happy as coming in to hear the turning of pages, a few clicks on a keyboard, and the murmur of patrons chatting.

At the desk Clara had a pile of papers in front of her and I wasn't sure what she was sorting through.

"Morning, Clara." I set my backpack and tea down on the counter.

"Good morning," she said with her usual perkiness. "How are you holding up with two days to go?"

I chuckled and ran a hand over the smooth skin of my head. "It's weird. There's a lot to do, possibly too much, and somehow this morning I'm feeling okay about it all."

I had a fantastic team around me with Olivia, Wade, and Mickey, and the rest of the volunteers made an enormous difference. Then there was Ethan. I couldn't discount the impact he'd had on solving a couple of the recent issues that had cropped up.

A feeling stirred in my heart and head—Ethan and I could solve anything together.

I shoved that idea to the side to consider later. "How's everything with you?"

"It's all good. I'm planning to get some more Pride decorations up. I'm also starting the display for the authors coming in for Friday's event, and you know I love to put up a display."

"I can't wait to see it." She had a knack for making any topic into a fantastic visual arrangement. "What's all this?" I pointed to the stack of paper and envelopes on the desk.

Clara's eyes lit up. "I had to empty the box where we were collecting the community letters in support of the Freedom to Read award nomination. It's only been a few days, but the response has been huge. Far more people are bringing in letters rather than sending emails."

It was incredible that the community had so much to say about this place and the banned books program. "Seriously? That's incredible. I can't thank you enough for handling all of this."

She waved off my thanks. "It's been my pleasure. I'm eager to find out how it all turns out. There's one thing for you..." She hesitated, her hand hovering over a folded paper that sat by itself. "I know you said you didn't want to see any of these, but... This wasn't in an envelope and I've been flattening out and straightening the papers so I can package them." She looked at the paper and back at me. "Of course I saw what some of them said... Anyway, I made a copy of this one and you should take a look."

My heart skipped a beat or two as she held out the paper. "Is everything okay?"

"Oh, don't worry," Clara said as she caught my concern. "It's good, I promise. I just think you'll want to read it."

Relieved but curious, I took the paper and gathered up my things. "Thanks. I'll give it a read. I'm going to go get some emails done and prep for my meeting with Bo in community development to make sure everything's a go from the city's point of view. You know where to find me if you need anything."

She nodded and turned to check out someone who'd come up with a couple of books.

As I headed toward my office, I nearly bumped into Mrs. Landry, one of our regulars. Her face lit up when she saw me.

"Andre. I hoped to run into you." Her eyes were bright behind her glasses. "I finished that book you recommended last week—the mystery set in 1950s San Francisco. I didn't figure out who the killer was until just before the detective did. It was so good. I've already picked up the next in that series." She held up the book to show me.

Her enthusiasm was infectious, and I smiled. "I'm so glad you enjoyed it. You'll like that sequel too."

"Do you have any other recommendations? After

this, I'd like to mix things up with a biography or two maybe."

My mind raced through the possibilities and what I knew Mrs. Landry liked. "There's a biography about the artist Keith Haring. It dives into his creativity and the huge number of works he made but also life in the 1970s and '80s in New York and his activism for queer rights. I couldn't put it down."

"That sounds good. I like his art. My son has a couple prints of his hanging in his living room."

"Another I'd recommend is the memoir by Harvey Fierstein. It's a look at his upbringing, how he got started in theater and became a playwright, and it's got so much about the plays and musicals he's written."

"Wonderful. I love *La Cage*." She jotted down the titles in her small notebook. "I'll be getting them both. Thank you so much."

"You're welcome. I look forward to hearing what you think of them."

She smiled and headed off to find the books.

This was why I loved this job. I never got tired of connecting people with stories that could open up new worlds for them, challenge their perspectives, or simply bring joy.

When I got to my office, I closed the door and sank into my chair. Once I got my tablet from my pack and got the folders of festival stuff as organized as possible on my desk, I took a sip of tea and unfolded the document Clara had given me.

My heart nearly stopped when I spotted the signature at the bottom: Ethan Gallagher.

Ethan had written a letter for the award nomination? Curiosity and surprise swirled around my brain at the thought that he'd taken the time, with everything else he had going on, to do this.

I started to read.

To the Freedom to Read Award Committee, I'm writing to express my full support for the Maplewood Library and Andre Thompson's nomination for the Freedom to Read Award. As someone who grew up in Maplewood and experienced firsthand the impact of our local library, I can't think of an organization, or librarian, more deserving of this honor.

A wave of emotions washed over me, moved by his sincerity.

The Maplewood Library has always been a cornerstone of our community. When I was a kid, struggling with reading and feeling like I'd never get it, the library was a safe place for me to put into practice what I learned at school and from my parents. As an adult, I've watched the library continue to reflect the inclusivity that Maplewood stands for. The shelves don't just hold books—they hold stories meaningful for every person. No matter who they are or where they come from, anyone can walk into the Maplewood Library (or browse the digital collection) and find books that speak to them. That kind of inclusivity is rare these days, especially in smaller towns like ours.

My vision blurred as tears formed. This was what I'd always hoped the library would achieve. That Ethan not only noticed but appreciated it enough to write this meant more to me than I could put into words. The impact of his letter deepened the connection I'd started to experience with Ethan, making me want to know him much better than I did.

In the past few years, Andre Thompson has taken that mission even further. His work to bring banned books to the forefront of our library's collection has been nothing short of extraordinary. In a time when too many communities are restricting access to books that explore diverse experiences and identities, Andre has ensured that the Maplewood Library is a place where no story is silenced.

I grabbed a tissue from the box on my desk. Ethan's words were beautiful, and I couldn't believe he wrote them about the library's work. This letter confirmed what I'd realized in the past few days working with him. His caring nature, compassion, and dedication to causes was crystal clear, and I had been blind to it.

I reached for my phone but hesitated to unlock it. The urge to text Ethan was overwhelming, but I shouldn't have read his letter. The message was intended for the award committee, not for me.

With a sigh, I set the phone down. I would find a way to thank him, even if he couldn't know exactly what for.

A knock on my office door startled me out of my thoughts. "Come in," I called, composing myself.

"Sorry to interrupt." Clara opened the door and then stepped back. She wheeled in the dolly stacked with packages. "Several boxes came in and it's too many to keep up front. I'm guessing these are for the author event."

I got up to help. "Probably so." I looked at the box on top and saw it was from Kendrick. "We can set these with the other boxes that are piling up in here." I moved one to the stack.

At this point so much had arrived at the library, I could build a fort if I wanted to.

My thoughts drifted back to Ethan as we stacked boxes.

The coffee meeting at Special Blend had started it all. We'd shared so much in a short time and there'd been a moment there, when our hands had touched, that I'd felt... something.

At the time I'd brushed it off, telling myself it was just the intensity of the festival planning. But now I wasn't so sure. While there was the reality that he didn't live here year-round, there were also a lot of possibilities.

My phone buzzed with a text and as soon as we had the dolly emptied and Clara had left, I checked it. My heart did a little flip when I saw it was from Ethan.

Ethan: *Hey, just wanted to confirm our meeting this afternoon to go over the judging criteria. Still on for 3pm?*

I typed so fast most of the words got autocorrected.

Andre: *Absolutely! Looking forward to it. See you then.*

As I hit send, anticipation stirred in me. The prospect of seeing Ethan again was undeniably exciting.

I settled back at my desk, trying to focus on the stack of work. But my mind kept wandering. Would I see more glimpses of the thoughtful, passionate man who'd written that letter? Could I continue to build a friendship, or more, with him?

ELEVEN

ETHAN

I arrived at the library fifteen minutes early, carrying a paper bag from Special Blend containing four scones. As I stepped through the doors, I immediately noticed Clara at the front desk looking frazzled and glancing anxiously at her watch.

"Clara? Is everything okay?" I asked, approaching her.

She looked up, relief washing over her face. "Oh, thank goodness. We have a bit of a situation."

"What's going on? Can I help?" The words were out of my mouth before I even knew what the problem was.

Clara sighed. "Our storyteller for the children's reading hour is stuck in traffic and won't make it in time. I'm the only staff member here since Andre's not back yet. I can't leave the desk unattended. And the kids usually want someone besides the parents to read to them."

My heart rate picked up as I realized what she might

be about to ask. I'd rather try to figure out how to check a book out for someone than have to read in public. But I'd already offered to help, so there was no going back now.

"Is there anything I can do?" I tried to keep my voice steady.

Her eyes lit up. "Would you be willing to read to the kids? I'm sure they would love you filling in."

I swallowed hard but nodded. "Of course."

Relief flooded Clara's face. "Thank you so much. You're a lifesaver."

As we walked toward the children's section, I focused on my breathing.

In for four counts.
Hold for four.
Exhale for four.

Calm was essential. I repeated the exercise, willing my nerves to settle. By the time we reached the group of waiting children, I was marginally more prepared to face this unexpected challenge.

"Everyone," Clara announced to the kids. Their chatter quieted, but whispers and pointing erupted as I stepped in beside her. "Miss Patterson is running late, so we have a special guest reader. This is Ethan Gallagher, and he's going to read to you."

"Mr. Ethan!" A little boy, maybe five or six, in a Maplewood Bears T-shirt bounced where he sat. "I can't wait to see you play Saturday! It'll be so much cooler than just watching on TV."

"And you're a Bears fan, I see." His enthusiasm helped ease my stress a bit.

"Yeah! I want to play for them. I'm on the Cubs now."

"That's where I started."

"I know. Coach tells us stories about you and Ryland Zervudachi all the time."

Liam coached the Cubs and the Bears, and the fact he invoked my name and Ry's as an example of players from Maplewood who had succeeded wasn't surprising. I found it a little embarrassing sometimes, but it was good there were players that young people could take inspiration from.

"I'm going to leave you with this bunch." Clara smiled and mouthed *thank you*. "Now, you all be nice to Mr. Ethan, okay?"

"Yes, Miss Clara," many of them chorused.

Their focus turned to me.

"Okay." I paused, willing calmness. The bookshelves held brightly colored covers with all kinds of illustrations. "What would you like me to read?"

"I know the perfect one." A girl with curly dark hair got up and went to the shelf. "It's new and it's about Pride." She brought me a book.

I took it, looking at the smiling boy on the cover standing in front of a rainbow. The title read *Finding My Rainbow, A Journey of Courage, Acceptance, and Pride*.

Settling into the reading chair, I opened the book. Larger, easier-to-read text and colorful illustrations made it less daunting. Extra space between the lines meant I didn't need to run my finger under them.

I read the words to myself a couple of times, trying not to take too much time. "In the small town of Cullman, Alabama, there lived a boy named Josh," I began. "Josh had a secret that felt as heavy as the summer air that hung over the corn fields."

After reading the first two pages, I turned the book so everyone could see the illustrations of Josh standing on his block and with his friends in front of his school.

A few adults, likely parents, had phones out taking pictures or filming. I tried to ignore that and focused on the young audience before me.

But I had a fear, even with this being easier to read, of messing it up. An idea struck. "Who wants to help me read the next page?"

Several hands shot up.

"Me! Me! I can read!" The curly-haired girl waved her arm enthusiastically.

"Come on up here. You picked out the book, so it's only fair you should read some of it for us."

I moved to the floor, sitting cross-legged so she could sit next to me.

"Hi there. What's your name?"

"I'm Marta."

"It's nice to meet you, Marta. Shall we see what Josh does next?"

She nodded and I handed her the book. Marta read the next two pages, then turned the book and described the illustration. It was a nice touch, and I wondered if that was what I should've done or if it was her own particular flair.

Absorbed in the reading, I didn't notice Andre's arrival until I looked up during Marta's explanation. He leaned against a bookshelf, arms crossed, watching us with a soft smile that made my heart flutter. Our eyes met briefly and his smile widened, sending warmth through my chest.

The moment stretched until one kid asked, "What's on the next page?" bringing me back to the present.

"Should I turn the page?" Marta asked.

"How about we see if anyone else wants to read?" Marta smiled and nodded, which I appreciated since I didn't want her to be disappointed.

The young man in the Bears T-shirt got his hand up first, so I called on him.

"I'm Bart," he said as he sat down.

"Good to meet you, Bart." We traded fist bumps before he took the book, read two pages, and talked about the pictures. I for sure had messed up not doing that, but it didn't seem worth going back since everyone seemed entertained.

My earlier anxiety faded to background noise. Everyone seemed to have a good time—some readers even did voices for the characters. Andre remained too, his constant smile directed at me even though he must have a thousand things to do.

I also realized that I desperately wanted to kiss his smile.

Luckily, that didn't hit me until we reached the book's last page just as Miss Patterson arrived.

"I'm so sorry," she said, unpacking the puppet theater, "but thank you so much for filling in."

Some older kids helped her set up, which was apparently a routine.

"Thanks for being such a wonderful audience," I said to the kids. "I enjoyed reading Josh's story with you all and learning about someone who lives in a different small town. And thanks to each of you who read too."

"Thank you, Mr. Ethan," they said collectively. A couple of kids even came up for fist bumps or hugs.

"You're welcome. Have a great time with Miss Patterson."

I joined Andre as the children settled in for the puppet show.

"That was impressive," he said in his soft library voice as we moved away. "Thank you for filling in. I know that couldn't have been easy."

"You're welcome. It was one of the scariest things I've ever done, but the kids being so good helped me stay calm."

"Want to head to my office? We can talk about the judging."

"Let's do it. I need to pick up one thing at the desk."

Andre raised an eyebrow, and I replied with a grin.

As we approached, Clara held up the bag. "Thanks so much for that last-minute help."

"My pleasure." I took it and gestured for Andre to lead the way to his office.

Boxes were everywhere, some stacked in a corner or other available spaces.

"These are for you," I said, holding out the paper bag. "From Special Blend. I remembered you liked their maple pecan scones."

Andre's eyes lit up. "Thank you so much. Perfect afternoon snack. I can't believe you remembered that after that one visit." He accepted and pulled out a scone. "You're having one too, right?"

"I'd love to." I sighed. "It's occurring to me now that I should've brought drinks too."

He held up a finger. "I've got it covered." He pointed behind me to a small refrigerator. "There are some bottles of coffee in there. Want to grab a couple?"

He'd stocked up with several flavors. I took two mochas, thinking they'd pair well with the scones.

As I turned and held out a drink, we laughed, realizing our hands were full. Our fingers brushed as we traded a pastry for a drink, sending that familiar spark through my chest just like the other day.

"So." He settled behind his desk, sounding flustered. Had that touch affected him too? We stared at each other, his smile giving me goose bumps. "Let's talk judging criteria. We can start with the crafts fair. We've got four criteria: Creativity, originality, use of a maple element, and relevance to the Pride theme."

I took a seat, moving closer to the desk. "Theme incorporation?"

He'd taken a bite just as I asked the question. He held up a finger and exaggerated the chewing motions as if trying to hurry up, making me laugh again. It already felt so easy to be around him.

"Each entry needs to incorporate something related to Pride or the LGBTQ+ community." Andre grabbed his tablet and started swiping. "Remember last year's winning entry? The huge handwoven tapestry featuring interwoven maple leaves transforming into all the colors of the Progress Pride flag?"

"Yes! That was amazing." The image of that gorgeous piece flashed in my mind as Andre held up his screen, displaying a picture. "Is that from The Wild Palette?"

"Good eye. The artist had a small show after the win, and that was the centerpiece. It's still there." Andre closed his tablet and put it aside. "Olivia arranged to have it as an ongoing display. The artist will be one of the judges this year too."

"Great. I can rely on them for guidance."

"You'll do fine. I..."

Andre's phone buzzed, interrupting our conversation. His expression grew concerned as he read the message. "We've got a situation at the park. The vendor tent setup isn't going as fast as planned, and we're short on volunteers."

"I can help," I offered immediately. "And I bet some kids from camp might be willing to pitch in. Let me text Liam."

"You don't have to."

"I want to." I pulled out my phone. "What time do you need people?"

"Now?" Andre sounded apologetic as he winced.

"We need everything set up before tomorrow's vendor check-in."

"Consider it handled." I hit the microphone button on the messaging app and dictated a text explaining the situation.

My phone buzzed with Liam's response, and I played it out loud. "We're wrapping up the session. I'll bring whoever I can, and we'll be in the park in a half hour or so."

"Thank you. You're helping so much today."

"I'm glad I can."

Before I could stop myself, I reached across the desk, grabbed his hand, and squeezed it—partly to show support but mostly because I ached to touch him. Electric sparks shot up my arm and straight to my heart, making it speed up. When he smiled broadly, my whole body hummed with an intensity that threatened to short-circuit my brain.

"Uhm, we should... Um... I need to get to the park. I don't—" Andre sounded as discombobulated as I felt.

"Yup." I snapped back to the task at hand but still squeezed one last time before letting go. "Let's get going."

TWELVE

ANDRE

The walk from the library to Maplewood City Park gave me a moment to process the last hour. Ethan reading to the children had revealed yet another side of him. He'd handled the situation beautifully. His genuine smiles and the way he'd engaged the kids made my heart swell. Watching him with the children, no one would've known the anxiety that moment held for him.

And he'd brought me scones!

That charged moment when he'd reached for my hand still lingered, so natural even as it set off fireworks under my skin. I was falling for him, hard and fast.

But there was a festival to run, and I needed to focus. I tried to direct my thoughts to tent layouts and vendor assignments. My mind had its own agenda, flashing back to the warmth in Ethan's blue eyes when our gazes had met across my desk.

"Andre?"

"Sorry. Thinking about the vendor layout." I hoped that explanation would cover my distraction. "What were you saying?"

"No worries," Ethan said as we crossed Maple Street. "I asked who's the third judge for the craft competition?"

I welcomed the distraction from my racing thoughts. "Olivia will be, along with you and Trevor Hals, who created that winning tapestry."

"I'm glad to have expert help." Ethan chuckled. I appreciated he was trying to lighten my mood.

"Olivia's excited to see who might top Trevor's tapestry."

As we neared the park, my mood plummeted. What should have been a mostly completed orderly setup of tents forming around the fountain in the park's center was a disaster zone. Only three of the twenty tents stood, and those looked like a strong breeze would topple them.

Sarah, the team leader for getting the vendor area set up, zipped between groups of people trying to assemble tents. She gestured frantically at a duo working with a tangle of metal poles and canvas.

"No, no—that's not—" She cut herself off with a visible wince as someone dropped two support poles with a loud clang. "Those pieces don't go together."

Another confused duo kept turning an instruction sheet around between them. At this rate we'd be lucky to have half the tents up by nightfall.

"Oh no." I kept my voice low so only Ethan could hear. "This is worse than I imagined."

"Hey." Ethan's gentle grasp on my arm was welcome.

"We'll figure it out. And Liam's bringing rein-forcements."

I took a deep breath, grateful for his steady presence. "Thanks. I just..." I couldn't help but chuckle. "This wasn't in the plan."

Sarah spotted us and hurried over. "Thank goodness. We're so understaffed, and these instructions might as well be in Sanskrit." She thrust a crumpled paper at me. "These aren't like the tents we've had the past few years."

"More help's on the way," I assured her, scanning the document. These were worse than any furniture instruc-tions I'd ever seen. "And we're here now, so put us to work."

"Let's get you two started on that tent." She pointed to one that was still in its box. "I'll keep working to sort out these teams."

Ethan and I approached the box, and he started opening it. I made a mental note to ensure we got easy-to-assemble tents in the future. He handed me the instructions.

"Okay, so it looks like we need to..." I trailed off as Ethan began efficiently sorting the poles and canvas.

"Start with the frame?" he finished, holding up two pieces. "Want to work from opposite ends?"

We fell into an easy rhythm, with me following his lead as we pieced the frame together. I tried to focus on the task but kept getting distracted by the way his T-shirt stretched across his broad shoulders as he moved.

A bead of sweat rolled down his cheek, and I nearly dropped the end of the structure I was holding.

"You good?" He caught my eye with a hint of concern.

"Yeah, just... trying to make sure we're doing this right," I lied, feeling heat creep up my neck that had nothing to do with the afternoon sun.

The frame was nearly complete, and we started securing the canvas. I was on my tiptoes trying to pull the fabric taut while Ethan worked on the other corner.

"Almost got it." I stretched as far as I could.

Something creaked.

I wasn't sure what, but I didn't let it deter me from trying to finish with this section.

"Andre!" Ethan called out but it was too late.

The tent came down around us in a chaotic tangle of metal and fabric. Ethan grabbed my arm, pulling me closer as we ended up huddled together under the canvas, surrounded by the collapsed frame.

"Well, this is dignified," I said with a laugh.

"You okay?" His breath on my cheek made me shudder.

"Yeah," I managed to say, keenly aware of how his hand was gripping my arm. "Though we might need to start over."

Now he laughed too. "You think?"

I tried to move but instead stumbled into him. His arms wrapped around me, steadying us both, and suddenly we were pressed together in the dim space under the canvas. My heart thundered in my chest.

Tension crackled between us. A fire blazed in his blue eyes as he locked his gaze on mine and his tongue darted out to wet his lips. I wasn't sure who moved first, but our mouths met and the gentle press of his lips against mine sent a charge throughout my body. The kiss began tentatively, both of us testing the waters, seeing if this was okay. But when Ethan let out a tiny sound and pulled me closer, deepening the kiss, nothing else mattered. My hands went to his broad shoulders, gripping the solid muscle there as he held my waist.

I felt like I was flying and falling at the same time.

The second kiss was confident, filled with all that had been building between us.

It was perfect.

Until the tent canvas was peeled away, flooding us with sunlight and the sound of gasps and some laughter.

"Well, well." Liam held the canvas to the side with a huge grin plastered across his face. "I see you two found a creative way to handle tent assembly."

We jumped apart, almost tripping over the poles on the ground. Ethan's face was red and I suspected mine was too. Behind Liam stood at least six teenagers from camp along with Dix, Oscar, and the other volunteers.

They tried to keep straight faces.

None of them did a good job.

"Perfect timing as always, Liam," Ethan muttered but he fought a smile.

"I try." Liam continued to grin, enjoying this way too much.

He helped Ethan step out of the mess we'd made as Mimi held the canvas. Ethan gave me his hand to help me up, and my heart somersaulted as he gave it a squeeze.

"These tents are evil." A young man spoke out loud and in ASL as he stepped next to Liam. "I helped my dad with these last summer. The instructions say two people can do this, but you really need four."

"Can you show us?" Ethan spoke and signed as well.

"For sure."

"Amazing," I said and then quickly turned to Ethan. "I'm afraid I don't sign. Can you, please?"

"It's okay." The teen shrugged casually even as he continued to sign. "My hearing aids are on, so it's all good."

"Andre, this is Milo, one of our campers."

"Very glad to meet you, Milo. Sounds like you're just the person we need to get this done."

"I'm happy to lend a hand. Let's start with one in the box and everyone can see how it's done."

My anxiety about the situation unclenched just a bit. "Let's do it."

"Tommy? Help us out?"

"Of course." Tommy also spoke and signed. When did he learn that?

Milo took charge with a confidence that made me instantly grateful he'd shown up. Milo and Tommy laid out the poles much the same way we'd done it before, but this time Milo added small paper tags using paper from a notepad he pulled from his pocket and rubber bands Sarah had.

After tagging everything, Milo explained the strategy. "My dad figured this trick out. Label each section before you start. Makes it way easier to keep track." He glanced at the mess Ethan and I had created with a sympathetic smile. "These things are like puzzles. But once you know how to do it, it goes pretty fast."

Milo directed Tommy, Ethan, and me through the assembly process as the other volunteers observed. The same corner pieces that had given us trouble came together smoothly under his guidance. When we reached the part where our tent had collapsed, Milo demonstrated how to brace the frame properly.

"See, you need someone here, here, and here." He positioned us. "The weight has to be distributed evenly while you attach the canvas or it'll fall apart."

Ethan caught my eye and grinned. "Maybe getting trapped under the tent wasn't entirely our fault after all."

"I'm choosing to believe that." I chuckled even as heat crept across my cheeks.

Within fifteen minutes, we had a perfectly assembled tent. No wobbles, no loose canvas, just a space ready to be occupied by a vendor. The difference between our earlier chaos and Milo's methodical approach was striking.

"That was incredible." I nodded at Milo. "Did everyone get that?" I looked at Sarah and the volunteers.

"I recorded it and I'm sending it to all of you." Sarah turned to the team. "Everyone good?"

The response was positive.

"How about we work on the ones that are messed up?" Milo looked between Tommy, Ethan, and me. "We can have them up in no time."

Milo continued to step up. Did he live in town and I

just hadn't met him somehow? I had questions but I held them since we had tents to build.

Ethan and I couldn't keep our eyes off each other as we worked. Each time it happened, my stomach did a little flip at the thought of the kisses we'd shared. The air crackled between us whenever we touched. Each accidental—or not so accidental—brush sent sparks of energy through me.

I wondered if Ethan had the same reaction.

The sun was setting by the time we finished, casting long shadows across the neat rows of white tents. Sarah was practically bouncing with relief as she checked off the last items on her list.

"I can't thank you all enough," I said to the group. "This was amazing community spirit in action with a great assist from our guests as well. Please let me buy you all dinner at Red's to show my appreciation."

There were cheers of approval, and people began gathering their things. I watched Ethan help Milo and Tommy organize the boxes the tents had come in, giving the young men fist bumps when they finished.

I wanted to ask Ethan to dinner.

Just him.

Somewhere quiet where we could talk about what had happened under that tent. But I hesitated, unsure if this was the right moment.

Ethan solved my dilemma by approaching me as everyone headed for Red's. "Hey," he whispered. "Would you maybe want to get dessert afterward? Just us?"

My heart soared. "Yes," I replied, possibly too quickly. "I'd like that."

His smile was bright. "Great."

I nodded, not trusting my voice. As we walked to join the others, our hands brushed again. This time, I let my fingers intertwine with his for a moment.

THIRTEEN

ETHAN

The diner buzzed with chatter as volunteers celebrated wrangling the tents into place. Mickey graciously accommodated us, likely past the seating capacity as some people stood at the counter. If anyone from the fire department happened by, we'd no doubt be told to disperse.

Andre moved from group to group, thanking everyone personally for their help. I watched, admiring how gracefully he handled his organizer duties, while remembering his lips against mine. My heart swelled with happiness every time he glanced my way and threw the sweetest smile in my direction, though joy tangled with an undercurrent of anxiety.

Excitement about someone I'd regarded as almost an enemy just days ago felt dangerous. Part of me wanted to temper these feelings, to protect myself from getting in too deep, but every time Andre's eyes met mine, that resolve evaporated.

"You're mooning." Liam's teasing voice pulled me from my thoughts.

"I am not." I shifted my gaze to my friend, who'd slid into the booth across from me.

"Uh-huh." He grinned. "So, about that tent..."

"Liam." I groaned, dropping my head into my hands.

"Hey." His tone shifted, becoming soft. He reached out and gently pulled on my right hand. "You okay?"

I lifted my head, grateful that he'd picked up on my discomfort. "I don't know."

"Tell me." Liam leaned in, giving me his full attention.

I appreciated these moments with him. Despite his playful demeanor, I could always rely on Liam for honest conversation. It was comforting that we were always there for each other.

"I like him. A lot." I kept my voice low, even though I doubted anyone was paying attention to us with the cacophony going on. "And those kisses were amazing. But having everyone find out that way..." I sighed. "You know that's going to be in *Maplewood Matters*, probably with pictures."

"Getting caught making out under a collapsed tent is a pretty epic way to announce a new relationship."

"Not helping." I couldn't help smiling while I chided him. "We're going for dessert after this. Just us."

"Good." Liam nodded. "You deserve this, E. I haven't seen you this excited about someone since..." He trailed off. We didn't need to discuss Marcus, someone I'd eventually have to tell Andre about.

"That's part of what scares me." I traced a pattern on the tabletop with my finger. "This kind of spark is something I haven't experienced in years. The way my heart races, how a simple touch excites me. But what if I'm making too much of it? What if he's not as interested? Or if it's just a summer thing?"

"First off, there's nothing wrong with it being a summer thing if you both agree to it. And..." He paused and leaned in even closer. "What if it's a lot more?" His whisper gave the idea a reverence I hadn't expected.

"Then there's an even bigger problem. I have to go back to Seattle." The thought made my chest ache. "I've already been through trying long distance, and that was with someone I'd been with for a couple of years. Starting something new with that hanging over everything..."

"Listen." Liam leaned forward. "You've got a couple of months and that's plenty of time to figure out if this is something worth more than a summer."

"Since when do you have so much romance advice?"

"I watch a lot of rom-coms. Those have taught me that being afraid of what might happen keeps you from experiencing what could happen." He smiled and sat back, looking satisfied. "Look, man, you owe it to yourself to see where this goes. But you need to talk to Andre. Make sure you two are in the same place."

I glanced over at Andre, who was laughing at something Sarah was saying. As if sensing my gaze, he looked over and our eyes met. He winked at me and I swooned.

"Yeah," I said softly. "We definitely need to talk. Thanks for listening."

"Always."

Andre headed our direction, looking happy. He dropped into the booth next to Liam. "This was good. I'm glad we did this for everyone."

"Is this in the festival budget?" I had to ask, knowing how much the event had grown.

"Mickey gave us a discount, and I'll just sort it out later." Andre sounded less than convinced that he'd be able to sort it.

"Let me take care of it. No need to add more to the budget."

"No, I can't."

"Yes, you can," Liam and I said together.

"See, he thinks it's a good idea too."

Andre sighed and then smiled. "All right. Thanks. It'll be good not to have to discuss this unexpected expense with the committee."

"Are you ready to get out of here?" The talk with Liam had me even more ready for alone time with Andre.

"Yes, please." Andre stood and Liam and I did too.

"Thanks, man." I extended my fist to Liam, and he bumped it.

"Have fun, you two."

As we left, I stopped by the counter where Mickey was talking to some of the tent crew. I quietly told him to add everything to my bill.

"Will do." He looked between Andre and me and nodded. "Hope you two have a good night." He followed that up with a clap on Andre's shoulder. I figured he and Liam would trade notes once we were gone.

Was the entire town trying to make this happen between us?

We walked to Special Blend in comfortable silence, our hands occasionally brushing. Each touch sent tingles through my fingers, up my arm, and straight to my heart. When I gathered the courage to briefly take Andre's hand and squeeze it, the warmth of his skin against mine made my breath catch.

Part of me wanted to intertwine our fingers and never let go while another part held back, wondering if I was setting myself up for heartbreak by feeling too much too soon. But the smile I caught out of the corner of my eye made those doubts seem unimportant, at least for now.

Special Blend's windows glowed warmly in the twilight, a Pride flag crafted from painted coffee beans hanging alongside *Happy Pride!* painted on the window. Small multicolored twinkling lights around the window shimmered. There were only a few customers inside. Ideal for a private conversation.

The bell chimed as we entered, and the familiar scent of coffee and maple welcomed us. The cafe's lighting was softer than during the day, with small lamps on each table creating intimate pools of warm light.

"There's a nice, quiet corner." Andre gestured toward the back.

I nodded and followed him to the table, appreciating how the location offered both privacy and a view of the relaxed setting.

Clara's daughter Jenny was working and came over to

take our order. "No coffee?" she asked when we both ordered hot chocolate.

"Some of us actually want to sleep tonight," Andre replied.

"Fair enough. Although as much work as you both did with those tents, I suspect coffee wouldn't keep you up." She keyed our order into the tablet she held. "And for treats?"

"Two maple tarts," I said. "Perfect accompaniment to the cocoa."

"That sounds delicious," Andre added. "Same for me."

"Great choice. One of my favorite combos." Jenny headed off to get our order, and silence fell between us.

I took a deep breath, sorting out what to say.

"About earlier..." I started.

"The kisses?" Andre's voice was soft.

"Yeah. I wanted to apologize. I shouldn't have—"

"Don't." Andre reached across the table and took my hand in his. "I liked it. A lot. Actually..." He ducked his head slightly. "I've wanted to kiss you for a couple of days now."

My heart soared. "Really?"

"Really." He looked back at me, his hands enveloping mine. "Though I'll admit, getting caught by half the town wasn't how I planned our first kiss to go."

I chuckled. "Yeah. Not my favorite moment. Based on the looks we're getting, I suspect everyone knows by now."

"Oh, I think everyone knew before Milo labeled the

first tent pole." Andre's thumb traced circles on the back of my hand, sending shivers up my arm. "Speaking of Milo, I've wanted to ask. Does he live in town? I don't think I've seen him."

"No, he's from Montpelier. He came to camp because he found out Dix was coaching. Tommy's family is hosting him during the session."

"Milo and Tommy seem to have become fast friends. I didn't know Tommy signed."

"He's been learning."

"That's cool. They certainly worked well together."

"They do on the ice too." I smiled, thinking about the on-ice chemistry they'd built in just a few days.

Jenny arrived with our hot chocolates and tarts. The aromas of chocolate, maple, and pastry made my mouth water.

"Mmmm. So good." Andre dug right in and ended up with a small bit of custard on his lower lip. It took all my resolve to not lean across the table and kiss it away. "I'm thinking that couple energy is building between us. Is it too soon to say that?" Andre covered his mouth as his eyes went wide.

"So much has changed since I've been back." A small chuckle escaped me. "I dreaded having to work with you, and now... well, I enjoy not only doing the festival stuff but also just hanging with you."

His smile was gentle and intimate, something he shared with me more and more. This time it gave me goose bumps.

"God, and then you give me that smile and I swear I could melt."

His glance flicked down to the table, to the wall, and back to me. All the while, he scrubbed a hand over his head.

"So." Andre's expression turned serious and I braced for something bad. "I'd like to go on a proper date with you. Do something that's not festival planning or tent disasters."

My heart rate picked up. "I'd like that too. Actually..." I gathered my courage. "Would you like to come over for dinner? Either tomorrow to celebrate the evening before the festival begins or the next night to celebrate the first day?"

Andre considered this, his brow furrowing. Then his face cleared. "Tomorrow. I don't want to wait."

"Yeah?" My smile probably looked ridiculous, but I didn't care.

"Yeah." He squeezed my hand again. "It'll be great to hang out away from an audience too."

"Agreed. That's why I suggested coming over, to get us out of view."

We sat in silence for a moment, goofy grins plastered on our faces. I imagined that people sitting up front were texting about how we were sitting close in the corner.

"So, I've been wanting to break in the new kitchen. How does salmon with roasted vegetables sound? Or pasta with a light cream sauce?"

His eyes lit up as if surprised I could cook. "The salmon sounds perfect. I'll bring dessert. Any requests?"

"I'll leave that to you."

We finished our treats, talked about the festival opening, and traded stories about past events. When Andre's hand found mine again, it was so right. Joy flooded through me.

We said our good nights to Jenny and headed outside to the coolness that had settled in with the sun down. Without discussing it, we headed toward the library. I was parked nearby, and I imagined Andre was in the lot.

"I need to get some things from my office," Andre said when we got to the quiet building. "I know we shouldn't, given how fast news travels." He stepped closer. "But I want to kiss you good night."

I glanced around the empty street, then back at Andre. "And I want you to."

This kiss was softer than our first two but no less electric. When we parted, Andre's smile made my knees weak.

"Tomorrow?" he asked.

"Tomorrow. Seven o'clock?"

"Perfect." He kissed me once more, quick and sweet, before stepping back. "Have a good night."

"G'night."

As I walked toward my car, I heard music coming from the theater, no doubt a rehearsal for an upcoming show. I could stop and check it out and see my moms but decided against it so I could just bask in my time with Andre before having to answer any more questions about it.

FOURTEEN

ANDRE

"The live streaming setup looks good." Wade tapped their tablet, showing me the final layout for the festival events. "We've got all the key locations covered, and the crew is ready to go. We did streams from each location earlier today to verify the wireless was strong."

I checked off another item from our list. A shocking amount had come together in the last twenty-four hours. "And we're sure the network capacity will hold even with activity from the attendees?"

"Triple-checked it myself." Wade grinned. "Plus we've got backup hotspots if needed."

We sat in one of the library's community rooms, a comfortable space for the last planning meeting. Olivia sat cross-legged in an overstuffed chair, flipping through a final copy of the festival program she'd designed.

"These turned out amazing." She held up the booklet. "The printer really nailed the colors."

Mickey, who'd brought coffee for everyone, peered over her shoulder. "They did. The whole thing looks fabulous." He looked up at me. "What do you think about where we are?"

"For a moment I didn't think we'd make it, but we did."

Mickey cocked his head. "And?"

I shrugged, reluctant to voice my concern.

"I know your tells. What are you not saying?"

Wade looked up from their tablet and Olivia closed the program booklet.

I sighed. "Ethan mentioned needing help with his speech but hasn't asked me to look it over, even though I've seen him every day this week."

"You're worried."

"Maybe." The nagging idea pushed its way to the forefront of my mind. "He told me public speaking isn't his thing, and this is a big moment. I should've asked him about it before now."

"I'm sure if he needed help, he would've asked." Olivia sat up. "He seems to handle himself under pressure well."

"True." I recalled how naturally he'd handled the story time. "I just want to make sure he feels supported."

"Speaking of support," Olivia interjected with a sly grin. "How's the tent situation?"

Wade snickered before covering their mouth.

Heat crept up my neck as I fought back a smile. "The tents are fine. And that's all we need to discuss about that."

"Uh-huh." Mickey's tone was teasing.

"And with that, I need to go." I started packing up.

"Really?" Olivia sounded shocked. "I mean, it's good that you're not going to keep checking and double-checking for a few more hours, but this is something new for you."

"Yup. I'm calling it a day. You've all said everything is set, and that means there's nothing more to do." I couldn't help grinning.

Mickey stared at me. "Are you going to go hang out in the back corner of Special Blend again?"

"Not tonight." I debated if I wanted to say more. Since these were my closest friends, it was easy to continue. "But before you ask, I'll tell you that I'm having dinner with Ethan."

"Then go. Get out of here." Olivia made shooing motions. "It's all good."

"Thanks. You've all been amazing getting us ready to kick off tomorrow."

"Have a good night." Mickey's voice sounded sincere. "You deserve it."

Before showing up at Ethan's, I picked up dessert from Sparky's, another of Maplewood's diners, and went home to change. Khaki slacks and a polo felt too formal for a summer evening dinner. After considering a few options, I settled on a soft green T-shirt, light blue denim shorts, and sneakers. Much better.

Just before seven, I pulled up to Ethan's, excited but nervous about our first official date.

As I came up the stairs, carrying a pie box, the front

door swung open to reveal Ethan in a fitted gray T-shirt, dark shorts, and sandals. He looked both casual and unfairly attractive. The shirt clung to his broad shoulders and chest, making my mouth go dry. His dark hair was tousled, like he'd just run his fingers through it. His warm, welcoming smile made my heart soar.

"Hey." He opened the door wide and stepped aside. "Come in. Sorry about the boxes everywhere. I haven't had much time to unpack. I hadn't thought about that when I invited you."

Even with the boxes, it was obvious the house suited him. The floor-to-ceiling fireplace was stunning. I imagined how he might decorate it for Christmas. The open layout connected to the kitchen, and I understood why he wanted to try it out. It was decked out yet enough rustic charm remained that it didn't clash with the living room or what I saw of the dining room.

"Looks like you have your work cut out for you." I put my hand on top of a stack of boxes.

Ethan chuckled as he closed the door. "Yeah, it's a bit of a mess right now, but it'll get there. We threw stuff in boxes so I had what I needed before the streaming team moved in."

"I can already tell this is going to be a comfortable place to be."

"Thanks." His smile faltered. "Wait, did you bring a Sparky's box into my house? Does Mickey know about that?"

"Mickey knows I need to stay neutral in the diner

rivalry since I help organize events that might include both of them." I worried I'd messed up as Ethan put his hands on his hips. "Wait, are you fully Team Red's?"

"Depends on what's in the box." He smirked and I was less concerned that I'd wrecked the night before it'd even started.

"Maple cream pie." I went over to him and opened the box.

He leaned in, getting so close I thought he might end up with whipped cream on his nose. An image of me licking the cream off flashed through my mind, and I struggled to push the appealing thought away.

A low hum came from Ethan. "Mickey cannot know this was here." There was a seriousness in his voice.

"Duly noted."

"I love Red's maple custard, but Sparky's cream pie —oh man. I honestly love them both, but I'd be in so much trouble if that got around."

"Consider me your hookup." I winked at him.

"Hopefully, my dinner is worthy to serve before this." He closed the lid and took the box.

"I'm sure it will be."

"Keep me company while I cook?" He led me through to the kitchen. "Can I get you something to drink? Water, iced hibiscus tea, beer?"

"The tea sounds great." Did he know I liked that flavor or did he like it too?

I leaned against the kitchen island, watching as he moved confidently around the space. Despite the boxes scattered throughout, the kitchen seemed well-organized, with equipment and ingredients laid out just so.

"How were the final preparations today?" Ethan asked, handing me the tea before returning to the stove where he was working on the salmon.

"Good. Everything's ready." I took a sip of tea. "Wow. This is fantastic. And how about you? Ready for it? Like I said, I'm happy to help if you need it."

"I'm as ready as I can be. I've been practicing with my moms and Liam. I didn't want to bother you with it. You've already helped a lot with judging stuff."

Despite his words, his voice held a hint of tension as he checked the vegetables roasting in the oven. I felt bad that he didn't think he could ask.

"The offer still stands if you need it. But, having seen you in action this week, I'm sure you'll be wonderful."

He shot me a grateful look. "Thanks. Though right now I'd rather not think about it. I'll be anxious enough tomorrow. Tonight I'd like to focus on cooking a tasty meal and hanging out with you."

"It already smells incredible." I watched as he expertly flipped the salmon. "Can I help with anything?"

"Nope. You're my guest." He gestured at me to stay where I was.

We fell into easy conversation as he cooked, discussing everything from other summer festivals to hockey camp. He seemed so at ease, precise and confident in a way that reminded me of how I'd seen him move on the ice when I watched games.

"I was thinking we could sit outside. It's a pleasant

evening." He moved the salmon fillets onto plates and then pulled the tray of vegetables out of the oven.

"That sounds great."

"Do you want anything different to drink? Normally I'd offer wine with this, but I forgot to pick any up when I was at the store." He ran his hand through his hair, mussing it again. The way some fell over his forehead was ridiculously cute.

"No worries." I raised my glass. "The tea is perfect."

"If you'll grab my glass"—he gestured near the stove —"we can head out."

Ethan took the plates and I followed with his tea.

The view from the deck was amazing. Trees stretched out before us, framed by the rustic wooden rails. The edge of the lake shimmered in the evening light. In the soft breeze, leaves rustled and waves lapped at the lake's shore. This was an ideal place to relax.

"I hope you enjoy it," Ethan said once we were settled at the table, where he'd already placed silverware and napkins.

He'd perfectly cooked the salmon. It flaked at the slightest touch from my fork. "Wow," I exclaimed after the first bite. "This is amazing."

"Thanks." A slight blush colored his cheeks. "I got into cooking a couple of years ago. It's relaxing, you know? Following recipes, getting everything right."

"Well, I'm impressed." I gestured at my plate with my fork. "My cooking skills are more breakfast based."

"Oh, what's your specialty?"

"Frittatas with a mix of meat and veg."

"Yum."

"Breakfast at my place sometime?"

Oh man. I couldn't believe I'd said that. That implied a second date. Was that too much? Would it be a date that began the evening before or a breakfast-only date? I willed myself to keep my expression even.

"I'd love that." His smile was big and warmed me through.

We ate in comfortable silence for a few moments, enjoying the company, the food, and the view. Ethan's vibe kept me from needing to fill the space.

"Can I ask you something without getting us into a bad place?" Ethan's voice carried hesitation.

I put my fork down to give him my full attention. "Yes. Please ask."

"What were your plans for this place?" He paused and looked at me as if trying to decide if he should continue. "I've been curious ever since you mentioned wanting to turn it into a camp."

My temper threatened to flare, and I tamped it down. I hoped my face didn't telegraph that. He was interested, and there was no need to get mad at that. I took a sip of tea, gathering my thoughts.

"I wanted to create a summer camp for queer youth. Something small to start—a few weeks of the summer. Not everyone gets to grow up experiencing the inclusiveness we have here. A camp run by people who embrace all that Maplewood stands for would be great for anyone to experience."

Ethan nodded encouragingly, and the words began flowing more easily.

"I imagined arts programs, sports clinics, nature activities. I want to give kids a community where they are valued and supported and send them home with new friends they can stay in touch with." I shrugged, suddenly self-conscious. "It's just an idea."

"It's a beautiful idea." Ethan's voice was soft, sincere. "What were you looking at for funding?"

"I've got some money already promised if I can secure land. There are other grants I can apply for too. Plus I've been saving for years because I've had this in my head for a while." I smiled ruefully.

He reached across the table and his fingers interlaced with mine, sending that now-familiar spark up my arm. "Don't let the idea go. There are so many options. Maybe we could work on it together."

The possibility hung in the air. Before I could respond, Ethan squeezed my hand and stood up.

"Want to take a walk? This place is beautiful at this time of day, and I'd love to show you around."

"I'd like that." The idea of walking somewhere that wasn't around town with him thrilled me. And he'd raised the prospect of working together on the camp.

We cleared the dishes, working in easy synchronization. We agreed that the pie could wait as a post-walk treat.

The evening air was perfect as we stepped off the deck, a pleasant temperature with low humidity. Ethan led the way down a well-worn path, our shoulders occasionally brushing as we walked.

"I think I told you I used to come here all the time as a kid." He glanced at me sometimes as he talked. "We'd play hockey in the winter. And in summer, we'd spend hours exploring trails, swimming, and goofing off."

The path wound through a grove of maple trees, their leaves creating patterns of shadow and light on the ground. Without discussion, our hands found each other, fingers intertwining.

"It must feel surreal owning it now."

"A little, yeah." He squeezed my hand. "Good surreal, though. Like everything's coming full circle."

We emerged from the trees near the pond, where the setting sun painted the surface in shades of gold and pink. A pair of ducks glided across the surface, leaving ripples in their wake.

"I can see why you love it here." I watched the ducks dip underwater and pop back up. "It's peaceful."

"It is." Ethan turned to face me, his expression thoughtful.

He raised my hand and brought it to his lips, planting soft kisses on my knuckles.

"Oh." That was the only sound I could make.

"Is this okay?" He held my hand close to his mouth.

I nodded.

"How about this?" He gently lowered my hand, still in his, and leaned in. His lips found mine and we kissed.

"Even better," I mumbled, refusing to take my

mouth off his. There was the lightest scratch from his stubble. It felt great against mine.

"Hmmm" was his only response.

When we parted, staying close enough to share breath, Ethan's lips curved in a dazed, almost dreamy smile. "I could get used to this."

"Me too." I brushed my thumb across his cheek, memorizing the way he leaned into the touch.

FIFTEEN

ETHAN

The pond at sunset was a different world—quiet, golden, and ours.

Andre's lips moved against mine, gentle but insistent.

I hadn't felt this kind of spark in years, not since Marcus. Even at our best, I didn't think it had been like this.

Part of me worried I was getting in too deep. But the way he kissed me, like I was the only thing that mattered, made those fears seem distant.

Andre pulled me closer, and the tentativeness from earlier melted away. The kisses ignited a firestorm of desire within me.

I couldn't get enough. Shivers ran down my spine as his tongue explored my mouth. His hands roamed my back, and his arousal pressed against my leg, a hard reminder of how much he wanted this too. It was intoxicating.

"Oh God," I murmured, my voice barely above a whisper. "You feel so good."

He smiled against my lips. "So do you."

Our hands roamed without hesitation. I ran my fingers over his shaved head, feeling the scratch of fine stubble. I'd wanted to do this for days now, and I relished in it.

He traced the lines of my back and glided over my shoulders and down my arms, leaving a trail of goose bumps. Soft moans slipped from my lips. Each touch deepened the connection we'd been building all week.

Andre pulled back, his deep brown eyes locking onto mine. "Can I take your shirt off?" His voice was husky with desire.

I nodded, a mix of excitement and nervousness swirling in my chest. Sure, this wasn't my first time, but what if he didn't like what he saw?

The anticipation outweighed the doubt. "Yeah, go ahead."

He lifted the hem of my shirt slowly. Every nerve tingled as he pulled the fabric up, his touch grazing my abs. I raised my arms, letting him peel it free. The cool evening air kissed my skin, but it was his gaze that made me shiver.

His eyes roamed over me, hungry and admiring. My cock hardened, pressing against my shorts.

Holding my shirt, he glanced around.

"You can just drop it," I said, my voice rough with need.

With a smirk, he let it fall. His hands returned,

brushing my collarbone. He leaned in, his breath warm against my neck. "You're stunning," he murmured.

The way he seemed to memorize every inch of me made my heart race. "I love how you're looking at me." My voice trembled.

His fingers traced my pecs, lingering on the dusting of hair, then circled my nipples. A jolt of pleasure shot through me, triggering a moan that was sharp and needy. He grinned, pinching one gently, rolling it between his fingers until I gasped, my head tipping back.

"You like that, huh?" he teased.

"Yes." I stretched the word out. "Don't stop."

When his tongue flicked over one nipple—wet and warm—I gripped his shoulders when my legs buckled as pleasure surged through me. My cock throbbed, desperate for more.

He'd unlocked something in me with such ease, and I arched into him, chasing the sensation.

"You're so fucking hot," he growled, his voice vibrating against my chest.

I'd never heard Andre swear before, and with the growl, it was one of the sexiest things I'd ever heard.

"Can I take your shirt off too?" I asked, my voice thick with desire.

Andre hesitated, a flicker of insecurity crossing his face.

"What's wrong?" I paused, not wanting him uncomfortable. "We don't have to."

"It's just... I'm not as fit as you," he admitted softly. "You're a professional athlete, and I'm... not."

I cupped his cheek, forcing him to meet my gaze. "I've wanted to see you like this since that tent collapsed on us. You're gorgeous, and I'd like to see all of you. Please."

He took a deep breath and nodded, slowly pulling his shirt over his head. As the fabric fell away, I stared. His body was lean and toned, with smooth, dark skin. His chest had subtle definition. A sparse treasure trail led from his bellybutton into his shorts. He was perfect.

The sight of him, shy and vulnerable, made my heart ache with tenderness. I wanted to explore every inch, but I also just wanted to take him all in.

His hand trembled slightly as he let his shirt fall on top of mine.

"You're gorgeous." I ran my hands over his chest, feeling the warmth of his skin.

His breath hitched.

The intense connection between us almost short-circuited my brain. Did he sense it also?

I wanted to ask, but the words stuck in my throat.

Instead, I brushed my thumb over one of his nipples, curious if he'd react like I had. His response was immediate—he gasped, his body arching into my touch.

"Ethan," he murmured.

Encouraged, I leaned in and took his nipple into my mouth, sucking gently and teasing it with my tongue. His hands slid into my hair, pulling me closer.

"Fucking hell," he whispered, his breath ragged.

Knowing I could get these reactions with just a simple touch was intoxicating.

I switched to his other nipple, lavishing it with the same attention, and his moans grew louder. My need was almost unbearable, but I focused on him, wanting to give him as much pleasure as possible.

His hands roamed down my back, fingers digging into my skin with desperate urgency. He let out a low, guttural moan. "Ethan, please."

I met his gaze. The raw desire in his eyes mirrored my own. I nodded, understanding what he needed. As I moved lower, my hands and mouth explored every inch of his body as I went.

Every touch drew a new sound from him, a new tremble. I wanted to learn every sensitive spot so I could bring him pleasure again and again.

When I reached the waistband of his shorts, I paused. "Can I take these off too?"

"If you don't, I'm going to be really pissed."

"Good," I said, smiling. "Because I'd be pissed if you didn't let me."

He caressed the side of my face, his touch tender. I unbuttoned and unzipped his shorts and pulled them down, revealing light blue boxer briefs that hugged his form. I ran my hand over his cock through the fabric, relishing its hard length. He pulsed under my touch, expanding the wet spot that had formed.

But I wasn't ready to reveal everything just yet. Instead, I ran my hands down his legs, feeling the muscles of his thighs, the soft hair tickling my palms.

I looked up at Andre, silently seeking permission. Desire and trust filled his eyes. He nodded, and I dragged down his boxer briefs, freeing his cock. It was long and curved and made my mouth water.

I leaned in and teased the tip with my tongue. The salty tang of his precum hit me, sharp and heady, igniting a surge of desire.

Andre gasped. His hands settled on my head and his fingers wove into my hair. The raw, unguarded sound of his pleasure washed over me.

I took him deeper, savoring the sensation of him against my tongue. A soft moan escaped me, the vibration making his hips twitch in response.

My hands glided up the back of his thighs, grasping his ass to anchor us both. His muscles flexed beneath my touch and I kneaded them lightly, drawing him closer.

"Ethan," he breathed, voice thick with longing. "So good."

His words fueled me, and I settled into a rhythm—taking him fully, then easing back, my lips snug around him. Each time I engulfed him, his breath caught and his grip tightened in my hair.

His reactions—the tremble in his frame, the way he surrendered to my mouth—stoked my arousal to a near-painful edge. My cock throbbed in my shorts, but I pushed the sensation aside. This was for him.

I glanced up, catching his gaze. His eyes, heavy with lust, set my pulse racing.

"Your mouth is amazing," he said breathlessly. "Don't stop."

I hummed, the sound rippling through him. My tongue danced around the head of his cock, teasing the sensitive ridge before I plunged down again. His moans grew louder, edged with desperation, and his legs quaked beneath my hands.

The taste of him, the heat radiating from his body, the way he filled my mouth—I wanted to etch that into my memory.

Andre's hands shifted to my shoulders, clutching tight as his hips rocked, meeting my rhythm. I urged him on with another hum, my fingers digging into his ass, coaxing him to take what he needed.

His breathing fractured into short, ragged bursts, signaling how close he was.

"Oh god, Ethan," he whispered, his voice splintering. "I'm right there."

I eased my pace, savoring the buildup, wanting him to feel every pulse of this moment. Pulling back, I traced my tongue along his shaft, following the throbbing vein beneath his skin.

"Tell me what you need," I rasped, my voice rough with want.

His eyes, dark and dilated, met mine. "Just... keep going. Please."

I smiled, pressing a tender kiss to the tip before taking him deep once more. This time I gave everything —pulling him in as I worked him with my lips and tongue. His moans morphed into low, primal groans, his body coiling tight as he neared the brink.

"Ethan..."

One final hum sent him over. His hips jerked, and with a deep, guttural cry, he came apart. Release surged into my mouth, hot and sudden, and I took it all. Andre's body shook with the force of it, his hands digging into my shoulders to stay standing. I welcomed it, wanting him to cling to me.

When he stilled, chest heaving, I eased back. I looked up, a grin spreading across my face. Sweat shimmered on his skin, and his eyes remained shut.

Slowly, they opened and he reached down, tracing my jaw with shaky fingers.

"That was... unreal," he said, his tone quiet and awed.

He offered a hand, pulling me up.

I rose, legs wobbling slightly, and he drew me into a lingering kiss. His lips were gentle. We held each other close, our bare chests pressed together.

SIXTEEN

ANDRE

Ethan kissed me, his lips soft and warm, a gentle press that silenced the noise in my head. Festival planning and wondering about my relationship with Ethan all faded into the background.

Then came the hug.

And God, he could hug.

His arms wrapped around me, firm yet tender. I leaned closer, my cheek against his shoulder.

When we pulled apart, his blue eyes met mine and my heart stuttered.

My mind flashed to quiet nights here, mornings tangled in sheets, the discovery of who we might be together. Could that all happen before he had to leave in September?

Was long distance even possible for us?

I brought my focus back to him and let my hand drift down his chest, brushing his nipple lightly. He groaned, low and long, and I grinned, loving how he responded.

"Can I..." My voice came out raw, barely above a whisper.

He caught my hand and guided it to the bulge in his shorts.

"Can I make you come?"

He moved my hand against him, slow and deliberate.

"Yes. I want it." His voice was thick with need. "But fair warning. I won't last. Almost lost it getting you off."

I sucked in a breath, imagining it—him falling apart as I came in his mouth.

"That would've been hot," I admitted, "but I'm glad you waited."

I wanted to savor him, just as he'd done for me. A playful spark flared, and I pulled my hand back. "Let's see how long you can hold out."

My hand slipped into his shorts, wrapping around his shaft—warm, thick, pulsing. I stroked him slowly as I leaned in for a kiss. Ethan responded by wrapping his hand around my head and deepening the kiss.

Once I couldn't wait any longer, I pulled back and dropped to my knees.

Ethan shifted, hips tilting forward, offering himself up. I tugged his shorts down. The fabric dragged over his thighs until they bunched at his feet, leaving him in boxers. His cock strained against the cotton, a damp spot spreading where he'd leaked.

I ran my hand up his leg from knee to thigh, the muscle firm beneath my fingers, soft hair tickling my skin. My hand curved to his ass—tight and perfect.

"You're a tease," he said with a groan.

I smirked up at him, eyebrow cocked. "Patience."

My hand roamed higher, tracing the faint ridges of his stomach then up to his chest. I brushed a nipple and he jolted, grabbing my shoulder, his breath catching sharply.

"How's that?" I murmured, pushing him a little.

A loud groan tore from him as his beautiful eyes locked on mine.

My fingers slid down, outlining his cock through the fabric. He twitched, his groan transitioning into a whimper of desire.

I leaned in, my lips brushing the head through the cloth, the texture rough against my mouth. His hand landed on my head, pressing me closer. The urgency in his grip made my heart pound.

I worked my mouth over the fabric—slow, steady, feeling him throb with each pass. When I pulled back, he exhaled hard and I peeled his briefs down, inch by inch. His cock sprang free, heavy and veined, the tip glistening with precum.

I grazed its length, slow and deliberate, swirling the slick drop at the tip.

"You're evil," he rasped, "and I love it."

I kissed the head gently and traced my lips along his shaft. His body tightened, a deep sound breaking free as his cock nudged my jaw. I stood, nipping his nipple with my teeth, and he shook, muttering, "Yes, yes, yes," his hands gripping me hard, nails digging into my skin.

He leaned into me, unsteady, but I kept going. My hand closed around his cock, stroking slowly. I licked his nipple again before moving in for a kiss. Our tongues met, his moans vibrating against me. The kiss was all heat and hunger.

"I'm so close," he whispered, voice fraying like it might break.

His body tensed, one hand on my hip, the other clawing at my shoulder. I sped up, his precum easing the glide.

His hips forcefully jerked and with a sharp cry, he came. Warm cum hit my hand, my stomach, his stomach, up his chest. I continued kissing him deeply, coaxing out every shudder until he slumped against me.

I slowed, pulling him close, his sweaty skin sticking to mine.

"Stars in my eyes." His breath was ragged. "Never came like that."

I sank to my knees again, and he watched, dazed but curious. Smiling, I took his softening cock deep in my mouth, tongue circling the head. He moaned, soft and sated.

Once I'd cleaned his cock, I stood and kissed him deeply again.

"Quite a mess." He glanced down with a crooked grin.

I laughed, brushing damp hair from his forehead. "Should've sucked you off like you did me—less to clean up. Still, watching you lose it was totally worth it."

"What you did was perfect." He shook his head, awe in his tone. "We've got plenty of time for more." A blush crept up his cheeks.

I stepped closer, hands settling on his hips. "I want more too."

Relief softened his face, and he smiled. "Let me clean us up."

He grabbed his shirt off the grass, wiping my stomach, legs and hand with careful strokes. Then he cleaned himself, swiping at the streaks of cum that had landed on him.

"Better?"

I took the shirt from him, catching his puzzled look. "Got some on your back when I hugged you." He turned, a streak glistening across his spine, and I wiped it off.

We dressed slowly as the pond rippled nearby, dusk settling in.

Walking back to the house, I took his hand, my fingers lacing with his. He smiled, chest bare, and I couldn't tear my eyes away.

"Never talked pasts yet," he said, "but out here feels right to share something."

"Oh?" I tilted my head, squeezing his hand.

He stopped and glanced at the pond before focusing on me. "Had my first... thing in these woods. I was thirteen, and a bunch of us were here for a sleepover. We snuck to the far side of the lake, all nerves and fumbling, scared we'd get caught."

I burst out laughing and he raised a brow. "Sorry, that's not about your story," I said, still snickering. "Just picturing a camp here—how many kids would sneak off for their firsts, like us tonight?"

He laughed too. "Tons if my hockey camps were any sign. My first time was here, but camp was wild after—locker rooms, stolen moments everywhere."

"I missed out, skipping camp," I said, half joking.

"Maybe we make up for it now?" There was a promise lurking in his eyes.

My pulse kicked up. "Who was that lucky first?"

He started to answer, then grinned, sheepish. "No. Some info has to stay in the past."

I nudged him, pouting playfully. "Come on, who should I be jealous of? Give me a hint."

He dodged, shaking his head. "They'd kill me for telling."

"Fine, keep your secrets, Ethan Gallagher," I teased, letting it go with a laugh. "I'm glad we didn't have to sneak tonight."

His eyes gleamed in the dim light. "There's more we can do out here, you know?"

"Like what?" I leaned in, voice dropping.

A sly glint flashed in his gaze. "Skinny dipping. Pond's perfect when it warms up."

I pictured it—him dripping wet, water sliding down his chest, his eyes in the moonlight. "Just say when."

We paused by the pond's edge, the water a dark mirror under the deepening sky. Ethan turned to me, his hand still in mine.

We lingered and I stepped closer, resting my head against his shoulder. He tilted his chin to press a kiss into my skin.

The sounds of the woods enveloped us: the gentle

lapping of the pond, crickets coming to life, an owl hooting in the distance.

I jumped at a rustling noise that was louder than any other noise I'd heard since we'd come out here.

"Easy," Ethan said calmly as if nothing happened.

"What was that? Are you sure it's safe to be out here?"

"It's completely safe." Ethan kissed me. That and the fact he didn't seem worried helped me relax. "Sure, there are animals out here, but nothing that would hurt us. It could've been a branch falling out of a tree, which happens sometimes. Of course, it could be Mabel. Maybe we gave her a show." He chuckled.

"You don't believe in the myth do you?"

"Completely. I'm sure I've seen her a couple of times out here when I was a kid. I even helped build a place for her food. I can show you sometime."

I shook my head. I was surprised that Ethan not only thought Mabel was real but that he'd seen her. "I'm going to need to know everything about that sometime."

"Sounds like a story to be told on a summer night when we can have s'mores."

"Hmmm. That sounds nice."

He pulled me into a hug, making me feel safe from whatever might be out here. I wasn't sure how much longer we stayed by the pond, but eventually we turned back toward the house, our steps slow as if we didn't want to let the moment end.

On the deck, I pulled him into a tight hug, his bare skin warm against my shirt. He melted into it, his breath hot on my neck. "Shower?" he asked, voice soft. "Together or separate—your call. After that, time for pie."

"Already had dessert with you," I murmured, lips brushing his ear, "but pie's good. And let's shower together. I don't want to miss the chance to scrub every inch of you nice and slow."

He kissed me and then led me into the house, neither of us in any hurry to end the evening.

SEVENTEEN
ETHAN

The satisfying sound of my skates cutting through fresh ice echoed in the empty rink. For as long as I could remember, I'd loved that sound. I'd discovered it when I was around five or six when I'd arrive at practice early to work on stick and puck handling. All these years later it still calmed me, a constant no matter what was happening in my life.

After an hour of familiar drills, my head remained cluttered, thoughts bouncing between last night with Andre and today's speech.

Last night had been incredible. The comfortable dinner conversation, Andre's eyes lighting up as he described his summer camp plans, the electricity of the unexpected make-out session at the lake. Every hot detail played on repeat in my mind. A goofy grin spread across my face even as I lined up shots.

The puck hit the back of the net with a satisfying swoosh. I retrieved the dozen or so I'd shot and set them up again at the red line, determined to focus on the mechanics of the game rather than the memory of Andre's naked body.

Despite wanting to focus on pucks, I was wondering if he was awake yet and if a good morning text might seem too eager?

The kiss he'd given me when we'd said good night suggested otherwise.

I shook my head vigorously and skated full speed to the opposite end of the rink. I picked up the puck and shot it once I crossed the blue line. It went wide, the thunk against the boards reverberating loudly.

"Get it together, Gallagher," I muttered, skating back to try again.

The speech loomed large. And it was just a few hours away.

Despite having memorized every word, practicing it in the mirror and with my moms, butterflies still swarmed in my stomach. Letting Andre down—letting the whole town down—wasn't an option.

The next shot found the net.

The familiar rhythm of skate, shoot, repeat had some effect on quieting my mind, but I couldn't hide on the ice all day.

As I began another run, Andre's vision for the summer camp rose to the forefront of my thoughts. His dedication to creating safe spaces and supporting the community resonated with me. That kind of thing was exactly why I'd set up the Maplewood Foundation.

My property had more than enough space for what he'd envisioned...

The puck clanged off the post, making me wince. One date and already I was imagining our futures intertwined.

Some people jumped to the moving-in stage. I'd skipped ahead to starting a massive project.

I switched to defensive drills, carrying a puck as I skated backwards.

The sound of the rink's door brought me to a stop. The clock showed forty minutes before the morning session. Tommy and Milo stood at the open door, already geared up and carrying water bottles and sticks.

Tommy took a bottle from Milo so he could swipe on his phone. When Milo gave a quick nod, Tommy started talking. "We didn't mean to interrupt. We didn't expect anyone to be out already."

Milo's gaze moved between his phone screen and us.

"No problem. Just running some drills. You're welcome to join."

Milo's eyes lit with enthusiasm. "Really? That would be awesome."

"You working on anything specific?" Tommy asked as they came onto the ice.

"Just shaking off some nerves about the speech later." A partial truth, but appropriate for teenage ears.

"You're going to be great," Tommy said with absolute certainty—a confidence I desperately wished to borrow.

"I appreciate that. And I'm mostly sure you're right.

You know how it is when you have to do something you're not used to."

Tommy nodded. "Oh yeah, I hate having to get in front of the class to do a report."

"And this will be bigger than any classroom." I thought for a moment. "How about we do some two-on-one drills? See if you two can get past me?"

They shared a look loaded with unspoken communication.

"You're on," Tommy said.

They skated to the bench and put the water bottles and Milo's phone down while I gathered most of the pucks into the net. I shot one to the far end of the ice and they took off after it. I drifted into the neutral zone to see what they'd do.

What followed impressed me. Tommy and Milo moved with seamless coordination, clearly having practiced beyond regular sessions. They anticipated each other's moves, communicated through subtle signals, and slipped several shots past me.

After Milo faked a shot and passed to Tommy for a perfect goal, I couldn't hold back the praise. "That was beautiful," I spoke and signed as we got water at the bench. "The way you read each other's movements, that's the chemistry that makes great pairings."

They beamed at the compliment.

Milo dropped his gloves to sign while he spoke. "Dixon's worked with us on our passing game and what works well between defense and wings. He says the best plays come from trusting your teammate to be where they need to be."

"He's right." I grabbed another quick drink. "Want to try again? This time I'll be ready for that fake out."

We ran through several more drills, then switched it up so I'd play offense with each of them.

Fifteen minutes before the start time, more players arrived. We exited the ice and removed our helmets and gloves at the bleachers.

"Thanks, Coach Ethan," Milo said. "That was fun."

Liam walked in, coffees in hand and wearing his usual calm smile. "Starting the party without me?" He approached us.

Tommy and I simultaneously signed Liam's words for Milo, whose phone remained on the players' bench. Tommy's signing continued to get more confident every day.

"These two are showing me up," I said. "They've got moves we'll need to watch out for in the exhibition game."

Tommy and Milo exchanged excited glances. We hadn't officially announced the game roster yet, although we planned to make sure all the campers got some ice time with the guests who were coming in.

"Get yourselves ready," I told them. "See you back out there in a few minutes."

They nodded and returned to the ice, leaving me with Liam.

"Here." He handed me the second coffee. "If I'd

known you'd be here so early, I would've shown up with it sooner."

"No worries." The warm drink hit the spot. "Just needed some ice time. Ended up running drills with those two."

"While you've been skating, everything's fallen into place for today's arrivals. Caleb and Kyle are driving in from the airport together, arriving around ten thirty. Cole and Miles hope to make the opening ceremony if traffic cooperates. Everyone else comes in this afternoon and tonight."

"Perfect. So many coaches here at once will be amazing for the campers." I loved that friends took the time to come in for the game and to coach. Caleb and Cole played for New York alongside Dix. Kyle was in Phoenix, while Miles played for Kyle's former team in Detroit.

"This group is certainly getting the VIP treatment." Liam sipped his drink, then fixed me with an expectant look.

"What?" I asked when his stare lingered.

"Don't *what* me. I need details about last night."

A smile spread across my face. "It was amazing. The best date I've ever had."

"Yeah?" His grin matched mine. "Tell me everything. Well, maybe not everything-everything."

"It wasn't like that," I said, though memories of our time by the pond heated my cheeks. "Well, okay, maybe there was everything-everything. Far more than I'd ever considered doing with Andre Thompson." Liam's mouth formed an O, followed by an approving nod. "We connected. Talked a lot."

"That's how it is when it's right." Liam clapped me on the shoulder. "So what brings you here shooting pucks so early? That's your stress reliever move."

I sighed, watching the campers warm up. "We might be moving too fast. Plus the speech later, the festival, that the summer is short."

"One thing at a time, E." Liam's voice blended gentleness with firmness. His ability to talk that way was one thing that made him a fantastic coach. "The speech will be fine. We can run through it now if you want. As for Andre..." He paused thoughtfully. "Remember how everything seemed so intense and important at their age?" He gestured toward the skaters.

His point hit home. Those intense teenage feelings had contributed to years of Andre and me being at odds. "We're not teenagers anymore."

"Exactly. You're both adults who know what you want. Sometimes things move fast because they're meant to." He bumped my shoulder. "Stop overthinking it."

"Rom-com advice again?"

"You know it." His serious expression cracked into a grin.

I chuckled and drained half the coffee. "Let's hit the locker room. I'll practice the speech while you get your skates on."

He clapped me on the back as we started walking.

In the locker room, I stood a few feet away while he sat to remove his sneakers. "Okay, here we go." Deep breath. "Thank you, everyone, for that welcome. To be honest, when I was asked to be the grand marshal of this year's Pride festival, my first thought was, *you've got the wrong guy*. I've always been more comfortable... skating... uhm..."

Shit. Three sentences in and already floundering.

"Hey, you were doing great," Liam encouraged. "No rush. Remember what Elena always says about taking your time?"

I nodded and tried again. This time my voice betrayed me, shaking as I described what growing up here had taught me.

"Want to know what I think?" Liam asked when I stopped.

"Always."

"You're trying too hard for perfection. The town doesn't want perfect—they want you. The kid who grew up here, learned how to play hockey, and returned to share his experience. Messing up or your voice breaking doesn't matter." He finished tying his skates and looked up. "Talk to them like you talk to the camp kids, to me, to your moms. Be yourself."

"That simple, huh?"

"That simple." He stood. "Try again but imagine you're just talking to Andre."

The suggestion caught me off guard. "Andre?"

"He believes in you. Focus on him in the crowd. Tell him your story."

I closed my eyes, picturing Andre's encouraging

smile, the warmth of his hand as he'd squeezed mine. Steadiness replaced anxiety when I opened my eyes.

The words flowed naturally this time. I stumbled in places but it felt authentic, unforced. When I finished, Liam beamed.

"That's it. Try to do that this afternoon."

"Yeah?"

"Yeah. Now let's coach some hockey."

As we headed back, confidence replaced the morning's doubt. The butterflies remained—they always would—but now they were manageable. I could do this.

"Hey, Liam?" I paused before stepping onto the ice. "Thanks."

"Always got your back, E."

EIGHTEEN

ANDRE

"I'm happy to say nothing's changed from last night." Olivia beamed as she spread jam on her toast. "Everything's ready for today. The rest of the weekend is in good shape too."

We sat at our usual meeting table at Red's, having our traditional breakfast. The combination of anticipation and relief that we had pulled this off energized everyone.

"The live streaming setup is solid." Wade tapped their tablet. "The crew's already been out this morning for a last test of the outdoor locations. Testing for indoor locations will happen an hour before we're supposed to start broadcasting." They reviewed their tablet one last time. "We even have more crew than we need, so if extra hands are required anywhere, you can text the AV group chat and someone should be available."

I sipped my tea, appreciating that we had no pressing matters. The past few days had been a whirlwind, but they'd led the charge of the wider group of volunteers making this work.

The vendor tents stood ready, the art installations were complete, all the venues reported they were ready with the programming, and even the weather looked like it would cooperate for the weekend.

Mickey's voice broke through my thoughts. "You're being suspiciously quiet."

"Just going through mental checklists." I picked up a piece of bacon, masking my expression.

Olivia's eyebrows shot up. "Really? Because usually when you're doing that, you're rapid-fire asking us questions about every detail. This morning you seem..." She paused, studying my face. "Relaxed?"

"The festival starts in four and a half hours." Wade looked at me with mock concern. "Should we be worried that you're not more stressed?"

Heat crept up my neck. "Can't I be confident in our preparation?"

"Uh-huh." Mickey's tone was knowing. "I've been part of planning or watching you plan countless events. You're never this calm." He studied me. "Does this have anything to do with dinner?"

Wade's coffee cup hung in midair. "Oh yeah. You didn't tell us anything about last night."

"It was just dinner." My voice remained neutral despite the smile tugging at my lips. "You know that meal that happens in the evening?"

"But this was with Ethan?" Olivia leaned forward as Mickey nodded. "You have to tell us everything."

I should have known I couldn't keep anything from them. But the memory of last night—the conversation, the delicious food, the walk by the pond, what we did next to the pond—made me want to hold on to the details for myself a little longer.

"It was nice." I took another sip of coffee.

"That's all we get?" Olivia protested. "Nice?"

"I'm going to excuse myself here." Wade looked at their watch. "I've got some B-roll I want to shoot." They looked at me with a gentle smile. "I'm glad you had a nice dinner, though I think it sounds like it was a lot more than just nice. Don't let these two make you say more than you want to."

"Thank you, Wade. I'll check in with you later today. Let me know if you need anything."

"Will do. See you all later." Wade shook their head and a soft chuckle trailed after them.

"I'll head out too." Olivia stood, collecting her bag. "The Palette's staff is coming in early so we can prep some things."

As they left, Mickey settled back in his seat, crossing his arms. "So, now that it's just us..."

I groaned and scrubbed my hand over my face. "You're not going to let this go, are you?"

"Nope." Mickey's voice was gentle despite his teasing tone. "Come on, you're practically glowing. And it's not because the festival's ready."

I met his patient gaze. Mickey had been there through all my relationship ups and downs, offering support without judgment. If anyone deserved to hear about this, it was him.

"It was perfect." The words rushed out. "Not in a fancy way but in all the right ways. He cooked dinner, we ate on the deck looking out over the woods. And we talked about everything." I paused, remembering how comfortable the conversation had been. "He actually asked about the camp."

Mickey leaned forward. "How'd that go?"

"Better than I imagined. He suggested we might be able to team up." My heart sped up when I thought about that moment. "Can you believe that? After I basically attacked him for buying the land?"

Mickey's smile was knowing. "I had a feeling you two would click once you got past the high school stuff. Teaming up on an enormous project like that is beyond what I expected, though."

I traced the rim of my coffee cup. "We're more than clicking. We went for a walk along the pond after dinner and..." I trailed off as warmth rose in my cheeks. This wasn't the place for private details.

"Ah." Mickey's expression softened. "That good, huh?"

"Yeah." I wondered if Mickey had been the one Ethan had his first time with. They were friends back then. Of course it could've been anyone, but I kept trying to guess.

"You deserve a night like that. Have you heard from him this morning?"

"No." A hint of anxiety crept into my voice because I'd been back and forth on if the silence meant anything. "But he's probably busy with the hockey camp. And we're both swamped with the festival starting today. I haven't reached out either."

Mickey studied me for a moment. "But you're worried."

It was a blessing and a curse how well he was able to read me. "Is it crazy to be thinking about what happens after the weekend? After the summer? He does live in Seattle most of the year."

"Not crazy." Mickey's voice was steady. "But maybe don't get ahead of yourself. See how things develop in the near term first."

"I just... I really like him. More than I expected." I sighed as I leaned in. "And it's not only the physical attraction, though that's definitely there." My cheeks warmed again. I was thankful my dark skin made it more difficult for the blush to show. "He's thoughtful and kind, and when he talks about the community, you can tell how much he cares."

"Have you told him any of this?"

"Not exactly." I shrugged. "Isn't it too soon?"

The buzzing of my phone cut Mickey off as he started to respond. I glanced at the screen, expecting a message from Ethan. Instead, it was an unknown number from Burlington.

"I should see who this is," I said as I tapped the connect button. "Hello. This is Andre."

"Mr. Thompson, hello," a crisp, professional voice said. "This is Maya Bristol from the Burlington Free Press. I'm hoping to get some information about the Pride festival's live streaming initiative to put up on our website."

I sat up straighter, shifting into what Mickey called my library director voice. "Yes, of course. We're very excited about the streaming initiative."

As I listened to the reporter's questions, Mickey mouthed *need to go* and gestured toward the diner's counter. I nodded, giving him a grateful smile as he slipped away.

"The live streaming allows us to share Maplewood's Pride festival with people who might not be able to attend in person," I explained, mentally thanking Wade for their thorough briefings. "In particular, we're happy we can share with anyone who may not have a Pride cele-bration where they live, as well as those who may not be comfortable or feel safe attending Pride."

"That's fantastic," Maya said. "I'm going to be there this afternoon for the opening ceremony. I'd love to talk to you and Ethan Gallagher. Would you both be available?"

My heart did a little flip at the mention of Ethan's name. "I'll need to check with him, but I don't see why not. The ceremony ends at twelve thirty—would twelve forty-five work? I'd also like to have you talk to Wade Connor. They're our streaming coordinator. Without them and the volunteer crew they put together, we wouldn't be able to do it."

"I'd love to get some comments from them too." She paused and I heard typing in the background.

After arranging a few more details, I ended the call and checked the time—eight forty-five. The morning was slipping away fast. I still needed to stop by the library to finish some things before heading to Maplewood City Park's amphitheater for final prep on the ceremony.

I swiped to my messages and hovered my thumb over Ethan's name. Should I text him about the reporter? Or say good morning?

Before I decided, Ingrid appeared with the check. "Mickey said to put it on the house, but he knew you'd argue about that."

"He knows me too well." I handed her my card. "Tell him thank you, though."

As I waited for her to return, I typed out a message to Ethan.

Andre: *Good morning! Thanks again for last night. I had the best time. Wanted to let you know that a reporter from Burlington wants photos and a quick interview after the ceremony. Around 12:45? Is that okay?*

I'd barely set the phone down when it buzzed. I fumbled picking it up, and it skittered off the table onto the floor, taunting me as Ethan's name flashed on the screen. Ingrid scooped it up as she returned with my card and the receipt.

"Looks like that was a soft landing." She placed everything on the table.

"Thank goodness." The phone appeared unharmed.

"Hope you have an amazing opening this afternoon."

I smiled and thanked her before she headed over to a group that had sat down a couple of tables over.

The phone buzzed again, urging me to read the waiting message. As if it was possible to forget.

Ethan: *Perfect timing. On a break from the morning camp session. 12:45 works. I more than enjoyed last night. Can't wait to see you later.*

He punctuated the message with a heart emoji.

It made me smile like a teenager with a crush.

"What's got you smiling, son?"

I looked up from my phone to find Dad and Sato standing next to the table. I jumped up to hug them.

"It's great to see you! I didn't expect to see you until the opening ceremony based on your late-night text."

"As exhausted as we were, we got hungry," Dad said.

"Um, no. Be honest, Ray." Sato cocked an eyebrow at Dad. "You got hungry and woke me up so you'd have company." He leaned in and kissed Dad's cheek.

"He's not wrong." Dad kissed Sato back. "Luckily he loves me so he came along with me. Good timing too, finding you here. Figured you'd be running around with final checks."

"Actually, things are in good shape."

"That's good news. It also means you can tell us what brought that smile to your face." He smirked at Sato, who also turned to me with a glint in his eye. "Could it have anything to do with the picture in *Maplewood Matters* of you and Ethan Gallagher under a tent?"

Of course they saw that. My cheeks heated and I hid my face in my hands.

"I think it is," Sato said.

There was no use trying to hide anything from these two. I waved Ingrid over to get their order along with another tea for me so I could give them a PG-rated rundown on what was happening with me and Ethan.

NINETEEN

ETHAN

It was a gorgeous day. Sunny, just a few clouds, comfortable temperature, and a pleasant breeze. A perfect early summer day.

The area was bustling with nearly every parking space filled and lots of people on the sidewalks. Maplewood wasn't a huge town, but people came out for the festivals. Today was no different. Most people were headed toward the park like me, with window shopping and lively conversations along the way.

I tugged at the hem of the Seattle Riptide Pride shirt I'd chosen to wear. I had other Pride shirts I'd wear during the week, but it seemed appropriate to start with this one. Dark denim shorts and my most comfortable sneakers completed what I hoped was the right first impression for the grand marshal.

"Ethan!" Mrs. Goddard waved as we approached each other in front of Special Blend. "Happy Pride."

"Happy Pride. How are you?" We traded a hug.

"Excited for Pride as always. Are you ready for the weekend?"

"As much as I can be, yeah."

"I know you'll do great." She patted my arm. "I better get in here and get my coffee so I can claim a good seat."

"I'll see you there." She smiled warmly before heading inside.

I'd only gotten a few steps farther when I caught sight of Mom and Momma. Their matching rainbow-colored Proud Moms T-shirts made me smile. They'd worn variations on the shirts for Pride as long as I could remember.

"There's our boy." Momma pulled me into a tight hug.

"How are you feeling?" Mom asked, giving my shoulder a squeeze.

I shrugged. "Like I might throw up."

"You've got this." Mom's voice carried the same steady confidence she'd used anytime I was unsure. "You've written a great speech and you've practiced. Most importantly, you're speaking from the heart."

Their support calmed some of the jitters. "I've got it printed out too." I patted the folded papers in the pocket of my shorts. They were my safety net. But even though they were in large print and in a font that was easier for me to read, I didn't want to rely on them.

"Remember, you did great at reading to the kids

too," Momma said as we crossed the street. "Everyone loved it."

"That happened so fast, there wasn't time to get stressed."

"Oh my, look how beautiful this is." The wonder in Mom's voice as she took in the decorations throughout the park ended the conversation. I was thankful for that. If we talked about it more, I suspected my anxiety would intensify.

The park was alive with energy and color. Pride flags fluttered in the gentle breeze as people streamed in. Attendees filled up the rows of chairs in front of the amphitheater stage while others gathered to stand behind them, and the vendor tents had already drawn people.

My heart swelled with excitement for all Andre and his volunteers had accomplished.

"I guess we should get backstage." Momma checked her watch. "I'll see you afterwards." She kissed Mom.

"I'll be cheering you both on," Mom said. "Love you both."

In the backstage area, the space buzzed with activity as people moved around with purpose. Mayor Axelrod reviewed notes while Mickey and Olivia had their heads together, whispering about something.

"Fantastic." Jenny, dressed in rainbow overalls rather than a Special Blend apron, came over to us as she tapped on a tablet. "Right on time. I've got you both checked in. Grace, you'll be speaking after Olivia. Ethan, you're up last as grand marshal. Andre will make the introductions and..."

Andre came into view and Jenny's words faded away. My attention locked on him, and I took in his outfit of pressed khakis and a crisp white button-down adorned with small rainbow polka dots.

He came over and the surroundings snapped back into focus just as Momma was thanking Jenny.

"Everyone's here and knows the plan, Andre. Wade also checked in and they're ready to start." She looked at her watch. "We've got about three minutes."

"Thanks so much, Jenny," Andre said, sounding calm.

She smiled and nodded before moving over to a podium next to the stage entrance.

"Hey." Andre turned to me. His smile was soft and private despite the surrounding bustle. "You ready for this?"

"As I'll ever be." I returned his smile.

Every muscle ached to embrace him, but the bustling backstage area held me back, although I suspected the town grapevine already knew about our date.

"It's going to be great." He squeezed my arm, the brief contact sending zings through me. He then turned to Momma. "Grace, always good to see you. I can't wait to see the program you've put together for the weekend." He leaned in close. "Don't tell anyone else, but the evening performances you've got are what I'm looking forward to the most."

She beamed. She'd been working on the lineup for months. "The response to it has been incredible."

"Andre," Jenny called to him.

"Looks like it's time. I'll see you out there." Before he left, he squeezed my arm again and my heart fluttered with happiness.

Momma waited until Andre was out of earshot before raising an eyebrow. "Last night was good?"

My moms knew about the date and my apprehensions and they'd admirably restrained their questions earlier. After witnessing the looks between Andre and me, though, Momma deserved some info.

"Yeah. Best date ever."

"I'm so glad." She squeezed my shoulder. "I won't ask more about it now, but Mom and I want to know as much as you want to tell us."

"We'll catch up. I promise. Though maybe not until the weekend is over."

"Of course." She smiled and gave me a brief hug.

We joined Mickey, Olivia, and Mayor Axelrod at the side of the stage so we could watch while we weren't on stage.

Andre stepped up to the microphone first, his welcome speech hitting all the right notes about community and inclusion. He made public speaking look effortless. I hoped I could channel some of that.

The crowd had grown considerably since I'd come backstage. Familiar faces dotted the audience. Liam sat with Mom in the front row, an empty seat next to them. Had they saved that for Momma? Tommy, Milo, Mimi, and others from hockey camp were a few rows back, with Dixon and Oscar near them. Caleb, Kyle, Miles, and

Cole had also arrived and were part of the standing crowd.

Olivia followed the mayor's welcome remarks. She offered details about the vendor marketplace, art installations, and crafting activities. Momma was up next, outlining the theater programming. Her passion for the arts showed in every word and even gave me goose bumps as she described what was ahead. Mickey's rundown of the food offerings had my stomach growling despite my nerves, which was the last thing I needed.

I tried to focus on what each speaker shared, but as each one of them finished and my time drew closer, I was increasingly worried I'd mess up. The folded papers in my pocket felt like they weighed a hundred pounds.

I made and released fists a couple of times, focusing on the movement as I counted through my breathing exercises.

I peeked out from backstage again, finding Andre, who stood at the back of the stage while the speeches were happening. His smile reminded me of Liam's advice to pretend I was only talking to him. I'd have to imagine it since he wouldn't be in my line of sight.

Suddenly Mickey was walking toward me, having finished. He stopped in front of me and put his hands on my shoulders. He said nothing as we locked gazes, silently calming me. I smiled and he nodded.

"And now it's my pleasure to introduce our grand marshal," Andre said. "Ethan Gallagher was born and raised here, learned how to play hockey here, and has played in the big leagues with several teams over the years.

He always comes back to Maplewood in the offseason to spend time with friends and family and run a youth hockey camp. And even when he's away during the hockey season, he supports this community in so many ways. Please welcome Ethan to the stage."

The walk to the microphone felt like skating through mud. Applause washed over me as Andre met me at center stage with a huge smile and shook my hand. His touch was even more steadying than Mickey's had been. Taking my place, I put my hands on the sides of the podium and worked to not grip it too tightly.

"Thank you, everyone, for that incredibly warm welcome." My voice cracked on the first words. I paused, took a breath, and found my moms and Liam in the crowd. "To be honest, when I was asked to be the grand marshal of this year's Pride festival, my first thought was, *you've got the wrong guy.*"

The words started flowing more naturally, just like they had during the practice sessions. I talked about growing up here, about my moms, about learning how to play hockey at school and at the place I now called home.

My voice broke again, though, as I talked about the camp where we brought so many young people together. This time it was pure happiness as I shared how proud I was of our players coming together across different languages and skill levels. I caught Milo's and Tommy's bright smiles as I took a breath.

As I talked about the library's work protecting access to books, I decided that was a reason to steal a glance behind me at Andre. His eyes widened, possibly surprised to hear his work mentioned, but it was important work for the queer community.

By the time I reached the end, my voice was steady and strong. "So, thank you for your support, thank you for standing together, and thank you for making Maplewood the incredible place that it is. It's an honor to celebrate Pride with all of you. Happy Pride, everyone!" I waved to the crowd.

The response was immediate and enthusiastic. My moms were the first on their feet, followed quickly by others until the entire audience stood cheering. Relief, joy, and satisfaction washed over me.

I survived it, and I thought I'd done pretty well.

Andre stepped up beside me, waiting for the applause to die down. "Thank you, Ethan. You'll find Ethan at many of our activities over the weekend. And you'll get to see him, some of his friends from the NHL, and the teens who are part of the hockey camp play at Saturday's charity game." He glanced at me with a grin. "But before that, we have one more important thing to do—planting this year's Pride maple tree."

Mayor Axelrod came back on stage to join us as volunteers brought forward a young maple sapling, a decorative pot, and soil in another pot.

"This tree represents our commitment to growing and nurturing our inclusive community," Mayor Axelrod explained. "Every year since Maplewood's first Pride march in 1970, we plant one during our celebrations, creating a living reminder. For this weekend the tree will be on display here in Maplewood City Park and then it will be transplanted in Pride Grove."

The mayor took the sapling and put it into the pot, which already had some soil in the bottom, and she held it as Andre and I took turns adding soil. As I patted the dirt into place, I thought about how this tree would grow along with Maplewood, becoming part of the town's story.

Once the ceremony concluded, people dispersed toward the vendor tents and other activities. I jumped off the stage to accept congratulations and answer questions about Saturday's game. My moms hugged me tight before heading to the theater to welcome people attending the afternoon film lineup.

"That was beautiful." Andre's voice came from behind me. I turned and found myself face to face with him. "Thank you for mentioning the library's work."

"I meant every word." I took his hand in mine. "Your work matters."

His brown eyes sparkled in the sunlight as he glanced at his watch. "We should head over to meet Maya, the reporter from Burlington. She's talking with Wade about the streaming aspect." He pointed to where the two were talking at one of the camera setups.

"Lead the way." We walked through the park, which was alive with chatter and laughter, with music playing through the speakers on the stage. "All of this is amazing, Andre. You and your team did an incredible job."

"We all did." He bumped his shoulder against mine. "I'm glad the opening ceremony's done and things are underway. What I'm really looking forward to is more time with you."

"I've got a lot of art to look at after the interview, but can we get together later? Check out some of the festival together?"

"Yes, to all of that. Let's touch base later in the after-noon and we can figure it out."

TWENTY
ANDRE

I sank onto a bench on Maple Street, taking a moment to catch my breath after a whirlwind afternoon. Everything had gone smoothly—aside from a brief tech hiccup when someone accidentally unplugged the sound system between panels at the history and educational sessions.

The two panels I'd moderated exceeded my expectations. The discussion about banned books drew an overflow crowd with passionate dialogue about the importance of representation in literature and protecting access to diverse stories. Several attendees gave powerful stories about finding themselves in books that others wanted to remove from shelves.

The second panel, focusing on Maplewood's Pride history since 1970, featured long-time residents sharing memories of the first march and how the celebration had transformed over the years. Mrs. Goddard's story about helping organize the first festival brought tears to many eyes, including mine. She spoke about how, even though there'd been no effort to promote that first Pride outside of Maplewood, more than a dozen people came to town that day so they could safely be themselves.

The other thing that made the day were the occasional texts from Ethan. He'd sent pictures of art pieces he was judging, and his commentary made me smile.

Ethan: *How am I supposed to judge when everything's so beautiful? You didn't include those instructions.*

Ethan: *Just saw the most incredible painting of two hockey players.*

Ethan: *Found the most amazing maple candy vendor! I'm saving you some truffles.*

I'd caught glimpses of him throughout the day, usually surrounded by people wanting photos or autographs. He handled each interaction with grace, especially with young people.

A social media post I'd seen earlier showed him with his NHL friends—Caleb, Kyle, Nick, Cole, and Miles—all of them grinning in their team's Pride shirts as they posed near the maple tree we'd planted. The caption read, *Ready to coach, play, and celebrate Pride in Maplewood.*

My phone buzzed with a new message.

Ethan: *Art walk winner announcement at 6:30. Meet you there?*

I smiled as I typed back.

Andre: *Wouldn't miss it. I'm already on a bench near The Wild Palette.*

It didn't take long for me to spot Ethan approaching. He wore a different shirt, a Maplewood High Bears hockey Pride shirt with the team logo in Pride colors. Despite the fatigue in his features, his blue eyes lit up when he saw me. He dropped onto the bench beside me with a long exhale.

"You look like you've had quite a day." I resisted the urge to smooth his tousled hair, which was drooping down across his forehead.

He leaned back, our shoulders touching. "It's been amazing. But I'm not used to talking to so many people in one day. Not to mention having to decide which art was the best."

"You seemed to handle it well."

"Thanks." His smile was soft. "Texting with you helped. I was so glad to hear about the panels. I want to watch those once this is all done." He glanced across the street to the vendor area. "So, I stashed the truffles at the theater because I worried I'd leave them somewhere. Instead, do you want to grab some ice cream? I've heard good things about the Pride Berry Rainbow Swirl."

"Lead the way."

We wound through the crowd to the ice cream cart, where Ethan insisted on paying. The vendor created perfect swirls of rainbow-colored ice cream topped with edible glitter that sparkled in the sun. We wandered back toward the gallery as we ate.

"So many flavors," I said after my first bite. "Some blueberry and... is that raspberry?"

"Strawberry too."

Ethan had a small smear of purple ice cream on his chin. Without thinking, I reached up to wipe it away with my thumb, and the touch sent a small electric current through my fingers. He made a soft hum in response.

People smiled and nodded as they passed us, but no one interrupted our ice cream time. It felt both surreal and natural to share a frozen treat with Ethan while he told me about his favorite art.

"It was so difficult to choose a winner. I'm not sure how I'm going to judge anything else if everything is as good as the art." He paused to catch some ice cream that was melting down the cone. The way his tongue darted out was sexy and sent my brain reeling. "This hockey painting really got me. I think it could be based on Cole and Miles since it's got two centers at the face-off dot looking fierce and ready to go while hearts dance above their head."

His enthusiasm was infectious.

"I need to see that."

"I'll show you." He checked his watch. "Speaking of which, we should get inside. I don't want to be late." He finished his cone and tossed away his napkins. "You want to go to Red's later? I'm craving a burger." He paused. "Provided you want to join me, of course."

"I'd love to." No way I'd say no to more time with him.

The gallery buzzed with excitement as people gathered. Olivia stood at the microphone, clipboard in hand

and covered works of art on either side. Ethan made his way to join her and Justin Mayer, last year's winner. I found a spot near the wall where I could see everything.

"Welcome, everyone!" Olivia's amplified voice carried through the space. "We've had an incredible showing of art this year, with over fifty pieces submitted. They'll be on display all week and you can pick up a location map here so you can find them all. Now, before we announce Best in Show, each judge will share their personal favorite."

Justin went first. He unveiled a series of photographs capturing quiet moments of queer joy in Maplewood— two elderly women holding hands in Maplewood City Park's gazebo, teenagers studying together at the library, a group sharing maple cotton candy at last year's Pride.

"Ethan?" Olivia gestured for him to speak next.

He stepped forward, hands loose at his sides instead of fidgeting. "My choice is Team Passion." He unveiled the painting he'd described earlier. "The artist captured something special with these two opposing players ready to battle for a puck while also clearly in love."

Olivia nodded in agreement before announcing her own choice, a painting that at first glance seemed to be swirls of rainbow colors but after a closer look became a scene of Maplewood's Pride parade.

"And now," Olivia continued, building anticipation, "our Best in Show winner." She opened an envelope with the appropriate ceremony. "Tracey Childs for Team Passion!"

The crowd erupted in applause as a teenage girl with

a hockey jersey tied around her waist made her way to the front, looking stunned. Ethan's face lit up as he handed her the ribbon and plaque.

"Speech!" someone called out.

Tracey gripped her plaque tight. "Um, wow. Thank you so much. I... I was inspired." She glanced around and her eyes suddenly went wide. "Oh gosh. They're here!" She took another breath. "This painting was inspired by Cole Ackerman and Miles Robinson. They play on opposite teams, but their love doesn't affect their competitiveness. I saw them in a similar pose during a game, and I wanted to capture that because it's the game I love and, of course, who doesn't love a love story?"

More applause followed before people moved around the gallery, congratulating Tracey and viewing all the artwork.

Just as Ethan got to me, Miles and Cole also joined us.

"Oh my God, she painted us." Miles pointed to where Tracey was talking with admirers by the painting. "No wonder you texted us to make sure we were here."

"I'm glad you could make it. I didn't know she'd win the whole thing, but it was my favorite. It's so awesome that it's really based on you two."

Cole slipped his arm around Miles's waist. "Let's go talk to her. Catch you two later?"

"Yeah. We're going to go grab a bite."

They gave us a knowing look, one that could only pass from one couple to another. Were we starting to develop that?

We stepped out into the cooling evening air. As we walked toward Red's, two teens approached with hopeful expressions and Pride shirts in hand.

"Mr. Gallagher, would you mind signing these?" asked a lanky teen with braces who was wearing a Phoenix Pride hockey jersey. His voice cracked with nerves. "I'm Anton and this is my boyfriend, Clark. We're trying to get everyone's signatures."

"Of course." Ethan took the offered marker, his smile warm and genuine as he accepted the Maplewood Pride shirts from them. The shirts already had signatures from Dix and Caleb.

Clark, the shorter of the two, with glasses and a rainbow beanie, bounced on his toes. "Thank you for this! It's so amazing meeting all of you."

Ethan looked around, trying to decide what to use to write against, when Clark dug into his shoulder bag.

"Sorry," he said, handing over a copy of a Kendrick Sanderson book. "This will help."

Ethan nodded and put the shirt against the book. Then he carefully added his signature with deliberate strokes. "You can find Miles and Cole in the gallery down the block if you want to try to grab them now."

"Oh cool!" Anton exclaimed, practically vibrating with excitement.

"Are you coming to the game on Saturday?"

They nodded enthusiastically.

"We start camp in a week too." Clark clutched his signed shirt to his chest. "It's going to be cool learning from you and Kyle Pressgrove."

"Fantastic. I look forward to seeing what you've got on the ice." Ethan's genuine interest made both teens beam.

"Thanks so much." Anton held up his shirt like a trophy. Clark was already folding his, treating it like a precious artifact. "See you around!"

The boys hurried off, their excited chatter trailing behind them.

"You're great with them," I said as we resumed walking.

"They remind me of myself at that age." He laced his fingers through mine. "Though I didn't have out hockey players for mentors then."

The warmth of his hand against mine created a sense of connection that belied how new this was between us. We walked in comfortable silence, taking in the festival as we headed toward Red's.

"The usual?" Ingrid asked as she took us to the corner booth Mickey had set aside for us.

"Definitely," Ethan said. "I've thought about that burger all day. And a 27, please."

"My usual as well," I added. "And can we get maple bacon cheese fries to share?"

"Coming right up." She winked at us before heading to the kitchen.

"The usual?" I raised an eyebrow at Ethan.

"Just because I'm only here for two or three months of the year doesn't mean my likes change." He smiled sheepishly. "The best burgers in Vermont, and really in North America as far as I'm concerned, are right here."

"No argument there." I took a sip of the water Ingrid had left us, studying Ethan's face. He looked relaxed, happy. "How are you feeling with the first of the grand marshal duties behind you?"

"Exhausted but good." He played with his straw wrapper. "It's different from the physical exhaustion of hockey. The things I'm doing with the festival are more personal. And seeing everyone so excited makes it easier."

"You're doing an amazing job."

"Thanks." A slight smile played on his lips as he reached across the table for my hand. "Today's been great, but last night was extraordinary. I'm glad we took the time to hang out, talk, and, you know…"

I barely heard him since I was fixated on his hand on mine. He'd done that so many times today and didn't seem to care if anyone saw. I liked not hiding what might be happening, even if it would get us featured in *Maplewood Matters*. "Yeah. It was one of the most perfect nights I've had."

Ingrid arrived with our fries and drinks, and we reluctantly separated our hands to make room for the generous portion. The combination of crispy fries, maple-glazed bacon, and melted cheese made my stomach rumble.

"So," Ethan said between bites, "I briefly ran into Wade and they said the live stream numbers were more than expected."

"Very much so. We were going to be happy if we just had a hundred viewers." I paused to pull out my phone to refer to the info Wade had sent. "The opening ceremony had more than 10,000 views, peaking during your speech. The panels had between 3,500 and 4,000 each."

"Oh wow. Glad I didn't think about how many people could be watching."

"Your team had something to do with that because there was a post on the Riptide's social feeds about fifteen minutes before we started."

"I didn't know they did that."

"And the comments we've been getting..." I scrolled a bit in Wade's email. "Some of them are crap that the team's deleted, but so many messages about people being inspired about it and glad the team shared it." I set the phone on the table, screen down. "I'm so glad Wade made it work."

Our burgers arrived, looking scrumptious as maple-candied onions spilled over the edges. We fell into comfortable silence for a few bites.

"Can I ask you something?" Ethan set down his burger, his expression turned serious. "Where do you see yourself in five years?"

The question caught me off guard, but I also appreciated his interest. "Honestly? I've thought about that a lot lately. I love the library, love what we're doing here. And the idea of the summer camp—" I paused, gathering my thoughts. "I want to make a difference, you know? Create spaces where kids can be themselves, find their community."

"But?"

He knew me well enough already to realize I had more.

"Sometimes I wonder if I should be looking at bigger opportunities, different cities?" I met his eyes. "Basically, I don't know what the next five look like. There are things I want to accomplish, but I'm not sure what that turns into. What about you?"

"I've got a few good years left playing if I'm lucky. Is it five?" He shrugged. "After that, I want to coach. Not just summer camps but develop young players full time. And I want to do it here, or at least near here." He gestured around us. "Maplewood's home and I'd like to be closer to it."

The certainty in his voice made my heart skip. "You've really thought about this."

"I have." His fingers intertwined with mine across the table. "Buying what I hope is my forever home." He dropped his voice a bit. "Plus reconnecting with you, seeing how passionate you are about your work. It's made me think about what I want my legacy to be."

"Besides an impressive NHL career?"

He laughed softly. "The game is only a part of it. I'd like to be known more for what I do after."

My heart swelled at his words. The idea of him planting roots here, of creating something meaningful beyond hockey resonated.

I pushed my leg into his under the table. "Aren't you already doing it? Every time you connect with those kids, show them they can be both an athlete and authentically themselves, you're building something that will last far beyond your playing career."

He nodded, pulling back to meet my eyes. "Here's to

the future and whatever we do to realize those aspirations."

He raised his shake glass and I tapped it with my iced tea before we each took a big drink for the future.

TWENTY-ONE
ETHAN

The theater buzzed with excitement as people found their seats for the evening's dance program.

Where yesterday had been mostly about the festival, today had been a full day of camp. With the exhibition game tomorrow, coaches and campers had focused on that.

I'd seen Andre briefly as I met him and Wade to talk about streaming for the game, but that was it. We'd maintained a steady text stream, though. Every time the phone buzzed, I was eager to get to it because I knew it was probably him.

I'd saved Andre a seat between Dixon and me. Dixon was currently engaged in animated conversation with Cole and Miles, who were sitting in front of us, and the three of them were dissecting today's ice time.

"You should've seen how pumped our team was." Dixon leaned forward in his seat. "Tommy and Milo showed off some passing sequences that are going to crush you guys. And we've got these guys at center." He fist-bumped Cole and Miles.

"Dream on," I said, knowing how outstanding my team had been. "We worked on some moves that'll have your defense spinning. Plus I've got Caleb, and he knows exactly how you and Cole play. And don't forget who taught Tommy that backhand shot he loves."

"I'm not worried." Dixon puffed out his chest a bit. "Milo and I have great chemistry on D. Nothing is getting by us."

"Speaking of clicking..." Kyle turned around from where he sat next to Cole. "Is this date number two for you and a certain librarian and festival organizer?"

Warmth crept into my cheeks. "Maybe."

"And how is it going?" Cole prompted. "I get why you don't talk about it at camp around the kids, but we're all grown-ups here."

"It's good and that's all I'm saying." I grinned at their collective groan of disappointment. Besides, while we were all grown-ups here, there were plenty of people around who could overhear our conversation which would be even more fodder for *Maplewood Matters*.

"Come on," Miles said. "We've been rooting for you two since we got here."

"You've been here less than forty-eight hours."

"Exactly. And in that time, I've seen enough to know I need more details."

Before I could respond, Caleb spoke up in his captain's voice. "Leave him alone, guys. He doesn't need us badgering him. Though I gotta say, Ethan, it's nice seeing how happy you seem."

"Hello, everyone." Andre's voice washed over me, making my heart swell with happiness. He stood at the end of our row, looking handsome in dark jeans and a deep purple button-down with the sleeves rolled up.

A chorus of greetings went up as everyone shifted to let him through to his seat. As he sat down, his smile was warm and private. "Hi."

"Hi." I took his hand. "How was the book festival?"

"Fantastic. The discussions were engaging, and we had a great turnout." His thumb traced small circles on the back of my hand. "How was camp?"

"Busy with prep for tomorrow's game. You missed Dix's attempt at trash talk earlier."

Dix shot me a slightly evil look and then grinned, which made Andre chuckle.

"I'm looking forward to seeing you play."

The house lights dimmed slightly, and Oscar stepped onto the stage. He looked sharp in black pants and a fitted black T-shirt with rainbow piping at the collar and sleeves.

"Good evening, everyone!" Oscar's voice carried through the theater. "I'm Oscar Salazar and I'm thrilled to be your host for this evening as well as a performer in the closing piece. Welcome to what promises to be an incredible night of dance. We've got eight fantastic performances, featuring both local talent and some special guests."

Andre's hand warmed mine as the house lights

dimmed further and Oscar introduced the first act. Andre leaned close, his shoulder pressing against mine as we settled in to watch the performance. As much as I'd looked forward to this program, I wished Andre and I were at my place. Alone.

The first few performances showcased an array of talent and diversity. Each piece told a unique story, from an energetic hip-hop routine to a contemporary duet that had the audience holding their breath with all its tricks.

During a pause between performances, Liam called out to me from down the row and help up his program showing the pictures of the performers. "Did you see that Daniel June is performing?"

"Oh, look at that."

"I don't recognize that name," Andre said.

"He's from Burlington and was at camp"—I thought for a moment—"three years ago. He was so passionate about both hockey and ballet." I smiled at the memory. "We encouraged him to pursue both because there was no reason not to."

Oscar returned to introduce him. "Next up, we have Daniel June and James Martinez performing *Love Finds Its Way*, a waltz they choreographed together."

Daniel and James took the stage in matching navy blue suits. As the music began—a piano arrangement of a pop song I recognized but couldn't name—they moved together with fluid grace. Their connection was evident in every step, every turn, every lift.

"They're incredible," Andre whispered, his fingers intertwining with mine.

Words failed me. I remembered a teenage Daniel, uncertain about balancing his passions. Now he danced with such confidence and joy. When the piece ended, I was on my feet cheering with the rest of the audience.

"That's your impact right there," Andre said as we sat back down. "You and Liam encouraged him to be himself."

"We just listened to him. Gave him space to figure things out."

"Sometimes that's all people need." Andre's voice was soft, understanding.

The next piece was a group number featuring dancers from a local studio. Their energy was infectious, and my foot tapped to the beat. During the next reset, Dixon excused himself.

Andre looked confused but I knew what was happening.

Dixon stepped out on stage. "Good evening. I'm Dixon Cliff and it's my privilege to introduce the evening's final performance. First, I have to say how wonderful it's been being here in Maplewood the past few days, coaching at Ethan's camp and celebrating Pride with you all."

The audience applauded.

"The piece you're about to see holds a very special place in my heart. Earlier this year, I attended a performance of *Ballet Strong* when its tour stopped in New

York. That night I reconnected with Oscar after years apart. This piece, entitled *Time*, was a stunning part of that performance. Tonight is the first time that Oscar and his dance partner Nathaniel Mayer have performed it since the tour ended. I can't imagine a more perfect place for it than as part of these festivities. They are accompanied tonight by Maplewood's own Dmitri Fairchild on violin."

As Dixon left the stage, the theater went completely dark. When the lights came up again, they revealed Oscar on the left side of the stage and Nate on the right, both dressed in simple gray pants and white T-shirts. Dmitri stood on a small platform at the back of the stage, illuminated in a soft pool of light, violin at the ready.

The first notes Dmitri played filled the space—haunting, beautiful, full of longing. Oscar and Nate began to move, each in their own space, their movements suggesting searching, yearning. As the music built, they drew closer together, their paths crossing but not quite connecting.

Andre's grip tightened as the dancers came together in a breathtaking series of lifts and turns. Their strength and grace told a story of two people finding each other and falling in love. Our journey mirrored theirs in some ways—from our misunderstandings to where we were now.

Sitting here holding hands, watching the performance, our story was just beginning.

The violin's melody became more complex as Oscar and Nate moved through what was clearly the evolution of a relationship. Their movements spoke of trust, intimacy, and deep connection. There were moments of playfulness, tender touches, passionate embraces. Each gesture was powerful yet vulnerable.

I glanced at Andre. He was completely absorbed in the performance, his eyes glistening. When he noticed me looking, he met my gaze with a soft smile that made my heart skip.

We turned back to the stage just as the music shifted to a slower, more contemplative tone.

The dance continued, showing the depth of a love that grew over a life. Oscar and Nate moved as if they were one person, their synchronicity breathtaking. The violin sang out a melody that seemed to capture every emotion—joy, fear, desire, commitment.

As the piece drew to a close, the music became soft and delicate. The dancers' movements slowed until Oscar kneeled beside Nate, who lay still on the stage. The last notes of the violin faded away along with the lights, leaving the theater in darkness.

For a moment, there was silence.

Then the audience erupted in thunderous applause. Everyone around me rose to their feet in appreciation. As the stage lights came up, tears glistened in many eyes, including my own.

Oscar and Nate took their bows, then brought Dmitri forward to share in the adulation. The three of them invited the other performers on stage and everyone took a final bow before the house lights came up.

As people began gathering their things, I turned to Andre. "I've only seen part of that in a clip that Dixon shared. Watching it live and being so close to it was incredible."

He wiped at his eyes. "I don't think I've ever seen anything quite like it."

Around us, our friends discussed the performance with enthusiasm, and several tissues were passed out from a packet that someone had produced.

"Do you want to come backstage with me?" I asked Andre. "I'd love to say hello to Daniel and congratulate Oscar and Nate."

"Of course."

We excused ourselves and navigated through the crowds leaving so we could get to the stage.

Backstage was buzzing. We found Daniel and James first, still in their navy suits, talking with a group of performers and audience members.

"I'm sorry to interrupt." I came up next to Daniel, and he gave me a big smile.

"Coach Gallagher! I'm so glad you're here. This is my boyfriend, James."

"James, it's good to meet you. You two were incredible." I pulled Daniel into a hug. "I'm so proud of you."

"It's great to meet you, Coach Gallagher. Daniel has told me so much about you. He's quite the talk at school as the goalie who also dances."

"I love that so much. Daniel, James, this is Andre Thompson." Andre shook hands with them as I talked. "He's..." I looked to Andre. "We haven't figured that out yet, have we?" I chuckled nervously.

Andre laughed while Daniel and James looked amused.

"Nice, Coach!" Daniel said.

"You coming to the game tomorrow?"

"Wouldn't miss it."

"Great. Let's catch up after." I didn't want to take up more of his time here. "I'll let you get back. Congratulations again. You were spectacular."

I gave Daniel another quick hug, and we made our way over to Oscar, Nate, and Dmitri.

"That was spectacular," I told them. "I'd heard the original music in a clip Dixon showed me, but the solo violin—wow."

"It was all thanks to Dmitri," Oscar said, clapping the violinist on the shoulder. "He heard the recorded track we'd brought and approached us to play live instead. We only had two rehearsals, but it came together fast and beautifully. I'm going to share the live stream footage with the original choreographer. He may want to adapt that for the future."

"It was really something having moved from piano and guitar on the tour to Dimitri's solo." Nate took a drink from his water bottle. "It elevated everything."

Dmitri smiled modestly. "It was an honor to be part of such a beautiful piece. I think the violin part tells its own story alongside theirs."

Oscar and Nate agreed, and after a few more minutes of conversation, Andre and I excused ourselves so they could talk to more admirers.

"What are you up to now?" Andre asked as we headed into the main theater space.

I shrugged. "Have something in mind?"

"Could we go to your place? Hang out on the deck?"

"Absolutely." Happiness fluttered in my chest. Andre was comfortable enough to ask for what he wanted. I'd been planning to extend an invitation, but having him take that step thrilled me.

TWENTY-TWO
ANDRE

I longed for Ethan on the short drive to his place. After the emotional intensity of the evening's performance, even the brief separation pulled on my heart.

He was nearby, though, as his car was just ahead of mine. When we pulled into the long driveway, the motion sensor lights clicked on, illuminating the road and the front of the house in a warm glow.

I climbed out of my car as Ethan got out of his. "Thanks for letting me invite myself over."

"I'm glad you did." His smile was soft, intimate, as he walked over to me. "I wasn't ready to say good night."

"Me either."

The house was quiet as we entered, such a contrast to the energy from earlier in the day. Ethan led the way to the kitchen, flipping on lights as we went. The silence was perfect for processing the emotional evening we'd experienced.

"I'm still thinking about that last piece." I leaned against the counter. "The way Oscar and Nate told that story."

Ethan's voice softened. "Kind of like us. Far apart for a long time, and then coming together."

The vulnerability in his expression tugged on my emotions.

"Two people finding each other at the right time."

"Exactly." He reached for my hand and raised it up. I followed his lead and twirled around once. "Though hopefully with fewer complicated dance moves."

"Oh yes, much fewer." I brought myself in close to him. "I like to dance, but I have nothing like that in my repertoire. That spin was about as complex as I can get."

"At least you have a repertoire. I'm glad you knew what I was doing. That would've fallen flat otherwise." He kissed my hand and then went to the fridge. "What can I get you?"

"Let me guess." I moved behind him to peer over his shoulder as he opened the door. "My choices are water, hibiscus tea, and beer?"

He chuckled. "I really need to work on my hosting skills."

I placed my hands on his shoulders and he allowed me to move him, gently pulling him away from the fridge before turning him around. "There's something else I'd like first."

"Oh?" His voice was a mix of playful and hopeful.

I brought my lips to his. The kiss started softly but deepened as Ethan wrapped his arms around me. All the emotions from Oscar and Nate's dance poured into our connection. When we broke apart, we were both breathing heavily.

"Wow," Ethan whispered, his forehead resting against mine. "Have I mentioned that you're an amazing kisser?"

"You're also quite talented in that area." I brushed another kiss against his lips before stepping back. "Now, about those drinks?"

He laughed, the sound warm and rich. "Beer?"

"Perfect."

We headed out to the deck and settled onto a cushioned couch. I angled myself toward Ethan, one leg tucked under me, and he mirrored my position.

The night was clear and star-filled. A gentle breeze rustled the trees as crickets chirped. I sank deeper into the cushions, enjoying the peaceful setting and the company.

This was a place I could imagine spending countless evenings. Even though it was way too soon, the thought of actually living here someday flickered through my mind.

"Can I ask you something?" I sipped my beer, gathering courage. "It's kind of a weird question."

"Go for it."

"How is it we're connecting so well? Not in my wildest dreams did I imagine this would happen." My mouth became a desert, and I took a quick drink so I could keep going. "I mean, you're a pro hockey player, and I'm just a small-town librarian who was a jerk to you in high school."

"First, you're not *just* anything," he said emphatically. "You're passionate, dedicated, and making real change in people's lives." He paused. "And yeah, we had our issues, but we grew up." His expression turned playful. "Plus you're hot as hell."

I nearly choked on my beer. "Smooth talker."

"I try." He reached over and took my hand. "But seriously, watching you these past few days—how much you care. It's amazing. And when you smile..." He squeezed my fingers. "You are so adorable. In his books, Shawn would call it swooning."

Warmth spread through my chest as I idly traced along his fingers. "I should probably tell you about why my last relationship ended."

Ethan cocked his head and nodded.

I didn't talk about this often, but it needed to be said. "I was engaged once. To a guy named Denzel. We met in college, stayed together through grad school. He was getting his MBA while I got my library science degree."

The memories weren't as painful now but they still stung.

"We were a week away from our wedding when he ended it. He told me I'd driven him away because I was too intense, too controlling about how things should be done. Wedding planning became the last straw."

"Oh my God," Ethan said softly. "That must have been devastating."

His hand in mine anchored me.

"It was."

Emotions spilled out, and a tear slid down my face. Ethan was quick, brushing it away before I could.

"We don't have to talk about this if you're not ready." He cupped the side of my face as he continued to hold my hand.

"But we do. You're important to me, and I want you to know this."

He nodded and wrapped my hand in both of his.

"So, I get why he felt like he did. I was so focused on everything being perfect right down to how we loaded the dishwasher and organized DVDs." I gave a self-deprecating laugh. "There was a lot of time in therapy after we ended it. I learned... still learning really, how to recognize when I'm getting too caught up in my vision of how things should be."

"I've seen that a time or two these past few days," Ethan admitted gently.

"I know." I wiped at my eyes again. Tears were near the surface and while I didn't mind being emotional, I didn't want to lose my focus on the conversation. "And I hate that. Not just that I did it to you, but that I did it all. It happens less, but it still can."

His kind expression didn't waver.

"It's not like I don't have things I work on too. You do the work, that's what matters. I saw how you listened and adjusted and apologized."

"That's the work paying off." I focused on his thoughtful blue eyes. "I'm better at recognizing when perfect isn't as necessary as being present. And I want to apologize again for how I was in school. I know..."

"Please stop." Ethan shook his head. "You've already apologized for that. It's in the past, and we both understand each other so much better now." He was quiet for a moment. "My turn. I should tell you about Marcus."

"Oooh. Is that the guy from the lake?"

He had a confused look before he grinned and chuckled. "Um, no. You're not getting that out of me." He playfully slapped at my hand. "Marcus is my longest relationship. We met when I was playing in Nashville. He moved with me to Boston and later got an amazing job offer in Texas. We tried long distance, but..."

He sighed, and a look of regret crossed his face. It was my turn to take his hand in mine.

"It's hard when you're both building careers in different places. The time zones, the travel schedules. Just shy of our fourth anniversary, and a year of living in different cities, we broke it off."

"That can't have been easy."

"It wasn't." He looked out at the woods for a moment. "And that decision is looming for us."

I hesitated before asking, "Do you think long distance is even possible?"

"It is," Ethan replied thoughtfully. "I've seen it work. Caleb and Aaron. Dixon and Oscar are only a few months into their relationship, but they're going for it. Miles and Cole too." His eyes met mine. "Though they all had the advantage of strong friendships. But I believe it's possible for the right people."

I considered that for a moment before changing direction. "Have you dated much since Marcus?"

"I've gone on dates here and there, but I haven't

found the right person," he admitted. "What about you?"

"It's only been in the past few months that I've felt ready to try," I said. "It sounds like we've had the same kind of luck." I met his eyes with a small smile.

Ethan brought my hand up and planted kisses on my knuckles.

A moan escaped as his lips sent tingles up my arm. "I suppose we don't need to figure it all out right now."

"Nah. Plenty of time." He smiled. "Let's talk about something less intense but just as important. What would be your perfect date night here in Maplewood?"

I laughed, relaxing back into the cushions. "Really? That's your important question?"

"Hey, this is crucial information," he said with a grin. "I need to know what works for you."

"Okay, let me think." I took a long drink and looked up into the gorgeous night sky. "Dinner at Giuseppe's because their homemade pasta is incredible. Dessert and coffee somewhere with maple pie. Your choice for which diner we'd show up at. Catch some music at The Striped Maple." I turned to face him. "What about you? What's your ideal date look like?"

"Mine would start at the farmer's market on Saturday morning." I raised my eyebrows. "Hear me out. We'd pick up some fresh snacks, head somewhere for a picnic. I'd have to decide where that would be. Maybe go for a hike in the afternoon. Back to town, we finish up with an evening at the theater." He smiled softly. "Simple but perfect."

"I like it." My mind filled with images of us doing exactly that, our hands linked as we explored together.

He leaned in, and this kiss was different—slower, deeper. My free hand found its way to his neck, pulling him closer as his tongue traced my bottom lip.

When we broke apart, Ethan pressed his forehead to mine, the gesture becoming wonderfully familiar. His fingers traced patterns on my cheek. His heart raced against my palm where it rested on his chest.

After a moment, he tilted his head and captured my lips again, this time with featherlight kisses that made me sigh. I melted into him, savoring the sweetness of the moment.

We stayed like that for a while, trading kisses and being close. The night air had cooled considerably, but next to Ethan, I barely noticed.

Eventually, I couldn't hold back a yawn.

Ethan did the same. "Oh man, I tried so hard to keep that in."

We laughed, which triggered more yawns.

"It's been a long day." I untangled myself from his embrace. "I should head home."

"Or..." He looked suddenly shy. "You could stay?"

My breath hitched. "Yeah?"

"Yeah. Just to sleep," he added quickly. "It's late, and we both have another long day tomorrow."

The thought of falling asleep next to him sent a wave of longing through me. "I'd like that."

He stood, offering his hand. "Fair warning—I

haven't shared a bed with anyone in a long while. I might be rusty."

"Same here." I let him pull me up. "But I'm willing to risk it."

His smile was worth any potential awkwardness. "Me too."

TWENTY-THREE
ETHAN

The rink parking lot was nearly full when I arrived after judging the crafts competition.

I chatted with a few people who were looking over the T-shirts and jerseys for sale as well as autographed auction items.

Liam and I had hosted exhibitions during Pride over the past couple of years, usually featuring one or two special guests including fellow hometown boy Ryland Zervudachi, who played for Columbus. This year we were able to bring in several pros to play alongside some of our most elite campers.

"Coach Ethan!" Tommy's voice carried across the lobby. He and Milo were already in their gear except for skates, talking and signing. When I reached them, Tommy continued to speak and sign. "Ready for us to crush..."

Tommy stopped and looked at his hands with a frustrated expression.

"Crush." Milo chimed in, saying the word while putting one hand over the other, palms facing. Then he slammed the upper hand down on the lower and rotated the palm of the upper hand in a squishing motion.

Tommy nodded and turned back to me. "Ready for us to crush your team?"

He signed the whole question over. The quick tutoring session was completely adorable.

"Pretty confident there, aren't you?" I replied, signing as well.

Milo's hands flew in response as he spoke. "With good reason. Coach Liam stacked our lineup."

"Don't let them intimidate you, E!" Caleb called out as he and Mimi joined us, already mostly geared up. "Our first line is going to find the back of the net. A lot." He fist-bumped Mimi. "And the second will add even more. Plus we've got Zervudachi on deck as our third center."

Mimi nodded enthusiastically. "Yeah, Tommy. You might want to save some of that energy for when you're trying to get past Coach Ethan on D."

"All talk." Tommy flashed a playful smirk. "We'll see who's celebrating after the final buzzer." He and Milo shared a fist bump.

"I'm sure that's going to be us," Bellamy Jordan said as he arrived. He also fist-bumped Tommy and Milo.

"No way!" Ry came in close behind along with his brother Jason, who was also Bellamy's boyfriend. "Our lineup of centers can't be beat, right, Cap?" He looked at me.

"I'm staying neutral... until we're on the ice." I appreciated how everyone was keeping things light, perfect for a game with teens. Teaching good sportsmanship was crucial. "Bellamy, glad you could join us for the game and to coach this season too."

"I'm excited to do it. I've heard a lot about this from these two." He gestured to Jason and Ry.

"I'm so sorry I haven't had a minute to see you guys." The brothers and I traded quick hugs. "Once the festival's done, we've got to do a proper catch-up."

"Looking forward to it," Ry said.

"Alright, we all need to finish getting ready so we can open the doors. It looks like it's going to be standing room in here."

Fist bumps went all around as everyone scattered to prepare. In the locker room, Liam looked up from his phone as I came in. "Hey! We've got a slight change. Travis is out sick."

"Oh no, what happened?" Not only did this affect the goalie lineup, but Travis had been excited to go against the NHL players.

"A stomach bug of some kind." Liam's expression brightened. "The good news is Daniel June's still in town. He has gear at his parents' place, so he's subbing in."

"Oh, that's outstanding." I stripped off my shirt and shorts. "From waltzing to being in net in less than twenty-four hours."

"Yeah, it's pretty cool."

The locker room gradually filled with players from

both teams. The mix of experienced pros and eager campers created an infectious energy.

Once everyone dressed, we headed out to the ice together and got into warm-ups as thumping dance music played over the sound system. The special jerseys looked spectacular on the players and some members of the crowd too. The Maplewood Pride Exhibition Game logo in the colors of the Progress Pride flag on the front created a striking contrast on my team's dark blue sweaters and Dix's team's white ones.

After a few minutes, I retrieved a microphone from the scorekeeper booth. The packed stands hummed with excitement. There was a row filled with the pros' boyfriends and husbands—Oscar, Aaron, Jason, and Shawn among them. I was happy to see that Kyle's boyfriend Austin had made it after some flight delays.

Then Andre caught my eye. He was sitting with my moms near center ice and up a couple of rows. His small wave sent flutters through my chest, and I smiled and nodded in his direction.

"Good afternoon, everyone." No nerves surfaced this afternoon as I spoke. After being so far outside my comfort zone the past few days, it was possible that nothing could faze me now.

"Thank you all for coming out to support our fourth Pride exhibition game. Because of your generosity, we've already raised over seventy-five hundred dollars for the You Can Play Project and GLSEN." I paused for the applause. "And just a reminder that you can help us raise more. The merchandise and silent auction bidding will be open for thirty minutes after the game."

I took a breath and moved on to thanking all the professional players who'd joined us and announcing that we were each matching the total raised, along with additional donations from our teams and the league. My shout out to Daniel for stepping in as goalie after his performance last night earned enthusiastic applause from the crowd. He raised his goalie stick in acknowledgement.

"Alright, we're getting started. First up, we've got two skills competitions with fastest skater and accuracy shooting. That'll be followed by two periods of play. And yes, the rumors are true—whichever team loses, that captain will take a shift in the dunk tank at six. Make sure you head over right after the game to take your shot at Dix in the park."

The crowd laughed exactly as I'd hoped.

"Hey, no fair!" Dix shouted from across the ice before rapidly skating over to me. He snatched the mic from my hand. "He really means you all should stop by and dunk him after the game. My team will prevail."

"Gimme that." Liam skated over and grabbed the mic. "Excuse these two." He smiled and shook his head at us. "Let's just see what happens over the next couple of hours, shall we?"

He returned the mic to the scorekeeper as the audience cheered again.

Andre's amused smile from the stands beckoned me to come kiss him. I forced myself to go to the bench instead. We'd get to hang out tonight, and then there would be kisses.

The skills competition kicked off with the fastest skater challenge. Tommy edged out Kyle by a fraction of a second in an epic finish. Kyle, who'd lost the faster skater by a similar margin at the All Star Game a couple of years ago, took it graciously. He grabbed Tommy's hand and raised it in victory, encouraging the crowd to continue cheering.

During accuracy shooting, Andre's presence kept drawing my attention because I wanted to see what he thought of all this. His intense concentration on me shattered my focus. I missed two targets. His expression had gone straight to my heart.

"Getting distracted, lover boy?" Nick teased as he came out to shoot next.

"Shut up and shoot," I replied good-naturedly.

Ultimately, Miles won, prompting Cole, his ultra-competitive boyfriend, to demand another round.

The game blazed with intensity from the start. My team's first line—which included Caleb and Mimi—connected well early, creating several scoring chances, but Dix and Milo proved to be a formidable defensive wall.

While I was defending against a rush, Andre caught my attention again as he leaned forward in his seat, completely focused on the play. That momentary distraction gave Tommy the opening to slip past and feed a perfect pass to Cole for the game's first goal.

"Nice assist!" I called to Tommy as we reset at the

center face-off dot. He raised his stick in salute. Even scoring against my team, he made me a proud coach.

The rest of the first period whirled by in a blur of fast breaks and crisp passes. The campers held their own beautifully alongside the pros. Milo especially showed remarkable awareness on the ice, anticipating plays before they developed.

During a brief break between periods, I gathered my team for a quick strategy session. "Alright, we're only down by one. We're doing all the right things so we need to keep that up and find a way to—"

"Score more than them?" Mimi interrupted with a cheeky grin.

"And keep them from scoring." I laughed. "In particular, we've got to watch out for their defense, creating breakaway chances. Let's go get this win."

Everyone cheered as the players lined up for the face-off.

The second period started strong for us as we broke up several offensive plays. Then Caleb won a face-off in our zone, sending the puck back to me. Mimi broke free along the boards. My pass hit her stick perfectly, and she deked around Daniel before roofing the puck to tie the game.

The crowd erupted. Fighting the urge to search for Andre's reaction, I congratulated Mimi on her beautiful goal.

The teams traded chances as the period ticked on. Ry and Bellamy's competitive streak flared when Ry stripped the puck from Bellamy during a breakaway, only to have

Bellamy chase him down to recover it. Their battle ended when our goalie covered the puck.

With just under a minute left, Milo and Tommy showcased their skills on a breakaway. Tommy drew our defense to him before making a no-look pass to Milo, who sent a blistering slap shot past our goalie's glove.

The final buzzer sounded with Dix's team winning two to one. As we lined up to shake hands, my impending dunk tank appointment couldn't dampen my spirits. The joy radiating from everyone—especially the campers—made everything worthwhile.

After cleaning up and changing back to street clothes, I navigated through the crowd, accepting congratulations on a fun and successful afternoon. I found Andre in the lobby talking with my moms.

"There's our star player," Mom called out as I approached.

"Even if his team lost," Momma added with a teasing smile.

"Hey, we put up a good fight," I protested, accepting hugs from both of them.

"The kids were incredible," Andre said.

Mom nodded and gave me a meaningful look. "Just like someone I remember at that age."

"Though hopefully with fewer pucks through windows," Momma said with a laugh.

"That was one time." I groaned, though a smile escaped at the memory.

"I'm going to need to hear that story," Andre added.

My moms exchanged knowing looks before Momma

said, "Well, we're going to go grab good spots for the dunk tank."

"Oh no, you're not going to sit there and watch, are you?" I feigned mortification.

"Of course we are." Mom took Momma's hand. "Probably take some pictures too."

"Maybe we should live stream it," Momma said.

I shook my head as they happily headed out, loving them completely.

Andre turned to me with that playful smile. "So, was I that distracting?"

"I don't know what you're talking about." I stepped closer, lowering my voice. "But if I did, I'd say it was worth it. I'll have to come watch you work sometime so you know what it feels like."

"I don't think working with books qualifies as a spectator sport." Andre's voice had a seductive edge.

"I'm pretty sure you could make it one."

His chuckle warmed me through. "Ready to get dunked?"

TWENTY-FOUR

ANDRE

Spending Sunday morning, the final day of the festival, at Red's was a nice extension to the night I'd spent with Ethan. After his repeated dunkings and a pleasant evening of theater, we'd gone back to his place. It was my third night in a row being there, and talking and making out late into the night was my new favorite thing.

We'd come into town because he didn't have any food in the house other than a couple slices from the maple pie I'd brought over and three-day-old pizza.

"I promise to go to the grocery store tomorrow." Ethan offered an apologetic smile as we sat in a booth across from the counter. "There needs to be more than beer, tea, and water at home."

My heart fluttered at his casual use of *home*. Even if he didn't mean it as *our home*, it still triggered an emotional response. "The company matters more than what's in the fridge."

"Still." He reached across the table to squeeze my hand. "I should at least have coffee for the mornings."

"You say that like I mind coming here." I gestured around us at the energetic diner. "What's not to love?"

Ingrid arrived with our breakfast. I got a veggie omelet, and Ethan got eggs, turkey bacon, and an English muffin. She'd barely set down the plates before my phone buzzed with another parade update.

Ethan buttered his toast. "I appreciate you're trying to ignore your phone during breakfast, but it's parade day and people have stuff to tell you. It's okay."

I sighed and picked up my phone. "You're annoyingly reasonable sometimes, you know that?"

"Only when it's necessary." He winked, and I looked away before his adorableness distracted me.

The message confirmed the sidewalk barriers along the parade route were in place. I responded, then put the phone back on the table face down. "Everything's good. I'm all yours until I have to head to the parade for last checks."

Ethan swallowed a sip of coffee. "I'm going to stop by the rink, check in on the morning session."

"Just don't let them rope you into an impromptu practice session. Liam can be persuasive."

"Says the man who got talked into reading three extra stories yesterday." His eyes sparkled with amusement as he remembered my recap of the story time we had at the picnic.

"That was different. Clara needed to get food, and I can't resist sharing books with kids."

"I know." His voice softened. "It's one of the things I love about you."

My heart did that fluttering thing again, and I busied myself with my coffee to hide how much his casual mention of love meant. After how close we'd become, which had included sexy times in the shower this morning, I struggled not to blurt out how I felt about him.

And in the past few minutes, we'd each said the word *love* in different contexts.

But it was too soon for those three big words to be said directly to him, wasn't it?

My phone buzzed, saving me from my thoughts, and I stole a quick glance. Wade's message confirmed the live streaming setup was ready.

I drifted back to the memory of how Ethan had held me this morning. We'd woken early, tangled in his sheets, and shared slow, sleepy kisses before I accepted his invite to the shower. The memory of water cascading over us, of Ethan's gentle hands and softer words, made me flush.

"You okay there?" Ethan's voice brought me back to the present.

"Just thinking." I took another sip of coffee to hide my smile. "About this morning."

His eyes widened slightly. "Oh?"

I leaned forward, lowering my voice. "Specifically about how good you looked with water running down your chest—and other bits."

A light blush crept up his neck. "Andre..."

"What? I'm not allowed to appreciate the view?"

"You're allowed." He lowered his voice even more.

"But I don't think we want that detail in *Maplewood Matters*."

I laughed softly, enjoying how easy it was to make him blush. The tough hockey player had such an adorably bashful side. I wanted to discover every facet of his personality. Maybe once I knew all of that, it'd be time for the three words.

"Hey, guys, sorry to interrupt." Alex, Maplewood's photographer and social media coordinator, appeared at our table.

"Morning, Alex," I said.

"Hey, thanks for all those great shots of the game yesterday," Ethan said. "They were stunning. We'd love to get copies of some for the camp website and the players are all interested in copies."

"Of course. Just let me know what you need. I've got more too. I shot a lot." He pulled his phone out and swiped. "Let me send you the link where you can see them. You can share that with anyone that wants to download anything. If they use them, it'd be great if they could credit me."

In a moment, Ethan's phone buzzed and he flipped it over to look at the screen. "Cool. Thanks. I'll pass that along."

Turning to me, Alex said, "Since I caught you, I wanted to ask. Do you think we can D&D the second week of July?"

Checking my calendar quickly, I nodded. "Any evening that week looks good."

"Great. Three down, two to go. I'll confirm with you

as soon as it's locked in. I'll let you get back to your breakfast. Happy Pride!" Alex claimed a seat at the counter.

Ethan looked at me quizzically. "D&D? As in Dungeons and Dragons?"

"Yeah. A bunch of us have played together for more than a year now. We try to get together at least once a month."

He washed down a bit of his English muffin. "I would've never guessed you as a gamer."

"I got into it when I was working in Austin. There was a group who played at the library, and the storytelling aspect sucked me in." I pulled up the photos on my phone and found the illustration Olivia had made of my character looking resplendent in deep purple robes with golden runes glowing across the front and his spell book floating open in front of him. "Meet Baldwin Scriptoris. His friends call him Script. He's a badass Tiefling Wizard."

Ethan looked like I'd spoken a foreign language as he looked between the picture and me.

"You're purple. And have horns. And a tail."

"Like I said, I'm a Tiefling. Horns and tails are common."

"And yet this looks just like you in the face, with that thoughtful look as you read the book." He continued to study Olivia's drawing.

"You can come watch us play."

"People do that?"

"Sometimes, yeah."

"I would love to see this side of you in action."

I hadn't expected that to excite me, but it did. D&D wasn't for everyone, especially to watch, so that he wanted to check it out was meaningful.

My phone buzzed in Ethan's hand, but he didn't give it to me when I reached out.

"Okay, even though it's parade day, you're going to take a brief break."

He swiped on the phone's screen.

"Hey, what are you doing?"

He smirked as he talked into the phone. "Hi, awesome parade volunteers. This is Ethan. Andre's going to take a quick break from responding so he can finish his breakfast before it gets totally cold. I promise he'll be back in a few minutes." He tapped once more before setting the phone next to him and covering it with his hand.

I shook my head, running my hand over it at the same time. "I can't believe you did that. But thank you."

"Sometimes you have to save someone from themselves." He continued eating, keeping his left hand firmly on my phone as it vibrated.

We ate, trading occasional smiles. Only after I'd finished the last bite did he release the phone. When he handed it back, I placed it face down.

"My therapist is going to love what happened here."

"I can do that anytime you need me to." Ethan checked his watch. "I suppose we should go, though. We've both got things to do before eleven."

At the register, I took care of the bill. We'd fallen into

a good routine of trading off who paid without discussion.

"Thanks for a brilliant morning," I said as we stopped at the intersection where we'd part ways.

"I hope we have many more." He pulled me into a quick hug. "See you at ten forty-five. Try not to stress too much before then?"

I laughed against his shoulder. "No promises."

The walk to the parade's staging area gave me time to shift into coordinator mode. The morning air was pleasant and the sun shone brightly.

Perfect parade weather.

I checked my phone updates from when Ethan had confiscated it.

First aid stations: set.

Sound checks: complete.

Everything was running smoothly because my team was incredible.

Checking floats and talking with participants ranked among my favorite parts of the day. Beyond approving initial designs with the committee, I deliberately avoided seeing the floats until the lineup. Seeing everything finished and in formation was magical every time. The work businesses and individuals had put into these creations took my breath away.

While I was doing the walkthrough, a message arrived.

Ethan: *Kids say hi. They're wondering if it'd be okay to throw water balloons at me during the parade to keep the dunk tank theme going. I gave a firm no.*

I chuckled. He'd been such a good sport with the dunk tank yesterday, staying longer than scheduled as people kept paying for chances. He got dunked repeatedly as his friends, campers, and townspeople lined up. Grace, Elena, and I had watched, entertained as he tried to distract throwers from hitting the target.

Andre: *Tell them hi from me. And absolutely no water balloons. Can't have the inside of the loaned car getting wet. If they want another shot at you, we can just put you back in the tank.*

I capped the message with a winky face.

He sent back a surprised emoji.

I arrived at the starting line at 10:44, expecting to see Ethan. But he wasn't with the rainbow-festooned convertible he'd ride in.

"Has anyone seen Ethan?" I asked nearby volunteers. They shook their heads, and the first flutter of anxiety hit my stomach.

10:46. I texted him.

Andre: *Where are you? Everything okay?*

No response. No typing indicator.

10:50. I called, but after several rings it went to voicemail. "Hey, it's getting close to start time," I said after the beep, keeping my voice steady. "Please call me when you get this."

Had the festival suddenly become too much? He'd seemed fine at breakfast, excited even. Still, worry nagged that something was wrong.

10:52. I texted the volunteer thread.

Andre: *Has anyone seen Ethan?*

Responses flooded in, but no one knew where he was. I was the last person to get a text from him.

I sent another message to him.

Andre: *Starting to worry. Please tell me you're okay.*

10:55. I took the walkie-talkie off my belt. Not everyone had one, but several volunteers along the parade route did.

"Is Ethan on the route anywhere?"

Sarah responded first. "Not that I've seen."

"Not where I'm at," Olivia chimed in.

"Saw him about five minutes ago," Jenny said. "He was talking with someone at the Harmonic Circus float."

Relief flooded through me, followed by anger. He was socializing? Now?

"Jenny, can you see if he's still there and tell him he needs to be at the starting point immediately?" I struggled to keep my voice level.

"On it!"

I paced the starting area, checking my watch every few seconds. I felt the weight of everyone's questioning looks.

10:58. Still no Ethan. I tried calling again but nothing.

The frustration building in my chest surprised me with its intensity. Earlier I'd appreciated Ethan helping me to be more relaxed and holding back on reading messages as soon as they arrived. Now my agitation was building as it was clear we wouldn't start on time.

10:59. Jenny's voice came through the walkie at a whisper. "Ethan waved me off when I tried to interrupt."

"Why would he do that?"

"He's on the float in a corner, talking with Kirk. I don't know why."

"Take your radio to him, please." I didn't need to get mad at her. This was on Ethan for not being here.

"Will do." Hesitation rattled her voice.

TWENTY-FIVE
ETHAN

At the rink, I fell into the energy of the campers reviewing yesterday's game with video that Wade had provided. Liam and the coaches were breaking down the plays that went well and the ones that didn't. When it was time to head to the parade, everyone got into their rainbow best.

Once I'd changed into the special Maplewood Pride Grand Marshal T-shirt I'd been provided, we left the rink together: the coaches, their boyfriends, the campers, and me. Our first stop was the float the coaches and campers would ride on.

"Wow," Nick said as we reached it. "This is incredible."

The float exceeded the proposed design I'd seen weeks ago. Rainbow-colored hockey sticks arched over the flatbed trailer with panels featuring action shots from yesterday's game already mounted along the sides. NHL team logos and the You Can Play Project emblem adorned the base in Pride colors while a Hockey Is For Everyone banner stretched across the front. Even the stairs sparkled with Pride flag stripes.

"I've been on the league's float in the Thanksgiving Day Parade and that has nothing on this." Caleb snapped pictures, including a selfie with his husband, Aaron.

"It'd be so cool to ride with you all, but I've got to get up front." I hugged my friends as campers scrambled onto the float. "Thank you all for being here. I've loved celebrating Pride with all of you."

"See you on the other side," Kyle called as I waved goodbye.

Walking to my place in the lead car gave me a chance to appreciate the incredible floats. Usually I watched the parade with my moms outside the theater, but this perspective offered something special.

Andre had sent pictures earlier of the convertible at the starting point gleaming with rainbows and streamers, but I looked forward to seeing it in person. Maybe he could ride with me, share this moment together. After last night and this morning, experiencing the parade with him would feel perfect.

Was he allowed to do that? Could he allow himself to do it? I doubted it would surprise anyone if we did since we were being very open about our new relationship.

Greetings echoed around me as I passed by people on the floats or those on their way to stake out a place to watch. The sense of community wrapped around me like a warm embrace. Over the past few days, my nervousness about being grand marshal had transformed into embracing the honor that it was. This was my hometown and being asked to take a lead role in the festivities meant a lot.

I slowed down as I noticed that a tense atmosphere surrounded the Harmonic Circus float. Several people huddled near the back corner, speaking in hushed tones to Kirk.

I knew Kirk's dad from high school, and just a few days ago I'd bumped into them and Kirk had been beaming because he was going to play on the float. Since I didn't see JT anywhere around, I decided to check.

"Hi. Everything okay here?"

A younger kid holding a bongo drum blurted out, "Kirk's freaking out."

Kirk winced from his perch on the float's edge, his guitar across his lap, fingers twisting nervously in the strap. His face had drained of color.

"Let's give him some space, okay?" My step forward prompted the others to back away.

"Hey, Kirk. What's up?"

He looked up with glistening eyes. "Ethan. I... I don't think I can do this."

The fear in his voice echoed my recent anxieties. "Mind if I join you?"

Kirk scooted over, making room. I climbed onto the float and sat beside him, our shoulders nearly touching. His slight trembling was visible up close.

"What's got you worried?"

"There are so many people walking by." His voice

cracked. "And the live stream... everyone will be watching. What if I mess up?"

"You know, I get nervous before big moments too." I bumped his shoulder gently. "That speech the other day? Terrifying."

Kirk's eyes widened. "But you play hockey in front of thousands."

"I can get anxious there too, wondering what will happen if I make a mistake. But put me in front of a crowd to talk? Scarier than facing any forward. There's always a little fear when you put yourself out there for an audience."

He nodded thoughtfully. "I guess that's true. Usually, I just play in the store or at home and that's easier. My friend Charlie told me he got stage fright before he played at the music festival, but I didn't expect... This is... huge." His fingers traced the guitar's wood grain. "Dad says I should picture everyone in their underwear, but that's weird. And gross."

"That advice never worked for me either." I turned to face him. "Want to know what I do?"

He nodded eagerly.

"Take a deep breath, counting to four." I inhaled slowly. "Hold for four counts, then release for four."

We breathed together until his shoulders relaxed.

"Now remember why you're here. You love music, right?"

"Yeah." His grip on the guitar loosened. "I practice every day. It's what I want to do."

"And today you're sharing that love with others."

"Yes." He plucked a string. "And because it matters. Being part of Pride matters. I wanted to contribute this year."

My phone revealed several notifications from Andre. Already past 10:45. "I have a friend here who might be able to help too. He performs professionally. Want to meet him?"

Kirk's eyes widened. "Really?"

I messaged Dix, speaking into my phone.

Ethan: *Can you ask Oscar to come to the Harmonic Circus float? It's five floats up from where you are. Got a nervous guitarist who needs encouragement.*

"Mr. Gallagher?" Jenny appeared, anxious. "Excuse me."

I held up a finger.

Andre must have people looking for me. But Kirk needed me right now.

"Am I getting you in trouble?" Kirk glanced at Jenny.

"Grand marshals can't get in trouble on parade day." I winked despite my tightening stomach. I could imagine what my lateness was doing to Andre. He'd surely understand, though. "It's in the rule book."

My phone buzzed and the phone read it out to me.

Dix: *On his way.*

Andre had texted too. I couldn't focus on that.

Oscar appeared moments later, his confident energy bringing exactly what was needed. Kirk's jaw dropped—clearly recognizing him from Friday's performance.

"Kirk, this is Oscar. Oscar, Kirk's playing guitar during the parade."

"It's so cool to meet you. I saw you perform the other night. I'd love to play for a dance sometime."

"We might be able to arrange that." Oscar leaned against the railing. "I hear you're kinda nervous. I still get that way. Truth is on Friday I was jittery even though I've done that dance at least a hundred times between performances and rehearsals. I had a teacher tell me once that getting nervous means you care how it turns out."

"I do care. It's—" Kirk started.

"I'm sorry, Coach." Jenny's expression turned worried. "Andre insists on talking to you."

I slipped off the float since Kirk was in good hands with Oscar. Jenny handed me the radio.

"Sorry, Andre. Had to handle something. I'll be there soon."

"You need to get up here now." His sharp tone made me recoil and quickly lower the volume. "This is throwing us off schedule."

With others listening on the radio and nearby, I kept my voice even. "I know. I'm on my way."

I gave the radio back to a mortified Jenny and offered a reassuring smile. "Don't worry, it'll be fine."

The words rang hollow, but I refused to let Andre's outburst affect Kirk.

Back at the float, I found Kirk's mood improved. "I need to get up front. Oscar, thanks for coming over."

"Happy to help. I'm actually going to hang out here. Get enough hockey talk at home." Oscar winked. "Plus I want to hear Kirk play."

"Thanks, Ethan." Kirk's voice rang with newfound confidence.

I hurried toward the front, late but satisfied with the reason. Andre stood beside the grand marshal car, his expression rigid.

"Good, you're here. Get in so we can start." His voice came out clipped and professional—and it stabbed me in the heart. He was treating me like I'd failed him, just like he had in high school.

"Andre, let me explain—"

"Not now. We're behind schedule."

The dismissal cut deep. Words to defend myself rose in my throat, but with the crowd watching, I swallowed them. We didn't need more of a scene than we'd already had. I climbed into the car and plastered on my media smile while disappointment burrowed into my chest.

The car lurched forward. I waved to the crowd, their cheers failing to soothe me.

"Happy Pride, Maplewood!" I called, forcing enthusiasm into my voice. Children jumped up and down with rainbow flags, reminding me why I was here.

Andre's cold treatment seeped into my bones. In high school, his disappointment had felt deserved. Not anymore.

Staying with Kirk had been the right choice. His panic had needed immediate care, and sometimes being there for someone meant other things waited. Andre should understand that. Deep down, I knew he did.

"Coach Ethan!" Daniel June shouted from the sidewalk, James beside him, both waving frantically.

I returned their enthusiasm, grateful for the distraction. Memories of working with Daniel alongside Liam years ago further validated my choice to help Kirk.

The parade route curved past storefronts festooned with Pride flags and rainbow decorations. Outside the theater, my moms were there, and I blew kisses. Mom's slight frown caught my eye—she'd sensed my tension despite my efforts to mask it. It was impossible to hide anything from her, even at a distance.

"Looking good, Gallagher!" Mickey's voice boomed as we passed Red's. I flashed an extra-bright smile when his phone pointed my way.

Rainbow colors and familiar faces blurred together as the parade continued. My media smile remained fixed while emotions churned underneath.

At the park, the parade's end point, I exited the car and met up with Mayor Axelrod as she got out of hers. We headed toward the maple tree for our photo opportunity as the floats continued behind us.

"Biggest Pride crowd I've ever seen," she remarked as we took our positions.

"Completely different from being a spectator on the sidewalk. It was thrilling seeing everyone."

Andre wasn't here—still at the starting point as floats entered the route.

Alex positioned us expertly to get us pictured with the maple while floats passed behind us. Some other media people and parade-goers captured shots as well.

Home beckoned, but first I needed to retrieve my car from the rink—preferably without encountering Andre.

I needed a mental reset before any reasonable conversation would be possible. Plus tonight's hosting duties demanded a calmer state of mind.

"Ethan!" Kirk bounded over, guitar bouncing against his back, Oscar following close behind. "Thank you! I did it!"

"You killed it out there, Kirk," Oscar added. "The crowd loved you."

"And you danced! I couldn't believe when I saw you moving to the music." Kirk beamed before his dad called his name from across the park. "Gotta go, but... thanks again. I'll never forget what you two taught me. Happy Pride."

As Kirk jogged away, Oscar squeezed my shoulder. "You did a good thing, stopping for him. Some moments are more important than being on time."

The validation warmed me, but Andre's reaction still stung. "Not everyone agrees."

"Give him time." Oscar's voice softened. "You'll work it through."

"Hope you're right," I murmured as the coaches and campers spilled off the float that had just arrived.

TWENTY-SIX

ANDRE

I'd treated Ethan like I had in high school—demanding, dismissive, cold.

Exactly what I'd promised myself, and him, I wouldn't do again.

Part of me wanted to abandon my post at the start of the parade and chase after the car that was carrying Ethan.

But I couldn't—wouldn't—let down all these people counting on me to keep the parade running smoothly. Still, every time I waved another float or group into the parade, the weight of choosing responsibility over making things right pressed down on me.

Three times, when I had a few moments, I'd sent texts.

Andre: *I'm sorry.*

Andre: *Let's talk as soon as the parade's done?*

Andre: *Please.*

Sending more might be too much, but holding back felt equally wrong.

My phone sat like a weight in my pocket.

After the parade, people scattered to other festival activities. I headed toward the park, hoping Ethan might still be there after his photo shoot. Alex had already posted the shot on Maplewood's social media feed, so he'd finished with that.

People waved and called out congratulations as I walked along the sidewalk. I mustered peppy responses while my mind fixated on how I'd spoken to Ethan. So far, it didn't seem like word had circulated about my behavior.

Near Harmonic Circus, Kirk was talking animatedly with his dad. When he saw me, his expression clouded over.

Strange. From what I'd witnessed, he'd played brilliantly as part of a group on the store's float, though Oscar's presence there had puzzled me since he'd been scheduled to be with the hockey players. It had been a nice addition, though, because Oscar had moved to the music the young musicians played.

"Mr. Thompson?" Kirk approached as if he thought I'd lash out at him, which hurt my heart. "I wanted to say I'm sorry if I messed up the parade or got Ethan in trouble. He was just trying to help me." Kirk's earnest explanation made my chest ache. "I don't think I could've played if he hadn't helped me with my anxiety attack."

That was why Ethan was late.

The realization hit me like a punch to the gut.

While I'd been going on about schedules and responsibility, Ethan had been helping a nervous kid find his courage.

God, I was such an idiot.

I swallowed hard. "You didn't get him in trouble. I'm glad he was there for you. You played great by the way."

Kirk nodded, though he didn't look convinced. "Thanks, Mr. Thompson. It was a lot of fun once it got going. And I'm glad I didn't cause a problem."

"It's all good." I forced confidence into my voice.

"See you at the concert tonight?"

I nodded. "Wouldn't miss it. The show and the fireworks will be a great end to the weekend."

"It's been epic." Kirk's smile returned. "I'll see you around."

As he returned to his dad, I wanted to crawl into a hole and pull it in after me. How could I apologize enough, not only for my behavior but for refusing to listen to his explanation?

I passed a couple of hours helping volunteers, moving on autopilot, checking items off my dwindling list. The more time that passed, the more concerned looks I received, making it painfully clear that word had spread about the altercation.

Finally, I arrived at the library for the last story time of the festival. "Are you sure you're okay for this?" Clara asked as she joined me near the children's area. "We can cover it."

I sighed.

"Sorry." Her sympathetic look pierced straight to my heart. "You know how this town works."

"Yeah." I scrubbed my hand across my face and over my head. "I appreciate your concern. Hanging out with the kids for a while should be a pleasant distraction, though."

As the previous storyteller thanked their audience, I stepped in. A few kids headed back toward their parents but most stayed seated.

"Have you all liked the extra stories over the past few days?" I sat on the floor, forgoing the chair.

The couple dozen kids sounded off together.

"It's great!"

"Loved it!"

"It should be like this all the time," five-year-old Leslie declared at the end of the cacophony.

"We'll see what we can do about that." Their energy lifted my spirits. "So, who wants to pick what I read?"

A few hands shot up, and I picked Daphne, who'd raised her hand first. She went to the new books section and returned with *Finding My Rainbow*.

All the energy drained from my body. Of course it would be the book Ethan had read a few days ago.

She handed it to me, and I somehow managed to thank her with a smile.

I looked out at the eager faces and forced myself to focus. These kids deserved a great time, regardless of my personal drama.

A couple of kids who'd been here when Ethan read the book added foreshadowing to some scenes, encouraging Josh. Their investment in the story touched me. I asked what they thought might happen next, sparking wonderful discussions.

The children's enthusiasm proved infectious, and somehow, sharing this book that was connected to Ethan eased a bit of the tension in my chest.

Still, I needed to talk to him.

I headed to the office for a moment alone and dropped into my chair, pulling out my phone.

My texts to Ethan remained unread.

Since several hours had passed, I took a chance with a new message.

Andre: *Ethan, I know I messed up. And I know why you were late. Please let's talk.*

I stared at the screen, willing a response to appear.

Nothing. It stayed in *Delivered* status.

The silence cut deeper than any angry words could have.

Seeking distraction, I checked my email. Weekends typically brought few messages, just a few newsletters and junk mail. But one subject line jumped out.

Library Association of America: Opportunity to Discuss

I opened it immediately.

Hi Andre,

Sorry to bother you on a Sunday, and especially Pride Sunday. But I wanted to get this into your inbox. My staff and I would love to schedule a call with you tomorrow, if possible, to discuss an idea we've had. Please let us know.

Happy Pride!

Stella Bradley
Program Chair

My first instinct was to share this with Ethan. The email didn't specify whether it was related to the award, but it should've thrilled me. Everything was muted, though, since the person I wanted to show the email to wasn't talking to me at all.

After suggesting meeting times in my reply, I headed to Red's. Tea and food might help. Maybe a side order of perspective too.

Mickey looked up as I entered, his usual warm smile subdued. "Comfort food time?"

I nodded, sliding onto a counter stool rather than my usual booth. The diner was peaceful since it was still too early for the dinner crowd.

"I screwed up." I stared into the tea Mickey placed before me.

He stood across from me, hands on the counter. "I winced when I heard how you talked to him on the radio." He paused and I held his gaze, trying to encourage him to continue. "Brought back memories of high school."

Anger at myself welled up and threatened tears. "I promised myself I wouldn't do that again, wouldn't treat anyone like that. My focus was on getting everything so fucking perfect. I forgot what matters."

"Which is?"

"People." My breath came out shaky. "Ethan was helping someone who needed him, and I treated him like he shouldn't have taken that time. I wouldn't listen to his explanation. Now he won't answer my texts."

Mickey slid a plate with a grilled cheese in front of me. "Eat. I'm guessing you haven't had a bite since breakfast. Then we'll figure out how to fix it."

I picked at the sandwich, appetite gone. "What if it's not fixable? What if I just proved I haven't changed at all?"

"The fact you're sitting here beating yourself up proves you have." Mickey's voice came out gentle but firm. "The Andre from high school wouldn't have recognized he'd done anything wrong."

My phone buzzed, and my heart leaped.

I pulled it cautiously from my pocket.

Ethan: *I'll be at the amphitheater at 5:30 to host the concert.*

The formal tone was another gut punch. No emojis. No warmth. Just facts.

"He's still showing up to host." I showed Mickey the message. "That's something, right?"

"It's very Ethan. He won't let others down, even when he's hurting." He gave me a pointed look. "Which means you have a chance to see him and talk. Don't waste it."

"I won't. I can't lose him. Not when I'm falling in love with him." Taking a bite from the sandwich, I let it sink in that I'd just said that out loud for the first time.

Mickey's eyebrows shot up. "That's new. Have you told him that?"

"No. And now definitely isn't the time." I sighed. "I gotta fix it first."

Mickey and I talked intermittently as he worked the register and waited on customers. Sometimes people chatted with me about how wonderful the weekend had been. Just like the LAoA email, though, the accolades couldn't permeate the sadness.

By the time I headed to the amphitheater, I still lacked any brilliant ideas on how to make sure he'd talk to me.

Ethan arrived exactly at 5:30.

He looked incredible in dark jeans and a Maplewood Bears Pride shirt that made his eyes pop. He smiled as he talked to Brent, the stage manager. But when he spotted me, he turned polite and distant.

After giving him some time with Brent, I approached. My patience had run out.

"I'm sorry to interrupt. Ethan, can we talk?" I asked softly. "Please?"

He hesitated then nodded. We moved to a quiet corner away from the preparation bustle.

"I'm sorry," I blurted out. "This morning I was out of line. I fell into old patterns and that's inexcusable."

Ethan's expression remained neutral. "You're right. It's not excusable."

"Kirk told me what happened." My voice broke. "I should have trusted that you were doing something important."

"You didn't even ask." His quiet voice carried hurt. "You just assumed. Just like in high school."

The controlled pain in his voice made me ache. "I hate I made you feel that way."

Ethan ran a hand through his hair, gathering his thoughts. A few locks fell across his forehead, and I wanted to push them back into place.

"I can't do this right now. I have a show to host, and it can't start late."

Ouch.

"I understand." I longed to reach for him, but I held back. "Maybe after? Before you meet up with your friends?"

He was celebrating the end of the festival at Red's with the people he'd brought to town. I imagined he had removed me from his guest list.

"I don't know." He straightened his shoulders.

The words deflated me. "Well, I'll be around."

He nodded once, then returned to Brent.

Protective walls threatened to rise around my heart. I couldn't let that happen. I didn't want to push him farther away. An incredible future awaited if I could prove I wasn't that high school kid anymore.

But watching him charm the sound check crew with a smile that never reached his eyes, I feared he might be lost already.

TWENTY-SEVEN

ETHAN

This was the last event and I wouldn't let what was going on between Andre and me impact the finale of the festival.

Where I wanted to be was at the empty rink firing off a bunch of pucks to clear my head and work out my frustrations.

That would have to wait until morning.

I psyched myself up as if this was a media event for the Riptide. A little autopilot so the audience wouldn't be impacted by my problems couldn't hurt. Most of them probably already knew what had gone down, but they didn't need to see my feelings on display.

"Five minutes to go," Brent said.

"Thanks." I glanced at the card with information about the first performers. I'd already memorized this. Brent had also said he'd read me anything I needed him to.

I peeked around the edge of the stage. Festivalgoers packed the park. Blankets and chairs covered the grassy area right in front while others stood around the vendor booths. The vibe was pure happiness.

Directly across the stage on the side where the performers would enter stood Andre. Even from this distance, the tension in his face and shoulders was unmistakable.

He'd tried to apologize earlier, but I hadn't been able to hear it then. Maybe I never would. The way he'd dismissed me this morning had the sixteen-year-old that still lived inside me crushed and angry.

But I couldn't think about that now. I had a show to host.

Brent gave me the signal, and I stepped onto the stage. The crowd's enthusiastic response as the spotlight hit me pushed some of the heaviness from my heart.

"Good evening, Maplewood!" My voice carried through the sound system. "Welcome to the finale of what has been an incredible Pride festival. For those who don't know me, I'm Ethan Gallagher, and it's been an honor to be your grand marshal this year."

More cheers erupted, and despite everything I grinned.

"We've got an amazing lineup of talent ready to share songs of pride and songs of love with you tonight. And stick around as we cap off the festival with fireworks."

I introduced the first band, The Maple Keys, made up of a vocalist, guitarist, and cellist. As I exited the stage, they launched into a gorgeous acoustic version of "I Have Dreamed" from *The King & I*.

As the melody floated through the evening air, memories of holding Andre close and sharing quiet moments washed over me. Just this morning, everything had seemed possible.

"You're doing great." Brent appeared beside me with a bottle of water. "The crowd loves you."

"Thanks." I took a grateful sip. "How long until the next intro?"

"About ten minutes. They've got three songs."

I nodded, trying to keep my attention on the music rather than looking toward Andre. It wasn't easy. Part of me wanted to go to him and enjoy this, just like we had at the dance performance.

The band transitioned into another love song, this one slower, more intimate. Couples in the audience swayed together.

My chest ached at the sight.

Would Andre and I ever have that? Or had this morning proven that some patterns were too deeply ingrained?

The evening progressed with a steady stream of beautiful music. Each time I stepped onto the stage, I transformed into the upbeat host. Between sets, I watched the crowd, drawn to the joy radiating from familiar faces.

Tommy and Milo slow-danced. They'd found something special.

My moms swayed together to a cover of "In Your

Eyes," which I could imagine them listening to when they first got together. Mom's head rested on Momma's shoulder. They caught me watching and waved, their concern written across their faces. I gave them a reassuring nod, though I knew they wouldn't buy it.

"Next act in three minutes," Brent said, appearing at my elbow.

I nodded, grateful for the distraction.

As I waited for my cue, I found my friends in the crowd. Caleb and Aaron shared a blanket, and Aaron was feeding Caleb bites of something from a Special Blend bag.

Nick and Shawn sat nearby, their heads bent together as they talked, probably discussing how a scene would work in Shawn's next book. Kyle had his arm around Austin as they enjoyed the music. Miles and Cole, and Jason and Bellamy were dancing off to the side.

Everyone seemed to be paired up, sharing this romantic evening under the stars.

I'd planned to tell Andre, at some point tonight, that I was falling for him. I'd even considered using the L word. The parade debacle had blown all that up.

When I stepped back into the wings after the next intro, I stole a glance at the spot I'd been avoiding.

Andre was watching the performance, his body rigid with tension. Our gazes met briefly before I looked away. The hurt and regret in his expression made it hard to breathe. He looked as miserable as I felt.

The band started another song. Each lyric about second chances and forgiveness seemed aimed directly at me. I wanted to believe people could change, that the Andre I'd gotten to know over the past few days was who he truly was. But this morning had shown how quickly old patterns could resurface.

The sky had darkened. Pride-colored lights created a warm glow throughout the park. Soon it would be time for the fireworks, the grand finale of the weekend.

I should have been ready to hang out with Andre once our festival responsibilities were done.

Instead, I was caught between what my heart wanted and what my head warned me about.

"Ready for the fireworks?" Brent asked.

I nodded, mentally running through my last announcement of the night. The band finished their set with a flourish, and I stepped out one last time.

"What an amazing evening!" The crowd's energy remained high. "Give it up one more time for all of our performers."

Everyone came back on stage, and I moved to the rear to give them room to take their bows.

My voice caught as I continued. "This weekend showed why Maplewood is so special. We're a community that celebrates love, that supports each other, that makes space for everyone to be authentically themselves. It's been our pleasure to share this with everyone who visited this weekend, whether it was in person or through the live stream."

The audience cheered, several of them waving Pride flags high in the air, including a couple of oversized ones. The sight took my breath away.

"So, are you ready?" I looked over to Brent, who gave me the nod that the fireworks team was ready. "Let's turn off the lights and look to the skies. Enjoy the show!"

As I left the stage, the first firework exploded overhead. The crowd gasped in appreciation.

Under different circumstances, I might have sought out Andre so we could enjoy the show together. Instead, I thanked Brent and said good night before leaving to join my friends in the audience. We'd all planned to go to Red's after the show as a thank you for spending the weekend here.

Making my way through the crowd, I nodded and waved at various people. My moms pointed to the sky, talking about the patterns in the fireworks just like they had every year since I was little. I stopped and hugged them but didn't stay long enough for them to ask how I was doing.

As I approached the cluster of hockey players, Dix pulled Oscar close for a kiss as golden sparkles painted the sky.

"How are you doing?" Caleb asked.

I shrugged. "I'm okay, I guess."

"We still on for Red's?" His concern was evident, making it clear it was okay if I said no.

I hesitated, torn between escaping to home and being with these people I loved. "Yes, we're still on, though I can't promise to be good company."

"Then let us be good company for you." He squeezed my shoulder.

The short walk to Red's allowed me to decompress.

After the warmth of the stage lights, the air was cool and refreshing. The streets buzzed with jubilant people.

I'd pushed far beyond my comfort zone to take part as much as I had. And I had one person to thank for that nudge.

We brought a capacity crowd to Red's, so we divided ourselves up between the counter, booths, and tables in the back. Joe and Mickey were awesome staying open late and hosting us.

Liam pulled me aside before I sat down. He wrapped me in a tight hug and clapped me on the back. "You okay?" he asked quietly.

"Hanging in."

"Good. If you need anything..."

I nodded into his shoulder and he let me go with another back slap.

"Have a seat, everyone," Mickey said, loud enough to quiet the chatter for a moment. "We've got appetizers coming and we'll be around to take orders for drinks and food shortly."

I'd parked myself at the counter so I could swivel and see everyone.

"You missed lunch, right?" Mickey stood in front of me.

I shrugged. "You caught me."

He set a burger, fries, and a 27 in front of me. "I'm going to leave this right here."

The first bite of the burger, chased with a drink from the shake, was exactly what I needed.

"You know, Ethan," Kyle said, his tone casual but

purposeful, "you and Andre remind me of when Austin and I first started dating." He glanced at his boyfriend, who nodded encouragingly. "We almost didn't make it."

That caught my attention. "Really?"

"Yeah." Kyle stirred his ginger ale with a straw. "I had a streak like Andre. I'm a stickler for punctuality, keeping commitments. And Austin..."

"Was a workaholic who had trouble being on time," Austin finished. "We had several blowups over it."

"And I got traded in the middle of all of it, which didn't help."

"What changed?" I asked, though I sensed why they were sharing this story.

"We talked. A lot." Kyle made it sound so simple. "Not just about that specific issue, but about why it bothered each of us so much."

"Communication is key in any relationship." Shawn offered his perspective as an author of many happily ever afters. "But so is timing. Sometimes you need space to process."

I ate a fry, considering their words. "What if you're not sure you can trust things will be different?"

"That's valid," Nick said quietly. "But you also have to ask yourself if what you could have is worth the risk."

That question hit home.

"I was going to tell him I was falling for him." I stared into my shake glass, unable to meet anyone's eyes. "This morning, everything felt so right. And now..."

"Now you know you both have things to work on," Cole said gently. "That's not necessarily a bad thing."

"I guess I need that space that Shawn mentioned," I said finally. "Figure out if I'm ready to take the leap. Any chance you can script it all out for me?" I looked in his direction.

Shawn chuckled.

"Maybe you can make this story the basis of your next movie?" Nick raised his eyebrows at Shawn.

"Next movie?" This was news to me. "There's a first?"

"Yeah, I got to announce it at the book event on Friday. A Christmas movie I wrote got picked up and goes into production in a few weeks. It's actually shooting outside of Seattle, so I'll be there for a couple of weeks."

"That's very cool. Congrats."

"Thanks. I'm looking forward to seeing it come to life." He gave me a sympathetic look. "As for you and Andre, given what I've seen of him today, he wants to talk too. If it was really over, I don't think you two would look so miserable."

My friends nodded and voiced their agreement.

The conversation shifted to lighter topics—plans for the rest of the summer, things they wanted to do when they returned for their coaching stints.

As things wound down and people started heading out, Liam dropped onto the stool next to mine.

"You glad you came out?" he asked.

I nodded, surprising myself by meaning it. "Yeah. I didn't need to just go home and brood."

"That's what friends are for." He pulled me into a

quick hug. "You know where to find me if you need to talk." Liam headed out the door. "See you in the morning."

As I took a sip from my second shake of the night, an idea formed on something I could do to apologize for my silence.

TWENTY-EIGHT
ANDRE

Sleep evaded me most of the night. Every time I closed my eyes, I saw Ethan's hurt expression over and over—tensed shoulders, sadness in his eyes, forced smiles. The memory twisted my heart. Even my anticipation about the upcoming Library Association call failed to override my guilt.

Was this karma knocking me in the head? Getting professional recognition while my personal life shattered? The call had the potential to be life-changing for my career. But what good was success when I'd hurt someone I was in love with?

I rubbed my tired eyes and looked at my phone.

6:45 AM.

I could lie here for another hour, but what was the point? My mind wouldn't stop grinding anyway.

What should've been a soothing shower was filled with memories of warm water and tender touches shared with Ethan. I braced my hands against the cool tile and sighed. What olive branch could I extend?

Send him flowers at the rink? Too public. Write him an apology letter? Too much like something out of *Bridgerton* or Jane Austen. Cook him dinner? That might work, if he'd even agree to come over.

As the water ran cold, I stepped out and dried off, still turning possibilities over in my mind.

I pulled on a soft gray sweater and dark jeans—something that said *I care about my appearance, but I'm not trying too hard*. The outfit felt right for both the Library Association call and anything I might do later with Ethan.

My stomach growled as I headed out to my car, reminding me I'd barely eaten yesterday. Special Blend would already be open, so I headed that direction.

A light fog hung over Maple Street, giving everything a dreamy quality. City crews were already out taking Pride decorations down. Later this morning volunteers would pack away the tents, including the one we'd had our first kiss under.

I looked across the park when I got out of my car. We'd pulled off something really fantastic this weekend.

Jenny's cheerful expression greeted me as I entered the coffee shop. "Breakfast sandwich and tea?"

"Please." I studied the pastry case while she entered my order. The maple tarts looked perfect, golden brown and perfectly glazed. "And two of those."

Her eyebrows rose, but she didn't comment as she

boxed them. Two of his favorite treats might smooth the way.

"Have you seen Ethan this morning?" The question slipped out before I could stop myself.

"He was first in the door." Her expression gave away nothing about how Ethan might have been.

I kept my tone neutral. "Can I borrow a pen?"

She passed me a marker, and I wrote carefully on the pastry box. I wanted no mistakes when he had his app read it out. *Can we please have lunch today? Andre.*

It wasn't much but it was a start. Now I just had to get the box to him somehow.

A few more early-morning people arrived and there was small talk all around. I moved to hide the message on the box to help keep it off the gossip network. Jenny quickly had the rest of my order ready, and I paid her.

"Good luck," she said softly.

"Thanks."

The drive to the rink took only a few minutes. Camp didn't start until eight, so it was possible I'd catch him alone. Texting Liam was a possibility and I could pass the tarts off to him to put them where Ethan would find them. I didn't want to make a public spectacle of giving him the box.

Indecision held me in its grip as I parked my car next to Ethan's. I drank some tea, took a couple bites from my sandwich, and considered options.

In the rearview mirror, I saw Tommy and Milo get out of a car and unload their hockey bags and sticks from the trunk.

Problem solved.

I got out of the car with the box in hand. "Morning, guys."

"Hey, Mr. Thompson," Milo said, not signing since his hands were full. "What's up?"

"Could you do me a favor? Could you make sure Ethan gets these?" I gestured to the box in my hands.

They exchanged a look that was far too knowing for teenagers.

"Yeah, we can do that," Tommy said, sympathy in his voice.

"For sure," Milo added.

"Thanks." I handed over the box, my awkwardness mirroring how I felt. "I appreciate it."

"You're welcome." Tommy had compassion in his eyes.

I watched them head into the rink, hoping the tarts would help start a conversation. And the kids would eat them if Ethan rejected them.

The library was quiet when I arrived, with the Monday morning book crew already in the community room. Clara was working to take down one of the Pride displays to make room for the July themes. Democracy for the entire month. Ice cream for the upcoming festival.

She stopped as I approached. "Morning." She studied my face. "You look a little better than yesterday."

"Thanks. I think." I offered a small smile. "The festival was amazing, even with... everything."

She nodded. "It was incredible. I know you were worried about how much bigger it was, but it seemed to go off without a hitch. At least that's what I saw and heard from people."

It wasn't all without a hitch.

"Me too." I stayed focused on the actual festival. "All the feedback's been superb. And we were lucky that the few things that happened behind the scenes were resolved quickly. The team did outstanding work."

"Just promise me you won't try to expand again next year." She put some rainbow flags in a box.

"Oh, I swear to that. This one was already busting at the seams, so I don't think we can handle another growth spurt for a few years."

"So I have to ask." She stopped packing things away to focus on me. "I noticed a Library Association call on your calendar. Any hint what it's about?"

"Your guess is as good as mine. Yesterday's email mentioned an opportunity but didn't have details. I'll let you know as soon as I'm done."

"My fingers are crossed for something awesome."

I smiled and headed back to the office to settle in before the call. As soon as I walked in, I nearly dropped my tea because a Special Blend bag sat on my desk.

That hadn't been there yesterday.

Moving quickly to the desk, I set my breakfast down. The bag had a note written in block letters. It looked like Ethan had used the same marker I had.

Please have lunch with me. E.

With quivering hands, I opened the bag to find two scones.

A laugh bubbled up in my throat. We'd had the same

idea. Either Clara had let him in and hidden it from me or someone from the Monday morning club had, since a couple of their members had a key.

I pulled out my phone to text him.

There were already typing bubbles in our message thread.

Andre: *Yes. Special Blend or Red's or somewhere else?*

Ethan: *Yes. Red's or Special Blend or wherever.*

The timing of our messages was almost comical as we'd simultaneously sent them.

Ethan: *Special Blend works great. 12:30?*

Andre: *Perfect. See you then.*

My phone buzzed again.

Ethan: *BTW, the maple tarts were a nice touch. Tommy and Milo were very sneaky about delivering them.*

The extra message made my heart lift. It felt like progress.

Andre: *The scones were perfect too. Great minds...*

I set my phone aside, trying to focus on preparing for the call, but my mind kept drifting to lunch, hoping we'd leave there with a way forward.

At precisely nine, I took a deep breath and clicked to join the virtual meeting.

"Andre! So wonderful to see you." Stella Bradley's warm smile filled my screen. She wore her usual stylish glasses with frames that had a purple and blush swirl of color. Her salt-and-pepper hair was in a neat bob. "I hope I'm not interrupting your post-festival recovery too much."

"Not at all." I straightened in my chair. "I'm eager to hear about the opportunity you mentioned."

"I want to take just a moment to say I loved watching some of the festival live stream. You all had some fantastic programming, especially the history sessions on Thursday and Friday's author talks."

Oh wow, she'd seen the stream. It never occurred to me that someone from the association would watch.

"I'm so glad you enjoyed it. I'll let the team know. The stream was a project headed by some students from University of Vermont."

"A student-led project. That makes it even better as far as I'm concerned." She paused and adjusted her glasses. "So, let me get into what we've been thinking about. We've been impressed with your banned books initiative. The way you've engaged the community, created safe spaces for discussion, and have such an extensive collection is a remarkable achievement for a town the size of Maplewood. Then there's the work you've done to help other libraries launch similar programs."

My chest swelled with pride. "Thank you. I couldn't do it without the support of our staff and patrons."

"With your experience, we'd like you to come work with us." She leaned forward. "We want to launch a nationwide program to encourage and support libraries to develop similar initiatives. We need someone to lead it. Someone who understands both the practical and emotional aspects of this work."

I blinked, processing her words. "Are you saying..."

"We'd like you to head up the project." Her smile widened. "It would be a one-year contract based in Seattle with some travel to other regions. You'd be developing training and marketing materials, mentoring other librarians, scaling up what you've done in Maplewood."

Seattle. Where Ethan lived most of the time. Talk about a coincidence.

"This is... wow." I struggled to find the right words. "I'm honored. Can I ask about the timeline?"

"Of course." She pulled up what looked like a calendar. "We'd want you to start in September, which would give you time to transition things in Maplewood. The bulk of the work would be September through May, with more flexibility in the summer months. We imagine you could be in Maplewood for the summer, especially Pride month, since we know that's important to you."

My mind raced with possibilities. This was an incredible opportunity. And so much opened up if I was in Seattle during hockey season.

"Can I take a few days to consider everything?" I asked carefully. "This would be a big move."

"Of course." Stella nodded in understanding. "I'll send you more information as soon as we hang up. We can set up another call later this week to discuss more and answer any questions you may have. I do hope you'll say yes but understand it's a big ask."

After we said our goodbyes, I sat back in my chair, overwhelmed by the morning's developments. The project was exactly the kind of work I'd dreamed of doing. That it was in Seattle felt like the universe was either helping us come together or playing a cruel joke.

First things first, though. Ethan and I needed to have lunch in a couple of hours. Then, maybe, we could talk about what this might mean for us.

TWENTY-NINE
ETHAN

The locker room was silent as I toweled off after my shower. Most of the campers had already left, heading out to enjoy the lunch break.

After giving up trying to sleep around three, I hadn't been sure how I'd have the energy to make it through the day after an exhausting weekend. After working around the house for a few hours, I came in to shoot pucks a little after six.

My outlook on the day had only improved when Andre and I ended up with similar ideas for lunch invitations. The exchange of pastries earlier seemed like a positive sign, but we had a lot to work through.

I pulled fresh clothes out of my locker, dark jeans and a soft blue T-shirt—nicer than my usual camp attire of sweats—for our meetup.

"You're overthinking again." Liam's voice startled me. He leaned against the doorframe, coffee cup in hand. "I see it in your face."

"Maybe a little." I sat down to lace up my sneakers.

"So lunch with Andre?" He settled onto the bench beside me.

"Yeah." I got up to check my hair in the small mirror on my locker door, trying to make it just so. "We're meeting at Special Blend."

"Good." He nodded.

I waited, sure he had more to say. "No advice before I go?"

"Do you want any?" Liam asked, studying me.

I shook my head with a small smile. "I think everyone covered it last night."

"Exactly." He grinned. "You know I'm here if you need to talk after."

"Thanks," I said as I closed my locker.

He stood and clapped me on the shoulder. "Now go get your man."

I hoped that Andre wanted to be my man as much as I wanted that. Despite our history, including yesterday's blowup, I was more attracted to Andre than anyone else ever. When I wasn't around Andre during the past few days, I'd been searching for ways to be with him.

Even when we were in high school, while it had felt like he was bullying me sometimes, there was also the fact that I'd wanted to do the things he'd asked me to do. I wouldn't tolerate being berated or made to feel bad, but if we could communicate effectively like Austin and Kyle did, I believed we had a decent chance of success. Even if that chance had to play out long distance.

My heart started hammering as soon as I approached

Special Blend. Through the window, I saw Andre already seated at our table, reading his phone. He smiled at whatever was on the screen. Unlike yesterday's tension, happiness softened his features.

A good sign for our chat.

Taking a deep breath, I pushed open the door. The wonderful scent of coffee and baked goods wrapped around me as conversations buzzed throughout the packed cafe. Andre looked up at the bell's chime, and our eyes met.

I walked back to the table, and he rose just as I got to him. He stepped forward as I came closer, narrowing the gap between us.

"Hi," I said softly.

"Hey." His smile reassured me.

We moved in unison again, connecting in a brief hug.

It'd hardly been more than a day since breakfast yesterday, but I already missed these moments of connection. Still, I made sure to let him go as soon as he pulled back.

The contact brought up memories of touching more than just his arms.

"Thank you for the scones," he said as we separated. "They were perfect with my morning coffee."

"The maple tarts were wonderful too." I ached to kiss him. "Tommy and Milo were very smooth with their delivery. They could have a future as a spy team."

Several people glanced our way with poorly concealed interest. "Want to get something to go? Take a walk?"

Jenny took our orders with a bright smile but didn't comment beyond asking if we wanted our usual drinks as well. She'd had a front-row seat to us getting to this point in the day.

While we waited, Andre and I stood near the pickup counter, maintaining a careful distance.

"How was camp today?" he asked, his voice quiet enough that only I could hear.

"Good. This group has exceeded where we expected them to be at the end of the first week." I was thrilled for each of them. "This was already an advanced session, so it's thrilling. Liam and I are talking this afternoon about how much more we can throw at them."

"That's great. A testament to the coaching." Andre's smile set off flutters in my chest.

"I fear there's not enough of us. Kyle's staying this week instead of going home for a few days. Miles and Cole are coming back early too so we can have more support."

"Sounds like your camp is growing like the festival did."

He'd nailed it with that comparison.

Our order came up, and we headed out into the pleasant summer day. With Maple Street quieter, it was easy to stroll.

"The festival seemed like a tremendous success," I said as we headed out of the cafe. "How's the feedback been?"

Andre's face lit up. "Incredible. I met with Wade, Olivia, and Mickey earlier. The live stream numbers were beyond expectations with viewers from as far away as Australia and Germany. The vendors set up in Maplewood City Park were thrilled with the traffic and sales. We don't have all the info from the stores in town, but so far it seems all positive."

"That's fantastic." I smiled, enjoying his obvious satisfaction with what the team had accomplished.

I hadn't realized how much I missed talking to him about normal, everyday things.

We crossed the street into the park, and he stopped at a shaded bench. "Shall we sit?"

We settled, sitting on opposite ends of the bench. The remains of the festival surrounded us. Tent patterns were still visible in the grass. The tree we planted was still in its pot, a dolly next to it signaling that someone would soon move it for replanting.

Andre set his cup and the bag with his lunch down in the space between us and turned to face me. "Let me just start with my apology." His voice was steady but full of emotion. "The way I treated you at the parade... I fell back into old patterns, and I hurt you so much. I don't know how to apologize enough."

The sincerity in his words touched me. "Thank you." I sat my food next to his. "I know the festival was important, but..." I gathered my thoughts. "When you shut me down from explaining, it brought back all those old feelings. Of not being heard. Not being understood. Of my feelings being disregarded."

"God, Ethan." Andre's face crumpled. "That's the last thing I ever wanted to do, but I didn't stop myself in the moment either. When I found out that you'd helped Kirk through his anxiety... I should've known you were doing something important."

"It's not all on you," I admitted. "I should've let you know what was up. All I could focus on was someone who needed help. I know all too well the impact of anxiety."

Andre reached for my hand, hesitating before taking it. His touch was grounding. "You're amazing with young people, you know that? The way you connect with them, help them... It's beautiful to watch."

I squeezed his hand, grateful for the connection. "I had good role models. Mrs. Goddard, my moms, Liam—they all showed me what it means to really see someone who's struggling."

"I've been thinking about how we can avoid doing this again." Andre's hand flexed on top of mine. "Remember I told you I've been seeing a therapist?"

I nodded encouragingly.

"She's helped me understand where that habit comes from and how to manage it better." He looked away for a moment before bringing his gaze back to mine. "Clearly it continues to bere a work in progress. Anyway, I wondered... would you consider coming to a session with me? Talk about our history and how we can build something healthy?"

The suggestion caught me off guard in the best way. It showed how serious he was about making this work. "I'd like that." I maneuvered our hands so his was in mine. "Therapy's done a lot for me over the years too. So, yes, let's do some together."

Relief flooded his features.

"I want this to work. These past few days, despite yesterday... You're all I could think about last night."

His breath caught. "Me too. I..." He paused, seeming to gather his courage. "I'm falling for you, Ethan. And it terrifies me, but..."

My heart soared. "Oh, I think I've already fallen for you. Hard." A weight lifted as I admitted this. "That's what I wanted to tell you after the concert. Before everything happened."

"We're quite a pair, aren't we?" His smile was tender. "We almost allowed ourselves to lose this."

"Speaking of this." I raised our hands up. "Would you have dinner with me tonight? Somewhere nice?"

"I'd love that." His smile brightened. "Giuseppe's?"

"Perfect." The Italian restaurant was a favorite. "Seven o'clock?"

"Yes, seven."

Just then, both our phones buzzed. We moved to get them out of our pockets.

"It's Mickey," we said simultaneously.

Mickey: *Just an FYI. You two are the talk of every table in here. Expect a callout in Maplewood Matters since this is making the rounds.*

He'd attached a photo, one that had to have been taken from across the street, that showed us sitting close, with me holding Andre's hand.

Andre looked up, a mix of amusement and concern on his face. "Maybe we should rethink eating out?"

"Come to my place instead?" I suggested. "I can grab takeout from Giuseppe's on my way home. Same food. No audience."

"Perfect." Andre smiled, relieved. "Can you get me the chicken marsala? It's my favorite."

"Chicken marsala it is. And we won't have the entire town knowing what happens."

He glanced at his watch and sighed. "I should head back. I have a meeting about the summer reading program I can't miss."

We stood, gathering our uneaten food. Neither of us seemed eager to part, even though we'd be seeing each other in just a few hours.

"Thank you," I said softly, "for being willing to work through this with me."

"Thank you for the chance." He stepped closer, his eyes searching mine. "Can I kiss you?"

Instead of answering, I leaned in and pressed my lips to his. The kiss was gentle, sweet with promise, and I felt him smile against my mouth.

"That'll give the people in Red's something to talk about." Andre had the silliest grin across his face. "I'll see you tonight?"

"Tonight," I confirmed.

THIRTY
ANDRE

As I drove to Ethan's house, my mind raced with possibilities. The Library Association's offer opened up options for the fall. But would Ethan think that was too much too soon? Or perhaps not enough?

His front door stood ajar, inviting me in. The transformation in the house struck me immediately. Where boxes had dominated before, framed family photos now adorned the mantel. A small table by the door cradled a bowl holding his keys and wallet. The space breathed with life now.

"Ethan?" I called once I'd closed the door. The rich aroma of seasoned food got my stomach rumbling. It was almost like being in the restaurant.

"Upstairs!" His voice tumbled down, and I loved how much like home just hearing him felt. "Be right there. Make yourself comfortable!"

I wandered toward the kitchen, discovering new touches throughout the house. A collection of hockey memorabilia spread across one shelf caught my eye—photos of Ethan in his high school and college uniforms, trophies, and team pennants. Regret pinched my heart. What would really knowing him have been like back then?

I shoved that aside. Nothing was served by second-guessing that time.

The deck doors stood open, a comfortable summer breeze drifting in.

His kitchen had been transformed. A coffee maker and blender sat together on a spotless counter. Mugs and glasses lined the open shelves in tidy rows. Two place settings waited on the island, complete with wine glasses and cloth napkins folded into perfect triangles. A bottle of red wine breathed nearby, the deep burgundy catching the evening light.

Footsteps sounded on the stairs, drawing my gaze. Ethan descended, wearing dark shorts and a forest green T-shirt that intensified the blue of his eyes. His bare feet padded across the hardwood. The casual confidence in his stance and how completely at home he was in this space stole my breath.

"Hey," he said, voice low and intimate, a smile warming his entire face. "It's good to see you." He crossed to where I was standing, his proximity radiating heat against my skin. He gave me a gentle kiss and I returned it.

We didn't linger long, but it was the perfect way to start the evening.

"You too." The nervous flutter in my chest settled

with the kiss. "Italian food was the right choice. It smells amazing." I motioned toward the oven.

He pulled open the refrigerator door, revealing that he'd been to the store. "Finally stocked up. What's your pleasure? Hibiscus tea, wine, sparkling water, soda, beer..." His eyes found mine with a hint of pride. "Even decent coffee."

A warmth spread through me at the thought of him remembering my preferences, another sign of roots taking hold.

"The wine sounds perfect." The corner of my mouth lifted as he reached for the bottle already on the counter and poured with practiced ease.

"Thought we'd eat at the island," he said, sliding a glass across the granite surface. "Slightly easier between the meals, the bread, and the salad that's in the fridge."

His fingers lingered against mine, electric currents shooting up my arm from the connection.

"Perfect. Maybe outside later." I slid onto one of the stools. "The house looks wonderful—things getting unpacked and arranged. It's really becoming yours." The wine hit my tongue—rich blackberry and vanilla notes with a hint of spice. He'd chosen well.

"Insomnia has its uses." His lips quirked into a half smile. "Unpacked for a few hours, then consolidated the remaining boxes in one of the spare rooms. Needed something to occupy my thoughts besides..." He took a slow sip, blue eyes holding mine over the rim of his glass. "Yesterday."

The shadow from our blowup hung between us; then we broke the silence simultaneously.

"Actually, there's something—"

"I have news—"

Our laughter collided in the space between us, dissolving any traces of tension. We'd been in sync so many times over the past few days, like we'd had the same script. If only I'd trusted that connection yesterday.

"Tell me." Ethan gestured with his glass, lips still curved from our shared moment. "What's on your mind?"

My finger traced the delicate stem of my glass as I organized my thoughts. "I had a meeting this morning..."

Ethan leaned forward, eyebrows lifting with interest. "Good news?"

"Very good." The excitement that had bubbled inside me all day threatened to spill over, jumbling my words. "The Library Association offered me a leadership position. They want to take what I started and further expand our banned books program across the country."

His face transformed with genuine joy, eyes brightening as if the accomplishment were his own. "That's incredible! Congratulations! Tell me everything."

"Thanks." His enthusiasm warmed me more than the wine. "But there's something else..." My fingers tightened around the glass stem. "The position would be based in Seattle." The words tumbled out before doubt could silence them.

Ethan froze, the wine glass suspended halfway to his

mouth. Time seemed to slow down before he spoke. "Seattle? For real?"

"Yeah, starting in September. Some travel involved, but Seattle would be home base through at least May. The contract runs for a year, but in the summer they expect it to be more flexible on where I am." Each subtle shift in his expression—the widening eyes, the parted lips —telegraphed the emotions he was experiencing.

He set his glass down with deliberate care, a look of surprise still on his face. "You'd be in Seattle. During the season?"

"If I accept." Eye contact became both difficult and essential, vulnerability burning in my chest. "We're still finding our footing, I know. But when Stella mentioned the location..." My throat tightened around the confession. "It felt like some cosmic sign we shouldn't ignore."

The smile that bloomed across his face reached deep into his eyes, creating those corner crinkles he got when he was happy and enthusiastic about something. Two quick strides brought him around the island to my side. "This is beyond amazing—professionally and..." His fingers threaded through mine, his palm warm against my hand. "Personally."

"I'm glad you think so." Electricity zinged through my veins, my heart hammering against my ribs.

"Absolutely I do." His hand squeezed mine, his thumb tracing hypnotic circles across my knuckles. "Tell me more about it. It seems very out of the blue. And does this mean you're getting the award?"

"Not really." I took a drink since I was no longer

nervous about his reaction. "Stella's on the judging committee for the Freedom to Read Award and when she read the packet on what we'd done here, she was impressed that our smaller library had done so much." Ethan beamed at me as he listened. "Beyond that, the efforts in helping other libraries who want to do something similar caught her attention. She wants me to come there and help the LAoA make it a replicable program for libraries of all sizes. As for the award, this has no bearing on that. It won't be announced until August."

"I'm so proud of you." He kissed me again. "And to have you in Seattle so we can be in the same city to date and be a couple—as a superstitious hockey player, I very much believe it's a sign."

"Superstitious? You? I can't picture that."

"You haven't seen my game prep. The things involved and the order matters."

"I can't wait to see."

Ethan raised his glass. "Cheers. And congrats again."

I clinked my glass to his and we both drank.

"So since we had our conversation about possibilities, the future is something I've been fixated on."

My pulse stuttered. "How so?"

"Let me show you."

I couldn't imagine what Ethan had been doing to have something to show. He guided me toward the dining room, his hand warm around mine. Across the polished table stretched several sheets of paper taped together into one large document. There were several cut-out squares too.

As we approached, the aerial photographs of his property came into focus, overlaid with careful drawings and block letter annotations.

"After sorting through all the boxes, inspiration struck." Uncertainty threaded through his voice. "Your camp idea has rolled around in my head endlessly."

"This is..." Words failed as understanding dawned.

"Overstepping?" His fingers tightened around mine. "This was your project, after all."

"God, no. The opposite—you've given hours to something that matters so much to me." The renderings blurred as tears welled. "Tell me about this."

Ethan's hands danced across the drawings, enthusiasm building with each explanation. "The pond is perfect for summer activities—swimming, canoeing, maybe even fishing. If there's actually fish in there. I'm not sure there is."

His fingers raked through his hair, mussing it endearingly, dropping those adorable strands over his forehead.

"Here, cabins arranged in a semicircle create community. And this area"—his fingertip traced over careful lines—"becomes the center of it all: dining hall, performance space, gathering spot for everyone."

Nothing had been overlooked. He'd marked trails winding through woods. There were nooks sketched in that were close enough to the buildings but far enough away for small group activities. Each element had been carefully considered and placed.

"And this?" My finger hovered over a wooded area marked only with gentle shading.

"Room to grow?" A self-deprecating shrug lifted his shoulders. "These are just starting points. Your youth program expertise combined with the sports connections Liam and I have plus the artists in town..." His voice trailed off as he studied my reaction, vulnerability naked in his expression.

Something cracked open inside my chest. Ethan had transformed my dream into a potential reality. More significantly, he'd placed himself within that vision, building it alongside me. "I can't believe you did all this," I said as emotion strangled my voice.

A shy smile curved his lips as his hand settled against the small of my back, warm and steadying.

I pivoted toward him, heart overflowing at the magnitude of his gesture. My hands rose to frame his face, drawing him to me until our lips met.

The kiss began as gratitude—a wordless thank you—but transformed into hunger as Ethan pulled me against his chest. His hands slid up my back while mine gripped his shoulders. The blueprints of our potential future lay forgotten as we rediscovered each other. The solid press of his body against mine filled me with contentment and longing for more of him.

When we separated, Ethan rested his forehead against mine. Vulnerability shimmered in his eyes, turning them the deepest of blue. "The plans meet with your approval, then?"

A soft laugh escaped me. "I love them. I love that you created them." My fingers threaded through the hair at his nape, reveling in its softness. "That you recognized what this dream means to me and made it more concrete than it's ever been."

"We'll build it together. Whether from Seattle or here, we can create something lasting." His hands tightened at my waist, anchoring me to him.

The undisguised sincerity in his voice coupled with the security of his embrace sent waves of emotion crashing through me. "I want you... and that. Everything."

His mouth claimed mine again. My hands slipped beneath the cotton to find warm skin, drawing a husky sound of pleasure from deep in his throat.

"There's food waiting," I murmured against his mouth, even as my fingers mapped the contours of his back, committing every plane to memory.

"Food reheats." Ethan's deft fingers were already working my shirt buttons free with focused intent. His breath caressed my neck, sending shivers cascading down my spine. "Unless immediate nourishment is required?"

I smiled against his lips. "This hunger is a different sort."

He drew back just enough for our eyes to meet, his darkened with desire but illuminated by something deeper. "Upstairs?"

"Upstairs," I agreed, following where he led, fingers laced tightly with his.

THIRTY-ONE

ETHAN

The staircase creaked softly under our feet, each step building the anticipation. Andre's grip was steady and sure on my hand.

Electricity charged the air, a palpable mix of excitement and nervous energy pulsing between us. He'd slept here already, and we'd made out in my bed and in the shower. What was about to happen was more, it was making up and a celebration. Did Andre feel it too, like we were about to cement something?

His eyes widened as we entered the bedroom, taking in my personal touches that hadn't been here just two days ago. I'd added artwork from my other house. There were even knickknacks arranged on the dresser.

"How on earth did you get so much unpacking done and do the drawings?" He ran his fingers across a collection of hockey action figures, pausing at one in particular. "Oh wow. This one is a tiny you." He held it up, comparing it to me with a playful smirk.

"Seattle made figures as part of a giveaway last season." My miniature in his hands made my heart flutter.

"Hmmm. I like the life-size version better." He squinted against the harsh sunlight flooding the room.

I crossed to the windows and dropped the blinds. "That's better." The shades created a soft, intimate glow.

Our eyes met as I joined him at the foot of the bed. The air shifted, heavy with unspoken promise. I leaned in, pressing my lips to his in a perfect, gentle kiss. His hands found my waist, drawing me closer. My fingers traced across his shoulders and down his spine.

The urgent need to experience more of him overwhelmed me. I continued unbuttoning his shirt where I'd left off downstairs. Each unfastened button revealed more of his smooth chest. My fingers explored his warm skin, taking in every contour.

He hummed approval against my mouth, his hands venturing under my T-shirt. "You feel so good," he murmured, his touch raising goose bumps across my skin. He gripped the shirt's hem and slowly drew it upward.

"And you're driving me crazy," I admitted, lifting my arms to help him. He took his time, his knuckles grazing my skin in deliberate paths that quickened my breath.

When he removed my shirt and tossed it aside, his eyes locked with mine. My skin burned under his gaze, heat radiating between us.

He traced patterns across my chest. As his hands

moved lower, he paused at a faint bruise along my ribs. His touch turned gentle, questioning.

"What's this from?" Concern softened his voice. "I didn't see this the other night."

"Last game of the season. A puck hit just below my pads. It's nothing. It happens sometimes."

Andre's fingers delicately explored around the bruise. "Does it still hurt?"

I shook my head. "Not anymore. It just takes time to fade away."

He kissed his fingers and delicately touched the spot. I shuddered at the gentleness of it.

"I think you need more padding." He peppered my lips with featherlight kisses.

"What I need is to get you out of this." I hastily finished unbuttoning his shirt and pushed it off his shoulders.

It fell to the floor, leaving his chest bare. I paused to appreciate him—the subtly defined muscles and smooth skin I'd been yearning to explore again.

We stood before each other, breathing deeply.

"I could look at you all day," he said, voice just above a whisper. His gaze roamed over me like I was something precious.

I leaned in, pressing a kiss to his shoulder, then his collarbone, then the center of his chest. Each contact drew a soft gasp, his breath catching as I moved lower, my lips mapping a path to his waist.

"You're teasing me," he murmured.

Dropping to my knees, I looked up at him, waiting for his consent. He nodded, desire darkening his eyes.

"Do it. Please." Huskiness roughened his voice.

I worked to undo the button and slowly unzipped. His erection strained against his boxers, even more impressive than I remembered. I slid his pants down, my fingers tracing from his hips, down his quads, and then to his calves. He stepped out of the pants, kicking them forcefully to the side.

Then I pulled down his boxers to get to his hard and ready cock. Wrapping my hand around the base, I gave a gentle squeeze before taking him in my mouth. This time, my need kept me from more teasing.

"I love how much I make your cock twitch." I darted my tongue across his head between words.

His body tensed, his hips moving in rhythm with my movements. "Ethan," he gasped, fingers tangling in my hair. "Feels so good."

"Ethan..." My name became a mantra on his lips, each repetition filled with urgency. Every time he said it, the fire in me grew exponentially.

His thighs trembled beneath my touch as I continued sucking him down. But I didn't want him to come this way. Not yet. I wanted to stretch this moment out, discover everything there was about him.

Pulling back, I looked up, a smirk playing on my lips.

He chuckled, the sound intimate in our private space. "You're evil."

"Maybe," I conceded, pushing myself to my feet, my heart racing. "But I think you'll love it."

His smile stole my breath. Those brown eyes I'd been falling into for days held something new—something that thrilled me. "I do. I love you." He added extra emphasis on the "you."

The words hit me with physical force, making my heart soar. I'd circled this truth for days, so many times when the words had almost escaped. In this perfect moment, everything clicked into place.

"I love you too." Raw emotion roughened my words. "So much."

I closed the small distance between us, drawn to him like a magnet. Our kiss was transformed—different from all we'd shared before. Love poured out, honest and raw.

When we separated, I searched his face, committing this moment to memory—his eyes filled with the same emotion thundering through me. "You realize that's the first time we've said that?"

"I do," he murmured, cupping my face. "And I'll say it again and again. I love you."

We stumbled toward the bed, hands exploring everywhere, lips locked. As we fell onto the mattress, his hands were all over me, learning every curve of my body. I vibrated with all the stimulation, unable to contain my moans.

Breaking the kiss, he moved lower, his lips blazing a trail down my neck, chest, stomach. He paused at my hips, his fingers hooking into my shorts. His eyes asked the question. I nodded, lifting my hips so he could slide them off. He didn't think twice about tossing them to the floor.

Andre took me in his mouth, tongue swirling around the sensitive tip. A gasp escaped me, my hips bucking at the sensation. He sucked me deeper, finding a rhythm that unraveled me.

My fingers clutched the comforter as ecstasy built. I had no words—only guttural sounds escaped as tension coiled throughout my body.

But like I'd done to him, he pulled back before release.

"Payback," he murmured, a teasing smile on his lips.

I chuckled. "I suppose I deserve that."

"Mm-hmm." He crawled back up my body, claiming my mouth in a fierce kiss. Tasting myself on his tongue was electrifying.

Once Andre shifted to my side, I propped myself up on one elbow to face him. "Can we talk for a second?" We should've talked about this already, but before we continued, we needed to be on the same page.

He nodded. "Of course. What's on your mind?"

I caressed along his bicep, unable to stop touching him. "What is your opinion on protection? I haven't been with anyone since my last test. I'm negative and I'm on PrEP."

A slight smile curved his lips. "It's the same for me."

I leaned in to kiss him. "I trust you. Given our status, do you want to use a condom? I'm good either way."

Andre reached down and stroked my still very hard cock. His touch sent electricity through me, causing me to shudder. "I want all of you, all the time. No need for a barrier."

"That's the best answer. Give me everything."

I moved on top of him and pressed another kiss to his lips. Our erections pushed against each other, need building between us.

"I want you," I whispered, desire roughening my voice.

"Whatever you want. I'm yours." Andre's words vibrated against my lips.

I pulled back to see his face. "Fuck me?" There was no need to be indirect about what I wanted.

His eyes widened with surprise and excitement. "Are you sure?" His voice remained steady despite his rapid breathing. His cock pulsed against mine.

I nodded, offering a small smile. "Very." I pressed a gentle kiss to his lips. "It's been a while, but I want this. If I need you to stop, I'll tell you."

Sitting up, I positioned myself so my ass hovered over his cock. I slid gently back and forth, feeling his girth push between my cheeks. He quaked beneath me, eyes falling closed.

"Oh, Ethan." His fingers dug into my thighs.

When the head of his cock brushed my entrance, a loud moan poured out of me, making me grateful for my secluded woodland home.

"Please tell me you've got lube." Andre's eyes burned with urgency.

"Oh yes. I wouldn't have suggested this if I didn't." I rolled off him and crawled across the bed to the nightstand. "Unpacked that necessary item last night too."

When I retrieved it from the drawer and held it up,

his gaze ignited with desire. His cock stood proudly, waiting.

And I couldn't wait to take him deep inside me.

THIRTY-TWO

ANDRE

Watching Ethan crawl across the bed, his muscles flexing with each movement, sent a thrill through me. All that hockey practice had made his ass and legs stunning. He retrieved the lube from the nightstand, holding it up with a smirk that sent my heart into overdrive.

He started to open the bottle, but I stopped him. "Let me." I moved to him so I could take the lube.

I wanted to be the one to get him ready.

Ethan's eyes, filled with trust and anticipation, met mine. He nodded, handing me the lube before getting on all fours, presenting himself to me.

The sight of him, so vulnerable, made my breath catch. I ran a hand over his back, noticing how the muscles shifted beneath my touch. His skin was warm and smooth with a few freckles scattered across his shoulders.

"You're incredible." I pressed a kiss to his lower back. He shivered under my touch, his body flexing slightly.

I applied lube to my fingers, warming it between them before pressing a single digit against his entrance. He pushed back, eager for more.

I smiled, my free hand caressing the firm curve of his ass. "Patience," I murmured, circling his hole with deliberate, slow caresses as he tried to follow my suggestion.

The passion radiating from him struck me to my core. His openness built on the vibe we'd created earlier when we said we loved each other. How he gave himself to me in this moment was something I'd always remember.

Ethan let out a soft sigh, his body trembling as I eased one finger inside. I maneuvered slowly, always giving him time to adjust. His muscles tightened, then relaxed. My cock throbbed in response, making its desire—and mine —clear.

"You feel so good." My voice was low with want.

I added more lube, nudging a second finger in alongside the first. My other hand explored the strong, powerful muscles of his thighs and up to his balls.

"More, Andre," he gasped, pushing back against my hand. His voice fractured with need.

I obliged, scissoring my fingers gently, stretching him. His body responded, opening up for me. I leaned down and trailed kisses and soft licks across his back. Each touch and movement drew fresh sounds of desire.

"God, you're so sexy."

He turned his head, his eyes dark pools of desire. "I need you, Andre. Please don't make me beg."

His words sent heat surging through me. I slowly withdrew my fingers, circling one around his entrance.

He dropped his head and released a long, deep growl.

"Please. Please. Please."

I coated my cock with lube, the head already slick with precum. Positioning myself at his entrance, I leaned over him, one hand steadying his hip.

"Fuck." He drew the word out.

I draped myself against his back, my chest pressed to his spine as I peppered kisses across his shoulders. "How do you want to do this?" I asked quietly, my cock nestled against his waiting hole.

He turned his head, his pupils dilated with desire. "I want to sit down on you." His voice carried a mix of steadiness and determination. "Like before."

I nodded and scooted backwards, creating enough distance to stretch out. I stroked the full length of my cock while he watched. His hand joined mine and we stroked together. Each movement sent electricity racing through my veins.

He looked down at me, an adventurous smile playing on his lips. He swung a muscular leg over me, planting his knees on either side of my hips. His hard cock stood proudly above my stomach, leaking a drop onto my skin. I gathered it with my fingertips and brought it to my mouth, savoring his taste.

Ethan reached back, wrapped his fingers around my cock, and stroked twice, increasing my anticipation. He positioned me against his entrance. Gradually, he lowered himself.

A groan slipped from me as the tight ring of muscle yielded, enveloping the head of my cock in velvety pressure. The sensation transcended anything I'd imagined. His tightness turned every nerve ending into a live wire.

"Fuck, Ethan. So tight." Despite my desire to watch Ethan's face, my eyes fluttered closed as overwhelming sensations threatened to short-circuit my brain.

"You're so long." His breath hitched as he took more of me. "But fuck, it's good."

I looked to him and found concentration etched across his features, discomfort mingling with pleasure in equal measure.

I gripped his hips, steadying him as he moved. "Take your time." My voice strained with the effort of holding back. "There's no rush."

"Except I want to ride you. Feel you deep in me." He rocked, sliding up and down a small portion of my length, previewing pleasures to come.

Leaning over, he planted his hands on my chest so he could kiss me. I ran my fingers through his wavy hair, moaning into his mouth as our tongues met.

He rested his forehead against mine, that small gesture of connection becoming very familiar. "You know, between us, I've got the girth, you've got the length."

"And I can't wait to have all of that in me." I reached and grabbed for his thick cock, stroking it a few times. As I did that, his hole pulsed around my dick.

His eyes flashed with fire. "Good to know."

After another kiss, he sat back up. The shift in position relaxed his muscles, and I slid in further. We gasped in unison. The intense bliss overwhelmed me, making me slam my hand down on the mattress. Ethan balanced himself with a palm against my chest, head thrown back in abandon.

"Fuck, Ethan," I managed to say. "Everything okay?"

His eyes glistened, the blue almost consumed by black. "Yeah." The word came out breathless. "Just need a minute."

He took deep breaths. The pause benefited us both —I needed the moment to pull back from the edge.

"All the time you need." I traced my fingers along his cock, smiling as it jumped at my touch.

He began moving, and I let him maintain control until he found his rhythm. Ethan's hips rose and fell, taking my entire length. He'd almost release me completely before sinking down again. Each descent ratcheted up the intensity.

The measured pace was maddening in the most delicious way. Carefully, I started moving with him, thrusting upward as he descended.

He nodded, his eyes glazing as a sheen of sweat broke out on his chest.

"You like that?"

He grunted an acknowledgment. "Need fucking more."

Ethan leaned forward, gripping my shoulders. I increased both speed and force as he tightened and released around me. The sensations bordered on too much, but seeing how much he was enjoying this drove me forward.

His cock bounced against my stomach with each movement, leaving trails of slick across my skin. I wrapped my hand around him, stroking in rhythm.

"Yes." The word escaped as a whimper, his body trembling. "Harder, please."

He pushed back against me with greater urgency. I matched his pace, our bodies slick with sweat, breaths coming in ragged gasps.

My orgasm built, tension coiling tighter with each thrust.

"I'm close," I gasped, muscles tensing as I teetered on the edge of release.

Ethan looked down at me, eyes filled with love and hunger. "Come with me."

His hand joined mine around his cock, our fingers interlocking as we stroked together. His muscles clenched as he shattered. Ropes of cum shot across my stomach and chest as he cried out.

That sight pushed me over.

With a final thrust, I came, my body shuddering through the intensity. For endless moments, there was nothing but our joined groans and pulsing bodies as we emptied ourselves.

As the aftershocks subsided, Ethan remained where he was, smiling down at me. His face softened with satisfaction, flushed cheeks and half-lidded eyes making him look impossibly sexy.

"I suppose I need to move." But even having said that, he didn't try to shift.

I caressed his thigh. "I kind of like you right there. It's a nice view."

He glanced down at my chest and stomach. "Oh my god. I made such a mess."

"It was fuckin' hot. It just kept going."

He reached behind himself and adjusted so my cock slipped free. With a graceful movement, he rolled to the side and settled next to me.

"Even on your chin." He leaned in and licked it away.

I groaned at the intimacy and ran my hand across his back, and he rewarded me with a languid kiss.

He relaxed against me with a contented sigh. "I'm sure I've never come that much before." He wrapped an arm around me, ignoring the stickiness between us.

"That was..." I began, but words failed to capture what we'd shared.

"I don't think I've got the words either." Those blue eyes I could lose myself in forever looked into mine. "I love you."

I reached over, cupping his face. "And I love you." I pulled him to me for a gentle kiss, the kind I'd never tire of.

Ethan's stomach rumbled, demanding attention and breaking our peaceful moment. We laughed as he rolled his eyes.

"I suppose we should clean up and have that dinner," I said as my stomach growled in agreement.

He rolled off the bed and offered me a hand up. "Please stay over."

"I'd like that." I led us to the en suite. "Waking up with you the other day was the best. I'd like to do that as much as possible."

"Me too." He trailed kisses from my cheek to my mouth.

He opened the closet and pulled out a towel, setting it next to his on the rack while I worked to get the water temperature right—simple teamwork that felt like a preview of countless times ahead.

THIRTY-THREE

ETHAN

Andre and I pulled into adjacent parking spots in front of Special Blend. It'd only been a few minutes since we'd left my house, but my heart leapt at seeing him again. We grinned at each other through the car windows.

"Good morning." I kissed him, oblivious to any curious eyes behind Special Blend's windows. Somewhere, I imagined, phones were buzzing with texts confirming that we'd been spotted together and that we'd made up. "Again."

"Hi." His gorgeous brown eyes sparkled in the sun. "Please tell me we can have a relaxing morning when we get to the weekend."

"Sunday," I said as we both reached for the door. We laughed. "I got that."

Andre stepped inside, and I followed.

"This camp session ends on Saturday around noon, and then we don't start again until Monday."

The cafe buzzed with its usual morning crowd. Several patrons smiled in our direction.

"Good. I'm going to tell Clara the library is all hers on Sunday."

Jenny's face lit up when we stepped up to the counter. "It's good to see you here. Together!" Her hands were already reaching for cups. "What'll it be today?"

I decided to go for something different and ordered a sausage, egg, and avocado spread on a toasted everything bagel. Andre also mixed it up with egg, maple caramelized bacon, pepper jack cheese, and sun-dried tomato spread on a maple bagel. For our beverages, we both went for lattes.

Jenny nodded. "Grab your regular table. I'll get all this right out to you."

"Could you add a couple maple croissants too?" Watching them slide into the display case, I wanted to pounce on those because they never lasted long.

"Good call," Andre added.

We settled into our spot, our knees brushing under the small table.

"I like the constant smile that's been on your face since we talked last night." Andre took my hand.

"I'm not sure I've ever been this happy." I squeezed his fingers. "There are a lot of great people and things in my life, but I understand now what it means when someone says they found their person."

Jenny appeared with our drinks. "I'll have the rest out to you in a couple minutes."

Once she left, Andre took a sip of his latte, leaving a

bit of foam on his upper lip. I reached over and wiped it away with my thumb. He caught my hand and pressed a kiss to my palm. My heart stuttered, and I was sure his affections would always do that.

"I've never been happier. I'm glad we got past our... fight? Hurt? Whatever you want to call what went down." He bumped his knee against mine and left it there. "Let's not do that again."

"Hopefully, we learned enough to avoid it in the future. Couples' therapy should help. Keep us from reverting to our past selves."

The arrival of our breakfast paused our conversation. Jenny set down plates with our sandwiches, the croissants, and—surprisingly—a maple tart and maple scone. "Enjoy your breakfast and maybe the extras later in the day." She also offered a couple of to-go containers. "Just in case you need to take some with you."

"Aw, thanks, Jenny," I said, touched at the thoughtfulness of the goodies and the to-go boxes.

A perfect nod to yesterday and the foods that paved our path to reconciliation.

"This is quite the breakfast feast." Andre's eyes lit up as he surveyed the spread that had taken over most of our table. "Though I might steal a bite of your bagel. That avocado combo is calling to me."

"Only if I can get some of yours." I cut my sandwich in half and offered it to him. "Trade?"

"Yes!"

He halved his and we exchanged. I appreciated the comfortable domesticity of sharing food. These simple moments were things I didn't realize had been missing from my life.

After a few bites, Andre set down his sandwich and took a sip of coffee. "About this summer..."

I gave him my full attention.

"I'm going to read over all the Library Association materials again so I can go over all my questions with them," he said, breaking off a piece of a croissant. "And there's so much to do here before I'd go. The superhero-themed reading challenge starts next week and runs until Labor Day. The kids are already excited about earning capes and other goodies for meeting their reading goals. Plus we're doing evening story times in the park this year."

He paused, meeting my eyes with a slightly overwhelmed expression. "I need to transition my current duties. Plus I want to spend as much time with you as possible."

"We can probably spend most evenings together, and most Sundays should be ours too." I reached under the table to squeeze his knee since there was too much on the table to get to his hands. "And Seattle in the fall... well, that's perfect timing, isn't it?"

His eyebrows rose. "It is, yeah."

"It's going to make dating so much easier." I broke off a piece of the croissant and washed it down with coffee.

"What's your travel like during the season?" Andre asked.

I took an extra sip before answering. "Depending on

the month, I could be away ten to fifteen days. The trips could be as short as a couple of days, but sometimes I can be gone for a week. And when I'm home, there's practice and games. The team is great about issuing schedules so everyone knows exactly what to expect whether we're in town or traveling. Any idea about your travel?"

"Not yet. Since the program's new, they know there will be travel, but they don't know what yet." He took another bite of his bagel before he continued. "Do you think we could visit Seattle in the next couple of months if I accept? I want to see it through your eyes before I live there."

"Absolutely." Showing Andre around my second home would be so much fun. "I can figure out some time away from camp. Between reaching out to have more guest coaches here already and Ry and Bellamy being based here, it'll work."

He nodded enthusiastically. "Perfect. It can be part vacation, part fall planning." He paused, a slight blush coloring his cheeks. "And see your place. Check to see if it's big enough for two?"

My heart did a backflip. "You'd want that?"

"I know it's fast," he blurted out. "And we don't have to decide right now. But the idea of coming home to each other..." He trailed off, uncertainty in his eyes. "If I'm honest, I've loved finishing the day with you on the deck, going to bed, and then starting the day together."

"Yeah. It's been great." A shudder reverberated through me, and I wondered if Andre caught it. The happiness washing over me was nearly overwhelming.

"We could take the summer to figure things out, see how we mesh together."

"These next few weeks are going to be the best." He raised his coffee in cheers before taking a long sip.

"Speaking of places to live." I leaned forward. "Would you help me finish settling into the house?"

His face lit up. "I'd be thrilled to. I have some ideas already."

"Of course you do." I chuckled, remembering his comments on the small changes I'd already made. "What about having people over this week? Part housewarming, part festival celebration..."

"Part announcing us?" Andre finished with a grin.

"Exactly. Perfect time to celebrate with friends. How about Thursday night?"

"That sounds good, especially so we don't have to give up our together time on Sunday."

I glanced at my watch. "We should get going soon. I hadn't realized the time. Liam's probably wondering where his coffee is."

We started putting our leftovers into the boxes. I'd be set for snacks later.

Andre also checked the time. "And I need to learn more about the job offer and catch up from the festival." Andre took another bite and covered his mouth as he spoke. "Dinner tonight?"

"Of course." Though I hated for the lovely morning to end, at least I had the promise of seeing him again in a few hours.

"At my place?" Andre asked after a sip of his beverage. "I'll pick up dinner, and tomorrow I can make you breakfast."

"Yes, please. I've wanted to try out your breakfast specialty." I stood and he followed suit.

Jenny had Liam's coffee ready, with the *3* on the cup to identify it, when we reached the front. She wished us a good day as we exited. We walked to Andre's car, our hands linked. At his driver's door, he turned to face me.

"Thank you," he said softly.

"For what?"

"For giving us a chance."

Instead of words, I pulled him close and kissed him. His hands framed my face as he kissed me back, the world around us fading to nothing.

We reluctantly parted. Andre slipped into his car while I watched him back out and drive away, his little wave through the window making my heart flip.

"Well, isn't that just the sweetest thing?" Mom's voice came from behind me.

I turned to find both my moms watching with knowing smiles. "Hey! Breakfast?"

"We were headed that way," Momma said, linking her arm through mine. "And it looks like you've already had yours with a certain someone."

"Come sit with us for a minute," Mom said. "We'd love to hear how you're doing."

Liam would understand the delay in getting his morning fuel. We grabbed a table near the window, and Jenny brought coffee for my moms. She also took Liam's, promising to keep it warm.

"So," Momma said, stirring cream into her coffee, "you and Andre made up?" The lilt in her voice indicated she already knew the answer.

I nodded.

"Are you both being careful with your hearts?" Mom asked.

"We are," I assured them. "We're taking things slow, even talking about therapy together. But we don't want to miss out on seeing where this could go. Especially with his Seattle opportunity."

Momma's eyebrows rose. "Seattle?"

I explained Andre's potential position and our plans to take a summer trip there.

"That's wonderful that you'll be in the same city." Concern threaded Momma's voice even as she was acknowledging the good news.

"We're not rushing into anything permanent," I said to clarify. "We'll use this summer to get to know each other, discover how we fit together."

Mom reached across the table and squeezed my hand. "I'm glad you're on the same page."

"I've never felt like this before."

Their faces softened with understanding. After all, they'd known their own hearts quickly too.

"Just promise us one thing?" Mom asked.

"What's that?"

"Keep talking to each other. Especially about the hard stuff."

"That's the plan. We have a troubled history. The whole town witnessed that over the weekend, so we want to make sure we're communicating well so we don't do that again."

Jenny returned for their orders.

"Would you come to the house Thursday night? It's an impromptu housewarming and celebration of the Pride festival's success."

Mom's eyes widened. "Your first party together."

Heat rose in my cheeks. "Yeah. Just a few close friends and family."

"We'll be there," Momma said.

"I'm glad. There hasn't been time to have you visit yet." I checked my watch. "I should go. Liam will think I abandoned him."

"Love you," Momma said.

"Have fun with the kids," Mom added.

I kissed them both on the cheek before grabbing Liam's coffee and heading out.

THIRTY-FOUR

ANDRE

"I think that's everything." I stepped back from the kitchen island where I'd arranged the appetizers we'd picked up from our favorite places—Red's, Giuseppe's, and Special Blend.

Ethan's warm chuckle came from behind me as his arms slipped around my waist. "You've rearranged all that three times."

"I want it to be perfect." I leaned back against his chest, taking in the spread on the island and beyond into other parts of the house.

Over the past few days, we'd transformed this place into something that felt like home. Books now filled the built-in shelves, arranged by genre just as I'd suggested. Photos and art adorned the walls, including a stunning black-and-white print of the pond in winter that Olivia had given Ethan yesterday.

He'd hung it over the fireplace, and this morning I'd

come downstairs to find him standing before it, coffee in hand.

"There are so many memories tied to this pond." His eyes had shimmered with emotion. "I can't believe I live here now. We're going to create something amazing here."

Butterflies had danced in my stomach at his words—still digesting that we were making plans to build the youth camp here.

Ethan pressed a kiss to my temple, pulling me back to the present. "It's already perfect. The house looks amazing, the food will be great, and more importantly..." He turned me in his arms so I faced him. "We're doing this together."

Soft jazz floated from the speakers we'd set up inside and out, creating a peaceful vibe. On the deck, Mickey prepared the grill, having volunteered to be grill master.

I reached up to straighten his collar, though it didn't need it. His blue eyes sparkled as he kissed me gently.

The doorbell broke the moment. "Ready?" Ethan asked.

My fingers trailed down his arm as we separated. "Ready."

Grace and Elena stood on the porch, both carrying covered dishes.

"We know we're early," Grace said, "but we thought you might need help setting up."

"Perfect timing actually." Ethan took their dishes. "Andre was just about to rearrange the food again."

"I was not," I protested despite the obvious lie.

"You probably were, son," Dad said as he and Sato came up the stairs. Sato was carrying a couple of cases of beer.

"Hey now, no ganging up." I stepped forward and hugged them both.

Elena laughed as she hugged me. "Some things never change. You were the same way in school and with displays in the library."

I held up a finger, chuckling at the memory. "Only until Clara threatened me if I kept changing her work."

"Someone had to rein you in," Elena said, her laughter warm.

"Don't let them get to you," Sato said. "Someone has to keep the rest of us organized."

"He's been amazing helping me get settled." Ethan pivoted the conversation as we all moved to the kitchen. "How about a quick tour?"

"Yes, please," Grace said. "I've been excited to see how it's coming together."

"I'd love to see," Dad added.

Ethan guided our parents toward the living room while I placed dishes on the island, my fingers already itching to adjust the arrangement.

Another ring from the door stopped me, and I hurried to answer so Ethan could continue with our parents.

Wade and Olivia stood on the doorstep with two boxes from Special Blend.

"Jenny asked us to bring these since she's picking up an extra shift. She said these were mandatory." Wade handed the boxes over.

I couldn't imagine what Jenny had sent since we already had a selection of Special Blend savory goodies.

Olivia nudged him with her elbow. "Don't tease. Those pastries are practically responsible for this happening tonight."

The entire town apparently knew about the scones and tarts, though we hadn't picked any up since Mickey had brought pies for later. They were appropriate, though.

"Among other things," I murmured, catching Ethan's eye across the room where he was about to lead our parents out to the deck. His soft smile sent warmth cascading through me.

Clara arrived next, bringing a bottle of wine.

"The board is thrilled that you're taking the interim director position," I told her as I opened the bottle to let it breathe.

"Thank you for having the faith in me to fill in."

"You'll do a great job. Next week we'll get started on the transition plan. Tonight, though, no more work talk."

Clara's smile mirrored my own. "Understood." She gave me a quick hug. "It's great to see you so happy."

The arrival of Dixon, Kyle, and Liam fresh from hockey camp brought new energy through the house. They practically buzzed from an afternoon on the ice.

Dixon pulled me into a bear hug before he'd even

fully crossed the threshold. "Congratulations on Seattle! Oscar wants to visit when I'm out there for a game. Says we need to double date properly."

"Fair warning," Kyle said, "Oscar's idea of a proper double date usually involves dancing. Austin and I were not ready for that, so be prepared."

"Thanks for the heads-up," I said with a laugh, remembering how naturally Ethan had twirled me in the kitchen a few days ago. I'd be game for whatever Oscar had in mind.

Conversation and laughter filled the house, mixing with the music to create the welcoming atmosphere we'd hoped for. Our friends moved easily between the kitchen and deck, celebrating all the good things that had happened over the past couple of weeks.

Ethan caught my eye again, this time with a questioning look that asked if I was okay. I smiled and gave him a subtle nod. I was more than okay. Even though we weren't officially living together yet, this place already felt like home.

I drifted over to Olivia and Wade to see how they were doing.

"I wanted to ask you, those drawings on the dining room table—is that your camp idea?" Olivia asked.

"It is." My voice caught slightly as emotion swelled in my throat. "We're looking at giving it a go."

"I've got to see that." Wade stood. "I missed it earlier."

"Come on, I'll show you."

As we moved inside, I explained the concept. "We're planning to develop part of this property."

"We'll start relatively small to prove the concept." Ethan appeared at my side as we approached the table. "But there's room to expand while keeping the camp and the house separate."

Our friends gathered around, examining the plans with interest. Dixon pointed to the area we'd marked as a stage. "Oscar would love to teach up here. He fell in love with this place last week. He didn't want to go back to Miami."

"We'll definitely take him up on that," I said.

"If the pond freezes over, you could have winter hockey camps." Kyle's eyes lit up at the thought of outdoor hockey.

"Exactly what I've been saying," Liam added. "Plus having cabins out here will make it easier for people from further away to attend hockey camp rather than having to find a billet family. They could split their time between the rink and outdoor activities here."

Ideas flowed freely. Wade offered to set up a technology center while Olivia proposed art therapy programs. My pen flew across a notepad we had on the table as I captured each suggestion, adding to our already extensive list.

"When do you think you'll start development?" Clara asked.

Ethan and I exchanged glances. This topic had dominated our evening conversations since he'd shown me the drawings.

"There's a lot to organize," I explained. "Funding, permits to build what we envision, gathering input from the town."

"And there's probably a lot more we need to do that we don't even know about," Ethan said, seamlessly picking up my train of thought. "We want to do this right—create something truly sustainable."

Grace wiped at her eyes while Elena squeezed her hand.

"I'm just so proud," Grace said, her voice thick with emotion. "Of both of you."

"It's amazing what our boys are doing," Dad said, wrapping an arm around my shoulders.

Ethan crossed to his moms, wrapping them in a hug. "Love you both."

"Come here," Elena said, reaching out to me. "Big family hug."

I hesitated for just a moment before joining them, followed by Dad and Sato. The intensity of the support made me feel like Ethan and I could do anything.

"You're going to do amazing things here," Grace whispered, her voice wavering.

Later, as Ethan fell into a spirited debate with Kyle, Bellamy, Ryland, and Liam about the upcoming hockey season, I pulled Dixon aside. I led him to the far end of the deck where the setting sun had painted the pond in shades of gold and pink.

"What's up?" Dixon asked, leaning against the railing.

"Any advice for making a relationship work across thousands of miles?"

"First thing, Oscar would kill me if I didn't extend the official invitation to join our group chat." Dixon pulled out his phone, grinning. "We call it Love Across the Lines because hockey players are terrible at naming things. It's for couples separated by states during the season—me and Oscar, Cole and Miles, Caleb and Aaron, and now you and Ethan if you want."

"A support group?"

"Exactly. Travel schedules, different time zones, all of it." He nodded toward Ethan, who threw his head back laughing at something Liam said. "The distance is difficult sometimes, but it helps having people who understand the struggle."

"At least Ethan and I have Seattle together first, to build a solid foundation."

"I envy that." Dixon's gaze drifted toward the pond. "Oscar and I built our relationship while he toured and I played. We crossed paths in a few cities but mostly communicated by texts and calls. Once the season gets underway, he'll be in Miami and I'll be in New York, but we're confident we'll be ready for it."

"Miles and Cole have that deep friendship foundation that must help," I said.

"They do. Frankly, those two should've sorted themselves out years ago."

Our laughter mingled with the rest of the chatter on the deck.

"How do you handle the tough days?"

Dixon's expression softened. "Communication is everything. Oscar and I talk daily, share everything, and never go to bed angry. When we're not together, we have regular date nights, even if it's just syncing up the same movie over video chat."

"That's actually really sweet."

"The key is remembering you're both choosing this. Every day you're actively choosing each other. That matters."

"We're both all in on making this work."

"No doubt about that." Dixon bumped my shoulder with his. "Oscar said he knew we'd end up together the night we reconnected in New York. It's only been a few months for us, but I know he's right."

"I feel that certainty too, despite our rocky start."

Dixon laughed. "That tension between you two? Painful to watch."

Heat blazed up my neck. "We weren't that bad."

"Andre." Dixon fixed me with a pointed stare. "The entire town placed bets on when you'd finally get together. Wade created a spreadsheet."

"They what?"

"Oops." Dixon's eyes widened in mock innocence. "Maybe I wasn't supposed to mention that part." He squeezed my shoulder. "Coming from a much larger city, the way this town invested in your relationship was interesting to watch."

"It can be a lot sometimes having everyone know your business. On the other hand, it was pretty nice having so many people rooting for us."

Around eleven, our friends gradually began to leave. Each departure brought warm hugs and promises to do this again before our September departure.

Grace and Elena were the last to go, pulling Ethan and me into tight embraces.

"We're so happy for you both," Elena said, her eyes shining.

Grace nodded. "Come over for dinner soon? And, Andre, please extend the invite to Sato and Ray."

"They would love that. We'll figure out some dates and let you know."

After they left, Ethan and I stood in the quiet house amid the party's remnants—empty wine glasses, plates with crumbs, and the Special Blend box with a single maple scone left.

"Want to split this out on the deck?" Ethan asked, already reaching for it.

I nodded.

The night air had cooled to the perfect temperature. We settled into the cushioned loveseat, my body finding its place against Ethan's side as he broke the scone in half.

Comfortable silence enveloped us as we nibbled the treat and gazed at the stars.

"I see it so clearly," I said finally.

"See what?"

"Kids swimming in the pond, performing on the stage. Music drifting from the cabins." I turned to face him.

Ethan's smile softened. "I can't wait to create it with you."

My palm found his cheek, drawing him down for a gentle kiss that tasted of maple and possibilities. "That's going to be the best part."

When we separated, Ethan rested his forehead against mine. "I love you."

"I love you too." The words flowed effortlessly from my heart.

EPILOGUE

ETHAN

ONE YEAR LATER

The mid-June sun warmed my face as I stood at the microphone, Andre's hand steady in mine.

Familiar faces stretched before us—friends, family, and what seemed like half of Maplewood—gathered for the Rainbow Maple Camp groundbreaking ceremony. Rainbow banners fluttered from the trees as the audience chattered with each other.

My moms sat in the front row, smiling wide. Next to them, Ray and Sato looked ready to burst with happiness. Mickey and Liam gave encouraging nods from the second row. The local press had their cameras ready, and Wade did final checks on the live stream setup.

Andre's fingers interlaced with mine. The sunlight caught the amber flecks in his brown eyes. His gentle smile calmed my racing heart. Countless rehearsals hadn't prepared me for the emotional wave that hit as we prepared to make the official announcement.

"Good morning, everyone." Andre's voice carried through the speakers. "Thank you all for joining us today for this moment that means so much to us."

I picked up where he left off, our words flowing together naturally. "A year ago, this was just a vision— Andre's vision specifically. He shared it with me, and I couldn't stop thinking about it. He was right that this land was perfect for a youth camp. We imagined a place where queer youth could feel safe, supported, and free to be themselves."

"Not everyone comes from a place as inclusive as Maplewood, and this camp will allow more young people experience our corner of the world. A place to explore their passions, whether in sports, arts, technology, or a combination unique to them. It's about teens finding their own path. Thanks to the incredible support of this community, the Maplewood Foundation"—Andre shot a glance at me—"organizations like the You Can Play Project, the National Hockey League, the Vermont Arts Council, and several generous private donors, that vision is becoming reality. The Rainbow Maple Camp will welcome its first campers next summer."

The late nights we'd spent planning flashed through my mind. Andre's eyes lighting up describing cabins and programs. My excitement bubbling over while discussing possible activities. We'd hoped to open this year, but getting everything right meant waiting.

A winter session might be possible for pond hockey and other activities, but we'd decided not to mention that until we were sure.

"We've already had an overwhelming response since registration opened earlier this week," Andre continued. "Now, before the official groundbreaking, we'd like to thank our friends who helped make this possible."

We acknowledged everyone who'd supported us and their contributions: our parents' unwavering encouragement, Mickey's reliable sounding board, Liam's sports program expertise, Clara's educational components, Olivia's artistic vision, and Wade's technological mastery.

Mayor Axelrod stepped up next, speaking passionately about Maplewood's commitment to inclusivity. "This camp represents the very best of our community," she declared. "A place where every young person can be who they are without worry." Andre blinked back tears as she described how the camp would "enrich lives for generations to come, just as Maplewood has since its very founding." I gripped his fingers tighter.

Finally, the time for the ceremonial groundbreaking arrived. Mayor Axelrod, Andre, and I each took a shovel —rainbow-painted thanks to Olivia—and moved to the marked spot where construction would begin on the main building.

"Ready?" I whispered to Andre.

"Let's do it."

Together we pushed our shovels into the soft earth and turned over a patch of dirt. Cheers erupted from the crowd, camera flashes lighting up around us. Mom wiped away tears while Momma wrapped an arm around her shoulders. Ray and Sato stood applauding along with everyone else.

After Alex shot the official photos and we answered a ton of press questions, our friends gathered close. Mickey brought over glasses of sparkling cider from the refreshments table.

"Actually," Andre said, his voice taking on a nervous edge I didn't often hear, "there's something I'd like to say since so many of our friends are here." He turned to face me, and my heart hammered at the look in his eyes.

"Oh, I have something too," I blurted out.

Andre chuckled. "Why don't you go first?"

"No, you should—"

"But I really—"

We stopped, chuckling at our simultaneous starts and stops.

"You go—" we said together.

Liam's amused voice cut through our fumbling. "Since Andre spoke up first about having something to say, he should go. Otherwise, we'll be here all day."

I nodded, my throat suddenly dry as Andre took both my hands in his.

"Ethan." His voice wavered. "This past year has been the most incredible journey. From that tense meeting before the Pride festival to standing here making this camp a reality, you've helped me to understand what it means to truly trust and to love."

He released one hand to reach into his jacket pocket,

and my breath caught as he pulled out a small box. Around us, everyone went silent.

"The thing is," Andre continued, dropping to one knee, "I don't just want to build this camp with you. I want to build our whole life together." He opened the box, revealing a silver ring with a subtle pattern etched on the band that caught the sunlight. "Will you marry me?"

Tears blurred my vision as I reached into my pocket, pulling out an almost identical box. Andre's eyes widened as I kneeled down facing him.

"You know," I said, my voice trembling, "I had this entire speech planned about how you challenge me to be better, how you make me laugh, how I'm never more at ease than when I'm with you." I opened my box, showing him the ring I'd chosen weeks ago. "But really, it comes down to this. I love you, Andre Thompson, and I want to spend the rest of my life with you. Will you marry me too?"

Andre laughed, a sound of pure joy that made my heart swell. "Yes," we said in unison, and our friends erupted in cheers.

My hands shook as I slipped the ring onto Andre's finger and he did the same for me. We stood together, and I pulled him close for a kiss.

"I can't believe you planned to propose today too," Andre whispered against my lips.

I pressed my forehead to his, overwhelmed by how perfectly right this was.

Our private bubble burst as Mom and Momma

reached us first, wrapping us in tight hugs. Ray and Sato followed, both crying happy tears.

"Did anyone know about this?" Mickey asked, looking between us with an amused expression.

"I knew Ethan had the ring," Liam admitted. "But I had no clue about when he was going to pop the question."

"Clara was my coconspirator," Andre said, his thumb tracing over his new ring. "She helped me pick the perfect moment."

Clara grinned. "Though I didn't expect you both to have the same idea on the same day. I love it, though."

The celebration moved to the house, where someone —I guessed Clara—had laid out treats from Special Blend.

As the festivities continued, Andre and I found a quiet moment together, looking out toward the lake.

"We've come a long way from our high school days." Andre turned to face me.

I kissed him. "How are we going to decide whose proposal counts as the official one?"

"They both count." Andre's eyes sparkled with mischief. "Though I did ask first."

"Only by a few seconds!"

"Still counts." He kissed me again, ending that debate. "And it makes for a great story."

"What a year it's been. I'm glad we're back here. It's always going to be home. But between the brilliant run Seattle had this year and the work you did around the country on banned books, it couldn't have been better."

"I think your teammates would disagree. Getting the Cup would've been a great cap to everything."

"Still, great hockey was played. We lost in game seven, after all." I caressed his cheek. "Coming home to you, or being there when you got back from a trip—that's been the best part."

His smile softened. "Even when I reorganized your entire kitchen while you played on the East Coast?"

"Even then." I chuckled, remembering how he'd created what he called a "more logical system." "Though I'm still not sure why the coffee mugs needed to be color-coded."

"It makes perfect sense and you know it." He leaned into my touch. "I love you."

"I love you too." The words held extra weight now, with a ring on my finger.

Liam's voice carried over from the other side of the deck. "If you two are done having your moment, we're about to cut the cake!"

We joined our friends and family, our deck overflowing with life. Our parents were deep in conversation about wedding venues. Clara and Wade were talking about technology for the camp. Olivia was showing Mickey her sketches for the camp's common spaces.

The cake was a work of art—three rainbow-colored tiers decorated with maple leaves, books, and hockey sticks. The top featured two rainbow hearts with *Congratulations Andre & Ethan* in elegant script.

"To the happy couple." Liam raised his glass in a toast.

"To Andre and Ethan," everyone echoed as Andre slipped his hand into mine.

"Think we can handle planning a wedding while building a camp?"

I pressed a kiss to his temple. "I'm sure of it."

THE END

I hope you enjoyed your visit to Maplewood for its Pride festival, and Ethan and Andre's journey to their HEA.

But wait... there's more!

Ethan and Andre travel to Seattle six weeks after Pride so Andre can check out the city, and attend an award ceremony. Go to JeffAdamsWrites.com/MaplewoodExtra, leave your email address and I'll send you a link to the short story. You can also sign up for my news-letter while you're there.

Be sure to check out the other books in the *Love in Maplewood* series!

- Winter Wishes and Coffee Kisses by Ana Ashley
- Love Me Like It's Real by Rhys Everly
- A Touch of Maple by Amy Aislin
- Bee-tween the Music by Chantal Mer
- Can You Feel the Maple Tonight by Bix Barrow
- Scoop Me Up by Riley Long
- The Great Maple Mistake by Beck Grey
- Something Cryptid This Way Comes by Susan Scott Shelley
- Don't Clause a Scene by Lee Blair

A NOTE FROM JEFF

Thank you for picking up this installment in the *Love in Maplewood* series. I hope you enjoyed reading Ethan and Andre's story as much as I did writing it.

I must give thanks to authors Lee Blair and Riley Long for inviting me to be part of the *Maplewood* family. With all the chaos going on in the world, I loved escaping to this delightful small town where everyone is welcomed and embraced for who they are. Creating the town and its population alongside Ana Ashley, Rhys Everly, Amy Aislin, Chantal Mer, Bix Barrow, Beck Grey, Susan Scott Shelley—and of course, Lee and Riley—was so much fun.

I'm so happy I got to write Maplewood's Pride festival. Pride is such an important event. Of course, there are parades and parties—but more importantly, it brings the LGBTQ+ community together to remember our collective history, take stock of where we are now, and reflect on the work that still lies ahead in the fight for full equality and rights. As this book comes out during Pride Month 2025, that fight remains as urgent as it's ever been.

I often like to write the world the way I want it to be. With Maplewood, that was easy—it's a queer utopia, a place where people are embraced just as they are. But the real world peeks in through Andre's work around banned books. He's a fierce advocate against censorship and bans, and I wanted to highlight that through his library work.

The idea that the Maplewood Library makes all the banned books available was inspired by the Brooklyn Public Library's (BPL) Books Unbanned initiative, which allows young adults from anywhere in the U.S. to get a library card from BPL so they can access their ebook and audiobook collection. Access to books is so important and something we need to be advocating for on local, state, and national levels to push back against those who would seek to ban titles.

There's mention of a few books within this story that I want to take a moment to tell you more about. The book Ethan reads to the kids in chapter 11 is an actual book. *Finding My Rainbow, A Journey of Courage, Acceptance, and Pride* is by Josh Coleman, who grew up in a small Alabama town and is now a fierce advocate for LGBTQ+ equality in the state. Having spent my teenage and college years in Alabama, I know how important it is for young people to find themselves in books—especially in conservative parts of the country. Josh's is terrific and I'm thankful he allowed me to quote a small part of his book here.

Andre also recommends a few books to a library patron in Chapter 10. The mystery series they talk about is the *Evander Mills Mysteries* by Lev AC Rosen. The recommended biographies are *Radiant: The Life and*

Line of Keith Haring by Brad Gooch and *I Was Better Last Night* by Harvey Fierstein. Just like Andre, I wholeheartedly recommend these titles—they're all fantastic reads.

The Pride celebration was a great excuse to bring many of my hockey players together to help Ethan celebrate in Maplewood and also coach at the summer hockey camp he runs with his best friend Liam. If you're wondering where to find all their stories, they're part of the *Hockey Hearts* series. Caleb and Aaron are from *The Hockey Player's Heart*. Kyle and Austin's story is in *Keeping Kyle*. Miles and Cole turn their friendship into much more in *Taking a Shot at Love*. Nick and Shawn have their origin story in *The Hockey Player's Snow Day*. Dixon and Oscar find their happily ever after in *Skating Back to You*. If you haven't read those stories already, I hope you'll pick them up to read more love stories involving hockey players.

Stories like this one—and the entire *Love in Maplewood* series—remind us of what's possible when love, acceptance, and community come first.

- Jeff
June 2025

ALSO BY JEFF ADAMS

Hockey Hearts **Romance Series**

- *The Hockey Player's Heart* (co-written with Will Knauss)
- *The Hockey Player's Snow Day*
- *Keeping Kyle (*A *Hockey Allies Bachelor Bid* Romance*)*
- *Head in the Game*
- *Rivals*
- *Taking a Shot at Love*
- *Skating Back to You* (A *Hockey Hearts* and *On Stage* crossover)
- *Checked by His Teammate* (part of the *Bennett Brothers Duology*)
- *Pride by the Book* (A *Love in Maplewood* Romance)

On Stage **Romance Series**

- *Dancing for Him*
- *Love's Opening Night*

More Romance

- *Bicycle Built for Two*
- *Room Service*
- *Somewhere on Mackinac*

- *Summer Heat*

Young Adult

Codename: Winger series

Available in ebook, paperback, and audiobook (narrated by Kirt Graves).

- *Tracker Hacker* (includes the bonus short story *A Very Winger Christmas*)
- *Schooled*
- *Audio Assault*
- *Netminder*

More Young Adult

Available in ebook, paperback, and audiobook (narrated by Jason Frazier)

- *Flipping for Him*

Non-Fiction

- *Content for Everyone: A Practical Guide for Creative Entrepreneurs to Produce Accessible and Usable Web Content* (co-written with Michele Lucchini)

ABOUT JEFF ADAMS

Jeff Adams writes queer romance and young adult fiction —often with a hockey player (or two) at the heart of the story. He's been telling stories since middle school and became a published author in 2009.

Jeff lives in central California with his husband of 25+ years, Will (who writes as William Gayheart). He loves musicals, both the Red Wings and Penguins hockey teams, and reading (of course).

In his day job, he's a digital accessibility expert, helping companies build more inclusive online experiences. He's also the co-author of *Content for Everyone*, a guide for creatives who want to make their content accessible.

Find Jeff's books and join his newsletter—where you'll get a free *Hockey Hearts* novella—at JeffAdamsWrites.com.